Worth the Risk

By the Author

Worth the Risk

Harmony

Worth the Risk

by

Karis Walsh

2012

WORTH THE RISK

ISBN 10: 1-60282-587-4
ISBN 13: 978-1-60282-587-1

This Trade Paperback Original Is Published By
Bold Strokes Books, Inc.
P.O. Box 249
Valley Falls, NY 12185

First Edition: January 2012

Credits
Editor: Ruth Sternglantz
Production Design: Susan Ramundo
Cover Design By Sheri (graphicartist2020@hotmail.com)

Acknowledgments

I'd like to thank the authors and associates at Bold Strokes Books for their support and encouragement. I've had the opportunity to meet many of them this year, and they've become my extended family, my friends. I feel truly honored to be part of this organization.

Thank you to Radclyffe for striking the perfect balance between personal and professional. Between business sense and a deep love of LGBTQ literature.

And of course, a heartfelt thank you to my editor, Ruth Sternglantz, for the time, effort, and care she has invested in the editing process. This is as much her book as it is mine, and it's been my privilege to work with her and learn from her.

Dedication

To Frank
For your friendship

Chapter One

Jamie Callahan leaned back in the black leather chair and let her attention wander while her boss droned on about interest rates and the recent changes in the estate tax. She wanted to prop her feet on the conference table and take a short nap, but she decided that would be pushing it too far. Dave Randall accepted a large amount of familiarity and independence in private from his most productive investment analyst, but she knew better than to hint at insubordination in front of the other bankers. So she occupied her mind with math games, a habit she had cultivated since childhood, and blocked out the world around her with numbers. She was in the middle of multiplying a long series of fractions when she registered that the meeting had turned its attention in her direction.

"Could you repeat that?" she asked Dave, careful not to change her casual posture. She had no need to appear guilty since it was an accepted fact that she tuned out the portions of these meetings having little to do with her job.

"We have a couple of interesting loan requests, and I was wondering whether you wanted to research them," he said, with no sign of irritation at her obvious lack of attention. He was young for his position, but Jamie had learned he had an intuitive sense of his employees' abilities. He was willing to grant Jamie plenty of leeway as long as she continued to make their corporate bank plenty of money.

"Sure. Those initial portfolios for the Bennett execs are prepped and ready to go to an associate, so I have the time," Jamie said, accepting the assignment easily. She mainly handled high-end, lucrative projects for Dave, but occasionally he'd offer her some of the unique or more difficult to research requests. She enjoyed the chance to help small-business owners achieve their dreams, as long as they were carefully planned and financially viable. She viewed these individual loan requests as a hobby, although she never lost sight of the bottom line. Her involvement was never personal, but working these projects was fun and sometimes an opportunity to learn new things. "What are the details?"

Dave glanced at the folders in front of him. "One guy has an Indian restaurant and wants capital to open two others in nearby districts. The second is a request for sponsorship, so you can send your report to the PR department. The woman wants to buy a horse."

The group laughed along with Jamie. "A horse?" she repeated. "You're sure this isn't some kid who wants a hundred dollars to buy a pony?"

"Try one point five mil." Dave corrected her with a grin. "Apparently it's a nice horse."

He slid the folders along the table, and Jamie stopped them with a slap of her palm when they reached her seat. "As long as I get to stand in the winner's circle at the Kentucky Derby, she can have the money."

"Show jumper, not a racehorse," Dave said, leaving her to read through the applications while he moved on to other matters.

By the time the meeting ended, Jamie had filled two pages of her notebook with questions and terminology to research. The horse idea seemed ridiculous to her, but the application was carefully crafted and appeared legit. The restaurant owner seemed to have a good idea but not much business sense, and she would need to judge that when she talked to him in person, if the application made it to that point. She tried to keep an open mind in the early stages of research, and she made sure she understood all the facts before she let her intuition take over.

"Hey, Jenn," Jamie said as she paused by her assistant's desk on the way back to her corner office. "What's the name of the Indian restaurant on Burnside? I think there's one in Beaverton as well."

"Bombay Palace," Jenn Harris answered without hesitation. She rapidly entered a few keystrokes on her computer. "Here it is. They started with a street cart and now have three franchises around Portland. The two you mentioned and one in the Pearl District."

"Do they deliver?"

"Not personally, but they're members of the Portland Express system. Do you have a craving?"

"It's for research," Jamie answered with a laugh. "Order a variety of entrees for me before you leave tonight. I have to work late, so I'll eat in my office. Oh, and get Elaine on the line."

Jamie ignored Jenn's disapproving frown and shut herself in the large office. She had just settled at her desk, her back to the expansive views of downtown Portland and the Willamette River, when her phone buzzed. She picked up the receiver and pressed the button for an outside line.

"Elaine, Jamie here. Something's come up at work, so I won't be home for dinner tonight."

The other end of the line was dead silent for a moment. "It would probably be easier if you just called when you *were* going to make it home on time."

"I know, I know." Jamie sighed and attempted to placate her. "Tell Anna I'm sorry and I'll make it up to her."

"I'm sure you will. There's a new computer game she's been talking about, something to do with creating a pet store. I guess it will have to do."

Elaine hung up loudly, and Jamie sat staring at the phone for a few minutes before shrugging off her guilty feelings and getting to work. By the time her Indian food arrived, she was deep into her research and barely registered Jenn's entrance with several plastic containers of curried meats and vegetables. She ate the rather bland, Americanized version of Indian cuisine sitting alone on her leather sofa. The Bombay Palace had successfully done what her investment applicant wanted to attempt, and learning more about the local competition would help her to reach her decision. She tried to shut out the thought of how excited her niece Anna would have been if Jamie had taken her and her live-in nanny Elaine to the restaurant instead of settling for solitary carry-out. She took a few bites of runny rice pudding before she gave up on the meal and returned to her desk, where she lost herself in the data flashing across her computer screen.

❖

Shortly after eight, Jamie locked her office door and headed down to the building's parking garage. She dumped her leftover dinner containers into a trash can on her way to the car so she wouldn't leave the smell of curry in the office and walked through the nearly empty lot to her silver Mercedes. She sped along Highway 26 to Beaverton, the Portland suburb where she owned a large, ground-floor condo, and barely made it to Best Buy before they closed. Jamie moved through the store like her convertible hugged the road, stopping the first sales clerk she saw and asking for the game Anna wanted. In less than five minutes she was back in her car with the guilt offering in hand, nervously tapping her fingers on the steering wheel. It was past Anna's bedtime, so she wouldn't be able to give her the present tonight. Even if Anna would have been awake, Jamie didn't know what she'd say to her. She was apologizing for more than a missed meal, and the computer game wasn't enough. It never was. The deepest relationships Jamie could handle were business meetings and one-night stands. After only a few seconds of indecision, Jamie started the car and drove back into the city. Might as well play to her strengths. She found a parking spot near one of Portland's bars that catered to a large business clientele.

Jamie shrugged out of her black suit jacket, tossed it on the backseat, and straightened the collar on her boldly striped blue-and-white silk shirt. She headed straight for the bar and leaned against it as she assessed the patrons quickly.

"Laphroaig, neat," she ordered when the bartender came over. She knew she'd only be having one drink tonight, so she might as well make it worthwhile. She took a sip of the smoky scotch, rolling it across her tongue appreciatively as her gaze came to rest on a voluptuous redhead a few stools down. She let the judgments form easily. Young, early twenties. Fresh out of business school since she seemed stiff in her off-the-rack skirt and jacket. Still thrilled with her title of assistant manager and not jaded enough to realize it meant next to nothing. Flushed with excitement because that successful-looking butch was obviously hitting on her, but a little uncomfortable with how aggressively the imposing woman was leaning into her personal space. Probably a lawyer, Jamie labeled her competition instinctively. She was interrogating the redhead with the intensity due a hostile witness on the stand, not a potential date. Everything about her spoke of experience, from her well-cut suit to the posturing that was practiced and designed to intimidate. And she looked smart enough to recognize a losing case when she saw one. Jamie could poach on her territory and not expect to be challenged. Perfect, she thought. She took another drink of her scotch, waiting for someone in the crowd to move the right way, and then walked toward the pair.

She kept her eyes focused straight ahead, managing to arrive next to her target just as another patron passed on her right. She moved out of his way more than necessary, jarring the young businesswoman lightly with her shoulder.

"Oops, sorry," Jamie apologized, locking on to the woman's startled blue eyes. She held her gaze as she gently placed a hand on the redhead's upper arm. "I didn't hurt you, did I?"

"Hey," the would-be suitor said brusquely from behind Jamie. "Watch where you're going."

Jamie turned toward her competition and raised her hands. "Easy. It was just an accident." She met the redhead's eyes again with a slight raise of her eyebrows. "Sorry, again," she said quietly before continuing on her way. She made it several yards before a hand caught her elbow. A small grin played over her mouth as she turned to face the young woman.

The redhead looked flustered for a moment, so Jamie quickly took charge and held out her hand. "Jamie Callahan. I work at Davison and Burke."

They shook hands and Jamie registered the look of appreciation on the other woman's face. It was definitely the type of bar where you could use your company's name to help you get laid. Not that Jamie needed the assistance, but it did speed up the process.

"I'm Candace Markham. I just started at First Capital Bank," she told Jamie, almost apologetically.

"That's great. Lots of room for advancement with them," Jamie said before she glanced back at the fuming lawyer who, as Jamie had expected, stayed seated and made no defensive moves. "I didn't mean to interrupt your conversation back there."

"Oh, that was nothing," Candace assured her. "We just met."

"So did we," Jamie said with a smile. "And guess what we're going to do tonight."

Candace's eyes dilated instantly, her dark pupils almost blacking out the light blue of her irises. She stepped forward and trailed a finger over the buttons of Jamie's shirt. "What exactly do you have in mind?"

Jamie leaned closer and breathed her answer into the redhead's ear. "I'm thinking we'll go to your place so I can get you out of that suit and fuck you until you scream for more."

Candace slid her hand around Jamie's neck and pulled her face down for a searing kiss. "Sounds perfect," she whispered as she broke away. She turned and walked toward the door, leaving Jamie to swallow the last of her drink before she followed.

Too easy, she thought as she drove behind Candace's Prius and slipped into a parking space near her apartment building. Still, she played her part exactly as required, pushing Candace against the door as soon as they were inside and kissing her deeply, slowly stripping off her business suit. Jamie helped when Candace's trembling fingers tried to undo her own expensive black slacks. Jamie led Candace to the bed and then worked her way along Candace's body until she was begging for release. Candace's fingers tangled in her hair as Jamie expertly used her tongue and fingers to drive Candace screaming toward the promised orgasm.

Jamie slid back up to the pillows next to Candace, who clutched at her and kissed her hungrily. Candace's hand slid between Jamie's legs, but Jamie caught it and rolled on top of the other woman. She held both of Candace's hands captive above her head.

"Bend your knee," she demanded roughly as she straddled Candace's thigh and slid her crotch along it, pressing on her swollen clit and making herself come with a shuddering gasp. She collapsed on the bed and gently cradled Candace against her. She would rest just a few minutes, she told herself as she stroked the silky red hair that lay across her breasts, and then she would go home.

She managed to keep the guilt and loneliness away until the drive home through the dark, empty city streets. Why couldn't she communicate with her niece as easily as with a business client or a stranger in a bar? Desperately needing a shower and embarrassed by the new computer game that sat on the passenger seat, Jamie reached her condo a little after one in the morning. Just a few hours to go, she promised herself, and then she would be back at work and able to distract her mind from this empty life.

CHAPTER TWO

Kate Brown peeled off her dusty jeans, tight as a second skin after hundreds of washings, and tossed them on her bed. A faded yellow T-shirt, sweaty socks, and a frayed sports bra quickly joined the untidy pile. She replaced the familiar outfit with a carefully fitted gray skirt, pencil thin and hemmed to right above the knee. She had put more thought into that hemline than she'd cared to. Just enough leg showing to invite a potential investor's appreciative glance, but not enough to imply anyone could move higher.

Completely impractical, Kate thought with disgust as she slipped on a lightly padded bra and a blue silk blouse with fragile pearl buttons. And damned uncomfortable. Kate shifted the bra so its underwire wasn't digging in her ribs and buttoned the snug gray jacket. If she were the one with money, she wouldn't finance the equestrian in the tailored suit. She would back the rider who showed up at her office in scuffed paddock boots and old jeans with wear marks across the seat where chaps had chafed against the denim. But she wasn't the one with money, and she had to convince someone who probably knew nothing about horses that she was worth a million-dollar gamble.

Kate went into her bathroom and leaned toward the mirror as she picked pieces of hay out of her mussed hair. She brushed it until she had erased any sign she had spent the morning wearing a riding helmet and clipped it back in a smooth ponytail. She replaced her gold stud earrings with silver hoops that matched the barrette and stood back to appraise the finished product. The effect was cold and impersonal. Exactly the lie she wanted to project—that she was more at home in a bank than in a barn.

She stopped by the den and picked up her new briefcase, feeling a slender folder shifting inside. She could easily carry the few pages of projected expenses and competition schedules by hand, but she wanted the briefcase to complete her professional outfit. She shoved a few outdated horse magazines in the case, covering them with a stack of vet bills she pulled randomly out of the file cabinet. Kate put her meeting notes on top, snapped the briefcase shut, and hefted it in her hand. Much better, as long as no one dug through her papers. Her costume was complete, and all Kate had left to do was play the part.

❖

Jamie sat at her desk with pages of handwritten notes about horses, market values, and show-jumping statistics strewn over the glossy burl walnut surface. She was scrolling through the results of local horse shows when her intercom buzzed.

"Yes?" she said, cradling the receiver with her shoulder as she gathered her notes and tucked them neatly into a leather folder.

"Kaitlyn Brown is here," Jenn's professional voice announced.

"Send her in." Jamie slipped into her usual black suit jacket, buttoning it over a silky taupe blouse marked with bold black slashes, and rose to meet her guest. She didn't practice the cheap trick of keeping people waiting for appointments. She had no need to reinforce the fact that she held the power in this relationship by wasting everyone's valuable time.

Jenn entered the office, followed by a slender woman in a light gray suit. Jamie's carefully controlled expression revealed no sign of her appreciation of the woman in front of her. Although Jamie's normal standard of beauty tended toward curvy and soft, she was willing to concede that the athletic Kaitlyn definitely was feminine, with her small waist and incredible legs. Naturally platinum hair, held off her face by a silver barrette, combined with the cool tones of her outfit to give her a decidedly chilly appearance.

"Ms. Brown, I'm Jamie Callahan." Jamie reached out to shake hands and suddenly found herself lost in the warmth of Kaitlyn's mossy green eyes. The flecks of gold in them were in such contrast to her cooler hair and pale skin that Jamie momentarily lost her train of thought and held Kaitlyn's hand for a fraction of a second longer than she should have. She quickly stepped back behind her desk, putting more physical distance between them, and gestured for the other woman to sit.

"Thank you for taking the time to meet with me," Kaitlyn said as she sat across from Jamie and placed a navy briefcase on the floor next to her. The leather was unscuffed and the latches were too shiny, Jamie noticed reflexively. Probably bought just for this meeting, since her regular job wouldn't require it.

"Can I get you something to drink?" Jenn asked. "Coffee? Tea? Water?"

"Coffee would be nice. Cream, no sugar," Kaitlyn said.

Jamie nodded at Jenn before she left. Over the years she had come up with a series of small tests that had proved to be very effective at revealing a person's character, and Kaitlyn had just passed the first one. She had enough confidence to ask for something she wanted without needing Jamie to make the first move. Jamie quickly moved on to the second test while Jenn was out of the room.

"Five sentences," she said tersely, unbuttoning her suit jacket as she leaned back in her chair. "Tell me what you want and why."

Kaitlyn nodded and sat for a moment, looking slightly to the right of Jamie's head as she collected her thoughts. "I have the opportunity to buy and campaign an Olympic-caliber show jumper for one and a half million dollars," she started, meeting Jamie's gaze with those soft eyes of hers. "I have the talent and skills needed to ride him at the highest level, but I don't have the money to buy him or the fame required to get a big-name sponsor. This horse would help me break into the top tier of my sport and would give me a chance to qualify for the Olympic team three years from now. The investment would put Davison and Burke's name alongside the likes of Rolex,

Budweiser, and Hermès, and an animal-related sponsorship would help your public image. Finally, after a five-year commitment, your bank should see a strong return on its investment since this horse will still be young enough to compete, and his bloodlines give him great potential as a breeding stallion."

"Very good," Jamie acknowledged as Jenn reentered the room with two mugs. She had met too many people who wanted her company's money yet were unable to clearly articulate why. Kaitlyn Brown was doing well so far, and Jamie settled back in her chair again, eager to see how she would fare with test three.

Jamie accepted her coffee with a smile of thanks at Jenn, and she watched Kaitlyn take a sip of hers and grimace. She held the cup out to Jenn as she passed by her chair on the way to the door.

"I take my coffee with cream and no sugar," Kaitlyn said in a kind voice, but without apology. "This tastes very sweet."

"I'm sorry," Jenn said smoothly, taking the mug. "Let me fix that for you."

Jamie hid her smile by taking a drink of her own coffee. *Well done, Ms. Brown.* Most people in this situation were too nervous to correct Jamie's assistant, and they would politely drink anything Jenn brought them, no matter how disgusting. Politeness had its place, but she wasn't about to lend it large sums of money. Confidence and assertiveness were much better traits in those who were potentially to be trusted with the company's assets. She and Jenn had shamefully laughed over the miserable concoctions some people had consumed in her office, and she was willing to bet Kaitlyn's drink had been more sugar than coffee.

Jenn returned quickly with a perfectly made cup of coffee, and Jamie stood up and waved toward a sleek sofa that faced the floor-to-ceiling picture windows. "Why don't we get comfortable over here while I ask some questions I have about this venture," she suggested. The two women settled on the couch, and Jamie reluctantly dragged her eyes off the lean, muscular calves revealed by Kaitlyn's knee-length skirt. She never mixed business with pleasure, but the contrasts she saw in this woman were intoxicating. She was coolly poised and in control during the interview, but those warm eyes hinted at a sense of humor and a depth of emotion Kaitlyn carefully kept off her other features. Her porcelain skin and hair were almost too pale until a soft flush of heat colored her cheeks when Jamie moved slightly into her personal space on the sofa.

Jamie acknowledged it was a sense of attraction to Kaitlyn and nothing to do with her business evaluation that made her sit closer than she normally would. She tamped down what she decided was her body's natural response to a beautiful woman and shifted slightly away. There was no way she would give in and make this personal, although she might be persuaded to offer comfort to Kaitlyn if she had to deny her application. She shook herself mentally and forced her focus to return to the interview and away from thoughts of exactly how she would like to go about comforting the woman next to her.

Time to get back to business. Jamie rallied herself as she opened her notebook to a page of questions she'd prepared. While her first three tests were easy to evaluate, this one was more of a gut reaction. She wanted to see the rare mix of detached business sense and true passion that had marked most of the successful ventures she had recommended as investments.

"What if the horse goes lame or dies?" Jamie plunged right in with her usual pessimistic approach to questioning. She dredged up every potential problem she could find with the proposal and waited to see how the applicant would respond. Those with more passion than sense would sometimes crumble under this tactic since they tended to avoid looking at the negative aspects of their dreams. And if a candidate didn't really love the idea they were pitching, they could counter the downfalls, but rarely could they convince her of the reasons their dream was worth the risk.

Kaitlyn seemed to have anticipated the question. "I'd recommend Davison and Burke carry a full insurance policy on the stallion, including loss-of-use in case he's injured and no longer able to compete or breed." She pulled a folder out of her briefcase, snapping the case shut before Jamie had a chance to peek inside. She found it interesting to look through the documents and papers people carried with them, especially the personal ones, but Kaitlyn didn't seem willing to share.

"Here's a quote from my insurance agent," Kaitlyn said as she handed Jamie a large envelope and set her briefcase by her feet.

Jamie put the envelope aside. She would read it later even though she had already done preliminary research on equine insurance. "Okay, say we back you and you manage to keep the horse sound, what guarantee do we have that you'll win?"

"None," Kaitlyn said with a small shrug. "I can't promise we'll win every class or make it to the Olympics. But I trust the man who found the stallion in Europe and recommended him to me. And I know I ride well enough to take him to the top."

Jamie still could see too much potential for disaster in the venture, but she admired Kaitlyn's confidence. And some of her most superficially foolish investments had yielded the highest returns. Kaitlyn had obviously researched the elements of her plan that might be problematic, and she wasn't afraid to discuss them. Jamie backed off her negative line of questioning since Kaitlyn was echoing the details Jamie had already covered in her research. PR sponsorships were as much about personality and charisma as logistics. She might as well give in to her desire to know more about Kaitlyn.

"Tell me about your barn," she said, leaning back and draping her arm along the back of the couch. She wasn't touching Kaitlyn, but the gesture was too casual, too date-like. Jamie considered pulling back but decided the retraction would be worse than having put her arm there in the first place. Aside from her flushed cheeks, which could just as well be attributed to interview stress, Kaitlyn didn't seem fazed by her closeness, and Jamie's attention shifted from the conversation to the woman herself. Just a few inches forward and her arm would be lying across Kaitlyn's shoulders, her fingers would unclip the silver barrette and slide through Kaitlyn's hair…

"…and I contacted the developer when he was planning the housing community and got my stables included," Kaitlyn said. Jamie mentally shook herself and refocused, disturbed to realize she had zoned out while fantasizing about the woman she was supposed to be interviewing. Although she didn't care about the missed details since Kaitlyn had included the information about her barn in the application packet, Jamie was bothered by her loss of control, of focus.

"My outdoor arena is open to the public, so the homeowners' association pays for its upkeep. My farm is ten acres and I have access to a trail system that's maintained by the community."

Jamie nodded as if she had been intently following every word. Kaitlyn went on to describe her property, from the dimensions of her riding arena to the number of stalls in her barn. Dry facts, but no real substance. Once Jamie managed to rein in her wandering attention, she noticed Kaitlyn occasionally slipped out of her detached, businesslike demeanor. A fire lit up her eyes when she talked about riding and, especially, about the students she taught. She seemed to be carefully monitoring her every word, though, and she would pull back each time she started to talk and gesture a little more freely.

Finally, the two women stood and shook hands again. Jamie was struck once more by the contrast she noticed as she held Kaitlyn's hand. Her palm was slightly callused and roughened by work. Given the glimpses of skin she could see, Jamie's mind could easily imagine how smooth the rest of her would be to touch. She was impressed enough by the interview to agree to come and watch Kaitlyn ride, although she felt oddly uneasy with her assessment of Kaitlyn herself. She knew she was good at reading people and usually could get a strong sense of personality after a face-to-face interview, but this woman eluded her somehow. She had done the right things, said the right words, while still keeping part of herself hidden throughout their meeting. Jamie sat at her desk without working for a long time after Kaitlyn left. She was uncomfortably aware that she had personal reasons, unconnected to her analysis of the proposed business venture, to want to know more about Kaitlyn Brown.

❖

"Kate, over here," Myra Owens called to her friend as she passed through the history section of Powell's Books.

"Hey, Myra. Thanks for meeting me here," Kate said, giving her a quick kiss on the cheek. She had escaped the offices of Davison and Burke and taken the short ride on the MAX to the huge downtown bookstore.

"So, how did it go?" Myra asked. Kate could hear the concern in her voice. Myra knew her too well to miss the signs of fatigue and worry Kate tried to hide.

Kate shook her head as the two headed down the stairs toward the store's cafe. "She's a shark. I'm just lucky I made it out of her office without being eaten." She flushed slightly at the Freudian slip, as she silently conceded that it might not have been a bad thing. Jamie Callahan definitely oozed a raw sexuality, and even in her nervousness at the interview, Kate hadn't been immune to her attractive qualities. The combination of confidence and power was mesmerizing, and adding in her I-don't-give-a-damn-what-you-think attitude had made it difficult for Kate to drag her eyes away.

"Uh-oh, you're blushing," Myra observed with a laugh. "I take it your Ms. Callahan has looks as well as money?"

Kate shrugged. "She's okay, I guess. Tall and kind of severe. And it's the bank's money I need, not hers."

The two women got in line to order their drinks, and Kate added to herself that the word severe was probably not accurate. Jamie's clothes and attitude were definitely designed to make a statement of power and control, but the woman inside looked anything but cold. Her reddish-brown hair was short and a bit shaggy, and Kate couldn't decide if she paid a fortune to have it look as if she didn't care, or if she cut it herself because she really didn't. Kate was inclined to believe the latter. Jamie's soft brown eyes had glinted with humor during the whole coffee episode, and when she sat close to Kate on the couch there had been an overwhelming feeling of heat and strength coming from her. For a moment, Kate had been tempted to lean on her shoulder and just sob out the whole story of her failed attempts to finance this damned horse, begging for help. Then Jamie had moved subtly out of reach, and Kate had managed to control her ragged emotions long enough to finish the interview.

"So, tell me all about it," Myra prompted when they finally found a seat at a long, crowded table.

Kate sighed and took a sip of her Earl Grey tea before answering. "I felt like Indiana Jones," she said with a frown. "Like I had to make my way through a series of challenges in order to get out of the temple, and she was just sitting there watching me, waiting for me to fail."

"Challenges? What do you mean?"

"Well, her assistant got my coffee order wrong—I mean really wrong. And believe me, this woman didn't look like she would ever make a mistake. I think Jamie wanted to see if I would just drink it anyway, or stand up for myself."

"So it's *Jamie* now?"

Kate blushed again, silently cursing her too-pale skin for showing every slight embarrassment. "It helps to think of her that way. It's less intimidating."

"Hey, don't get me wrong," Myra said. "I know how much this means to you, and if you need to use those killer looks of yours to get the sponsorship, then go for it. Although that might have been a little too much cleavage for a business meeting."

Myra gestured at Kate's blouse and made her blush even deeper. Once she had left the office building, she had taken off the blazer and opened the top two buttons of her silk shirt. "Don't worry, I was properly clothed the whole time," she said. If there was one thing Kate knew well, it was how to fit into any situation, and the uncomfortable clothes had just been part of the charade. No matter how much of herself she had to hide, or how exhausting it was to keep pretending she belonged, this was the only way she could get what she wanted. And if she managed to finance her horse and make it to the international shows, then she would finally know she had arrived and could just be herself. She had to ignore the fact that on every rung of the ladder she had felt the same way, as if she was a fraud and those around her would know the truth if they managed to see beyond her mask.

"So what happens next?" Myra asked.

"She's coming to the barn tomorrow to watch me ride," Kate said. "So at least I've made it to the second stage. And even though she was negative, she asked a lot of good questions today, so she's taking me seriously enough to have done all that research. I just have to impress the hell out of her when I ride." And ignore the sexual energy that made it difficult to think straight. Jamie Callahan couldn't ever see her as weak. No one could.

CHAPTER THREE

Jamie's Mercedes ate up the few miles of I-5 between downtown Portland and the suburb of Wilsonville where Kaitlyn Brown's barn was located. She zipped in and out of traffic, downshifting for some of the tighter turns and enjoying the feel of her car as it gripped the road. She had initially wanted a Mercedes because it whispered wealth and power instead of shouting it like a flashier sports car. And she had chosen the E-Class eight-cylinder convertible because it was just damned fun to drive. She took the exit for Wilsonville and soon arrived at the Cedar Grove housing development. Kaitlyn's barn was located at the back of the development, and Jamie admired the initiative it must have taken to get her stables included as part of Cedar Grove when it was designed several years earlier. Jamie expected most small farms in the same situation would have sold out, moved on, and she was impressed by Kaitlyn's business sense and attitude. Even more, she recognized the same kind of creative problem-solving she had used to become successful in her own career.

Jamie stopped the car on the road leading to Kaitlyn's farm and took a few minutes to observe it from a distance and evaluate her first impressions. Next to the street, enclosed by a white panel fence, was the outdoor riding arena filled with brightly colored jumps. Everything looked freshly painted, and Jamie figured that was in anticipation of visits from potential investors, like hers today. The gravel driveway led past several paddocks, each containing a dozing or grazing horse, and Jamie knew from Kaitlyn's application that the road continued up to a couple of barns and an indoor arena. Kaitlyn hadn't spent a fortune on landscaping, obviously, but everything appeared to be well-maintained and tidy. The atmosphere was calm and the summer sun hadn't yet turned the green grass brown.

Jamie's mind conjured up a fleeting picture of Anna and her bedroom filled with model horses and animal books. She would have enjoyed coming today, but that wouldn't have been a good idea. No sense wanting what you can't have, Jamie thought bitterly as she threw her car into drive with more force than necessary. She pushed aside her brief flash of anger and drove slowly up to Kaitlyn's barn. She had been left feeling vaguely disquieted after her last interview with this woman, and she was determined to keep a professional distance today. Distance gave her perspective, and she had gotten too close to Kaitlyn. Almost close enough to touch. To care. The only thing that mattered to Jamie was her company's bottom line, and she could only protect it if she remained uninvolved emotionally. Her accustomed confidence in her ability to see through layers of personality and read another person had been shaken, and she knew it was because she was physically attracted to Kaitlyn.

Although Jamie had never before found herself in a situation quite like this, she had a good idea how to get out. She would be all business during the interview today so she could give her intuition a chance to do its job. After she evaluated this woman's proposal with a cooler mind, she could send her recommendation to PR and be done with Kaitlyn Brown. Follow up with a trip to one of Portland's gay bars, and she could find someone to help her take care of her body's needs. No problem. Balance restored.

Kate watched the Mercedes idle in front of her farm. She had expected Jamie to be early and had been ready for the visit for over an hour. At least she thought she was ready. Now she saw her barn through the coolly evaluating eyes of Jamie Callahan, and she desperately wanted a few more weeks to prepare.

The silver car came slowly up the driveway, and Kate saw how out of place it looked on her property. Her farm was functional and comfortable but not fancy. She was proud of her barn, but someone like Jamie would never recognize the qualities Kate appreciated. She would only see a ragged strip of grass lining the gravel drive where Kate could picture her students chatting while they let their horses graze after a lesson. Jamie would notice the old, repainted jumps in the arena, while Kate remembered the painting-slash-pizza party when all of her clients came over to help her prepare for this inspection. She hated the twinge of embarrassment she felt when she considered her barn based on the opinion of a stranger.

She turned and walked deeper into the shadows of the barn before Jamie's car got closer. She picked up a pot of half-eaten geraniums and shoved it in an empty stall. She had let her horse nibble on this one attempt to decorate her barn while she had been absently talking on her cell phone. She sighed as she latched the stall door, defeated before the interview even started. She couldn't impress Jamie with a few flowers. She had to use facts, from the height of the fences she jumped to the bottom line in her business accounts. Her emotional attachment to her horses and riding meant nothing, even though they were her strongest assets.

Kate zipped a worn pair of chaps over uncomfortably stiff new jeans and boots. She had spent enough money for a month's worth of hay on new outfits for these meetings, so she had to make the investment pay off. Pretending to be confident was as easy as putting on the right clothes. Kate pulled her shoulders back and pushed her doubts deep inside as she went out to meet Jamie.

❖

Jamie was early, on purpose, but Kaitlyn seemed to have been expecting that and was on hand to greet her when she stepped out of the car.

"Ms. Callahan, thank you for coming all this way," Kaitlyn said politely, reaching out to shake her hand.

"We're outside of the office, Kaitlyn. You can call me Jamie." Well, that was a good start on keeping a professional distance, Jamie thought irritably.

"All right, Jamie. And most people call me Kate. Come on inside and I'll show you around."

She turned to go into the barn and Jamie found herself staring at an incredible ass. She had thought Kate was beautiful in her business suit, but in jeans and a forest-green polo shirt she was stunning. Especially with those brown suede chaps that showed off her round bottom to perfection. *Jesus Christ, get a grip*, she scolded herself, dragging her eyes away from Kate's rear end.

They walked out of the sunlight and into the barn aisle where a stocky woman was grooming a large bay horse. Her short brown hair showed a few streaks of gray, and she was casually dressed in faded jeans and a plain white T-shirt. Jamie had intentionally dressed with more formality than was required, in designer jeans and a pressed pinstriped shirt, and she admitted she wanted to project an image of control and distance. Any observer would recognize her as the one who didn't belong here. Kate looked at home in a barn, but she was too carefully made-up and dressed for a regular ride and obviously intended to impress Jamie. Kate's friend was the only one who didn't appear to have an agenda, and she seemed perfectly at ease around the horse and unconcerned by the game Jamie and Kate were playing. She was like a stagehand walking onstage in the middle of a play, and her presence disconcerted Jamie.

"This is my friend Myra Owens," Kate introduced her. "She's here to help set jumps while I ride. And this is my horse Top Echelon."

Jamie shook hands with Myra and gave the horse an awkward pat on the neck. She wasn't much of an animal person, to Anna's chagrin, but she had a good eye for symmetry and beauty, and the horse seemed to possess both of those qualities. She had seen the horse's name listed along with Kate's at the top of local show results during her research.

"So, why can't you show this horse at the international level?" she asked, fighting off a twinge of jealousy as she watched Kate and

Myra work together to tack up the horse. They moved easily around each other, touching casually like old friends. Jamie had no doubt Myra was gay, but she was still unsure about Kate. The comfortable way the two had with each other suggested they might be lovers, and Jamie didn't like the fact that she cared either way.

"He's a great horse," Kate started almost apologetically as she rubbed the bay's neck. "But he's maxed out at five feet and really is more comfortable jumping four foot six. The fences in Olympic-level competitions will be over five feet high and wide."

Kate tucked her hair into a black riding helmet and buckled the strap under her chin. She seemed so calm talking about jumping, but Jamie couldn't imagine how insane you'd have to be to leap over fences on an animal with a brain the size of a walnut. "Half a foot makes such a big difference?" she asked. "Can't you just train him to jump higher?"

"Every horse has limits to its natural ability, and no matter how much training Topper has, he'll never be able to compete at the same level as the stallion," Kate said, shifting a little under Jamie's questioning. She was obviously more comfortable discussing her own riding, or the stallion she proposed to buy, than the performance of her own horse. "It's the same with people. If I ran a hundred meters, my time and that of a world-class sprinter would be separated by seconds, not minutes. But those seconds make a huge difference, and I could train every day and never bridge that gap."

Jamie shrugged. "Okay, I can see that. So those six inches add up to several extra zeroes on the horse's price tag."

Kate nodded, looking relieved that Jamie had finally understood her. She turned her attention to Topper's bridle, and Jamie watched her slender fingers as they adjusted the leather straps and straightened out the horse's black forelock. She had a quick vision of those hands running over her own body, and she continued her interrogation in an attempt to control her straying thoughts.

"So you're bored with this horse, with this level of competition," she said in an unintentionally challenging voice. Kate stepped between Jamie and her horse as if she were trying to protect him.

"No, I love riding him. But if I want to move forward, I need a horse with more talent and potential."

"What do you mean by 'move forward'?"

Jamie watched a slight frown crease Kate's forehead, although no such change of expression reached her eyes or her mouth. Jamie sensed she had found a trigger here, and she felt a childish sense of relief that she didn't have to be the only one uncomfortable in this situation. Her thoughts were too consumed with a desire to touch Kate, and if it hadn't been for Myra watching them with an amused smile she might have tried to simply move in for a kiss instead of challenging Kate verbally.

"If I want to advance to the next level," Kate clarified.

Jamie waved a hand dismissively at Kate's words. "You said that already. I just want to know what it is specifically you're looking for. Is it the thrill of jumping bigger fences, or the fame, or the money?"

"I don't care if the jumps are two feet high or six feet," Kate said in a clear voice, not backing down from Jamie's questions. "As long as I know I rode well and got the best out of my horse, I'm happy. But if I compete on the Grand Prix circuit, people will know my name. I'll have opportunities to teach, give clinics, train horses…"

"I thought you already did all of those things," Jamie observed, gesturing at the stalls around them.

"Yes, but not on such a large scale."

"Ah, I see," Jamie said with a smile, backing away a step to show her questioning was finished. "You'll be able to make more money than you do now. Why didn't you just say that in the first place?"

Kate glanced between Jamie and Myra, unsure whether she should argue with Jamie's conclusion or simply let the matter drop. She didn't mind talking about her ambitions and goals when she was in Jamie's impersonal office, but she had a difficult time pretending to be indifferent while she stood next to Topper and dissected his abilities and her small barn's potential. Her dreams were about more than simple dollar figures, but they didn't matter to Jamie. She only cared if Kate was a financially sound investment for Davison and Burke. Jamie had managed to bring the conversation back to meaningless numbers, and Kate had to remember she was nothing more than a column of projected earnings to her.

"Don't worry," Jamie said with a laugh, as if reading Kate's thoughts. "You didn't just make a deal with the devil. There's nothing wrong with wanting to be financially successful. In fact, it's a trait I admire."

Kate swallowed back her irrational desire to explain herself, to convince Jamie there was more to her than a driving need for wealth or fame. She didn't need Jamie's admiration—and she was angry with herself for wanting it—but she did need her approval if she had any chance of getting the sponsorship.

Jamie barely caught the glimpse of distaste on Kate's face before it was carefully masked again. She nodded at the horse. "Do I get to see you ride today, or are we just going to stand around and talk?"

Kate turned without a word and led Topper down the barn aisle with Myra at her side. Jamie followed the trio out into the sunshine, watching with irritation as Myra took hold of Kate's bent knee and vaulted her into the saddle. They walked to the outdoor arena and stood in the center of the ring while Kate trotted the horse around to warm up.

"Don't you usually bring a bright light to shine in someone's eyes when you interrogate them?" Myra asked casually as she leaned against a jump standard.

"I'm just doing my job," Jamie said, her voice neutral.

"Oh. So, does it actually say 'bitch' on your business cards?"

Jamie chose to ignore that comment. Myra was obviously feeling protective toward Kate, but Jamie still wasn't sure whether it was simply because they were friends, or more than that. "Have you and Kate known each other long?" Jamie asked, her eyes never leaving Kate as she watched her canter some circles and figure eights.

"We've been good friends since high school," Myra answered.

Jamie nodded, determined not to ask how good. "How good?" *Damn.*

Myra only laughed and gave her a shrug before she moved away to set a small jump for Kate. Jamie watched the rest of the schooling session in silence. Without knowing the technicalities of jumping, she was unable to do more than appreciate Kate's grace as she took the horse over a series of gradually higher fences. They made it look simple, and Jamie recognized that as an accomplishment in any sport. She still felt frustrated at her inability to see past the detached, impersonal façade Kate showed her, and it didn't help to watch Myra go out of her way to be teasing and intimate with Kate, laying a hand on her thigh while they talked about the horse's performance and bringing up personal references that made them both laugh. She figured most of it was an act, motivated by Myra's realization that Jamie had revealed a less than professional interest in Kate, but it still upset her. She was used to being the enigma in any situation, not the one who was too easy to read.

"Very nice. The two of you seemed comfortable together," Jamie said when Kate dismounted next to her. Her mind was still wondering about Kate and Myra's relationship, but the phrase sounded as if it would work for the horse as well.

"I've had him for five years," Kate said as she loosened her horse's girth and removed her riding helmet. She smoothed her blond hair carefully. "I did most of his training."

"Maybe your friend can take care of the horse while you show me around?" Jamie suggested as they started back toward the barn.

"Oh, um…sure," Kate said, turning to Myra. "Do you mind?"

Myra smirked at Jamie and reached for Topper's reins. "Glad to," she said easily, taking Kate's helmet. "Just stay out of the hay barn," she tossed over her shoulder with a grin.

Jamie glared at Myra's back, fully understanding the half-joking threat from one alpha female to another. As if a roll in the hay was what she had in mind. Although now that Myra had brought it up…

"There's nothing wrong with my hay barn," Kate assured her with a confused frown. "I'm not sure why she said that, but I'll be happy to show it to you if you want."

"Maybe later," Jamie said, fighting back a grin. It would have been more tempting if Kate had realized what she was offering. Instead, they veered off to the left and came to a small barn. Each of the stalls had a paddock attached.

"The stallion's name is Guns Blazing," Kate said as they walked through the barn and into a large stall. "He'll be out of quarantine in about a week, and then he'll come here to stay."

Kate went on to explain how horses imported from Europe were quarantined on arrival, and that the process was longer and more involved for a mare or stallion that could be used for breeding than for a gelding. Although Jamie had read about all of this while doing her research, she let Kate talk without interrupting. Reading about any subject rarely could compare with listening to someone speak in the lingo and shorthand of an expert in the field.

"My old trainer is brokering the deal, and that's why I've been given first chance at him. If I can't...If I don't buy him, Marty will board him here until he's sold," Kate said. She gestured toward the open door leading out of the stall and into the sunshine. "I took out a divider to make a double stall and raised the paddock fence a few feet."

"Why the maximum security prison? Are you afraid he'll jump out?" Jamie asked, noticing that the fence was not only higher than the others on the property, but it had been reinforced with extra panels.

"Yes. I have several mares here as well," Kate said with a shrug. "If one of them comes in heat he might try to get to her."

"Men," Jamie said, rolling her eyes.

Kate joined in her laughter. "I know. That's why I prefer them gelded."

Jamie met her eyes and they smiled at each other, sharing a brief moment of camaraderie at odds with the antagonistic tone of their earlier conversation. One question answered. But where did she stand with Myra? Not that it was any of her concern.

Kate showed her around the rest of the property. She even insisted on taking Jamie through the hay barn, as if she had to prove she wasn't running a sweatshop in there. They ended the tour in a lounge attached to the tack room. The walls were covered with bright ribbons and pictures of Kate and her students riding in shows, as well as posters of a funny cartoon horse. She pointed out some of her students to Jamie, a hint of pride evident in her voice as she listed their accomplishments.

"I'm taking some of my kids to a show on Saturday, if you're interested in coming to watch me compete," Kate said. "I won't be jumping any higher than I did today, and it's just a local show. But if you have the time…"

"I'm free Saturday," Jamie said. She usually spent her weekends working, but after looking at the photos of Kate riding in those tight breeches, with an expression of intent concentration on her face, Jamie decided she could definitely make the time to see more of her.

"I'll get the directions," Kate said. She went over to a corner of the lounge where she had a makeshift office and opened a drawer in her file cabinet. Jamie was tempted to follow and peer over her shoulder, but she walked around for a closer look at the pictures instead.

"Did you draw these?" Jamie asked, stopping in front of one of the posters. The horse was reeling around with an apparent concussion after a fall, and the poster warned riders not to forget their safety helmets.

"Yes," Kate said with obvious embarrassment, as if she wished she had removed the sketches before Jamie's arrival. She handed Jamie a schedule for the show. "They're silly, but the kids like them. Here are directions to the show grounds, and I've circled my classes. Just find the show office when you get there, and they'll tell you where my horses are stabled."

Jamie accepted the paper and the change in subject. She nearly asked Kate to draw a horse for Anna's room, but she quickly censored the idea. Those were two worlds that shouldn't meet, so she changed the subject instead.

"We still have a ways to go before we reach a decision about your proposal, but you have a nice place here and you seem capable of taking good care of the horse you want," Jamie said. Against her better judgment, she cast about for something to say to help her break through to a more personal side of Kate. This distant, collected woman didn't seem to belong in a barn that had walls covered with photos and handmade posters. "I'll bet your students will enjoy having such a high-caliber horse around the barn."

"Not for long," Kate said. "I'd keep him here for a couple of months until I can sell the farm, then we'll head to Florida for the winter circuit. After that, I'll be traveling most of the time and will probably be based somewhere on the East Coast."

Jamie looked at her in surprise. "But you said you wanted a chance to ride this horse so you could make a name for yourself as a trainer and teacher. I thought you wanted to expand on what you're doing here."

"Well, I do," Kate said, some discomfort showing through her carefully composed expression. "But my students only ride in local shows. I'll be able to teach at a higher level on the East Coast. The move won't hurt Davison and Burke's publicity, though, since the stallion and I will always be listed in programs as being from Portland."

"What about your horse?"

"Topper? He's for sale, too. I've had some interest in him already, but nothing's worked out yet."

Jamie suspected that for a more motivated seller, those deals would have worked out just fine. "So you're giving up all of this and starting from scratch with the stallion?"

Kate frowned and looked around, refusing to meet Jamie's eyes. "I'll miss this place, but I can't pass up the chance to be successful on a level I just can't reach from here."

Jamie heard a waver in her voice, a brief slip into a Southern drawl. She stepped closer, unsure whether she was drawn to the small sign of weakness or if she felt compelled to offer some comfort. Kate turned toward her again and her eyes widened as if surprised to find Jamie standing close to her. It was too easy to reach over and trail a finger down a strand of blond hair that had worked its way out of Kate's ponytail, to let the same finger trace along Kate's flushed cheekbone. Jamie watched as Kate struggled to maintain her composure, but although she could keep the distant iciness etched over her pale features, she couldn't hide the emotions flickering in her green eyes. Jamie leaned closer and frowned as she saw the subtle shifts in Kate's expression.

"You don't want to go," she said in surprise.

Kate shook her head slightly. "There are always sacrifices. But I want this."

"Be careful what you ask for," Jamie warned as she lowered her mouth toward Kate's.

"Oh, I didn't realize you were having a business meeting in here," Myra said from the doorway. Jamie didn't move, but Kate scurried a few steps away from her.

"We were having a private conversation," Jamie said coldly.

"It's all right, Myra," Kate said, her cheeks bright red but her voice calm and devoid of any hint of a drawl. "I was just telling Jamie about my plans to move back east."

Myra settled her shoulder against the wall and crossed her arms. "Then you don't mind if I hang out and listen. Your move affects me, too, you know."

"Actually I need to get going," Jamie said stiffly. "Thanks for showing me around, Kate. I'll see you on Saturday."

❖

"Damn," Kate sputtered when she heard Jamie's car door slam shut. Her eyes filled with unshed tears as she walked down the barn aisle toward her horse, leaving Myra behind.

"Hey, sorry I interrupted back there," Myra said when she finally caught up. She peered closer at Kate who was leaning against Topper's side. "Are you crying? What did she do to you?"

"She didn't do anything, but I did. I just blew my chance at her bank's money."

"How?" Myra asked, running a brush over Topper's sleek coat. "It looked like the two of you were getting along quite well."

Kate shook her head. The memory of Jamie's touch still burned. Once again she had felt a ridiculous urge to let her feelings show without monitoring her every word and move. "I let down my defenses a little bit and she could see I have mixed feelings about leaving here."

"Of course you do," Myra said soothingly. "You love your students and it's only natural you'll miss them. Your Miz Callahan can't be such an uncaring freak she'd hold that against you."

Kate smiled briefly at Myra's drawn out *Ms*. "If she has any doubt and thinks I'm not fully committed to this…"

"No one could, Kate." Myra assured her. "What did she mean about seeing you on Saturday?"

"She's coming to watch me ride in the show this weekend, so I guess you're right to say she hasn't turned me down yet."

Myra laughed. "She's not likely to turn you down no matter what you offer."

"Did she say anything to you about the sponsorship?"

"Not about that, but she was fishing for information about you. She wanted to know if we're lovers."

"She asked that?" Kate asked in disbelief.

"Not in so many words, but it's what she meant," Myra said, cleaning Topper's hoof with a metal pick.

"Very funny. You've seen the way she looks at me. There's no way she'd think of me like that."

Myra stood up and faced Kate. "How exactly does she look at you?"

Kate shrugged. For a moment, she had thought Jamie was looking at her with desire, but it was only in her imagination. She was letting her own attraction color what she saw, and she knew Jamie had no interest in her beyond her PR value. "Like I'm not worth her time. Compared with the other investments her company makes, the money I need is insignificant."

Myra moved on to Topper's next hoof and bent to clean it. "Just because she deals with multi-million-dollar investments doesn't mean she has that kind of money herself. And yes, I saw her car and clothes, so I don't think she's broke. But her interest in you has nothing to do with dollar signs."

Kate shook her head with a sigh. "You heard her. For people like Jamie Callahan, everything is about dollar signs. I just need to make her believe I fit in that world. It's the only way I can convince her I deserve the sponsorship, that I can handle it."

"Right. Because there's no way a woman would be into you for any other reason. It's not like you're beautiful or smart or funny."

"Say what you want, Myra," Kate said as she unclipped Topper from the crossties so she could lead him out to a paddock. "Our interest in each other is only business, not personal."

"And that's why she's calling you Kate and not Kaitlyn? The only people who call you that besides me are your students. Everyone who matters to you calls you by your legal name."

Although she said it in a joking tone, Kate knew Myra meant what she said. She stopped walking and laid her hand on her best friend's arm. "You matter to me. You know that, don't you?"

"In a way. But you want to move in a certain social circle and you think Kate doesn't fit in there. Neither does Myra, but at least she doesn't give a damn."

"My mom always hated it when people called me Kate Brown," Kate finally admitted with a small laugh as she turned Topper loose. "She said it was too pedestrian and the right people would never take me seriously."

"Well, Jamie didn't seem to find anything wrong with your name. And judging by the focus of her attention, she was pretty impressed with your ass as well."

Kate burst out laughing at the ludicrous suggestion that Jamie Callahan might think of her at all that way. She figured Myra's teasing was only meant to take her mind off the interview, and she squeezed her friend's shoulder in appreciation as they headed back to the barn.

❖

Jamie was still absorbed in work when Jenn came into her office after five. She had restaurant trade journals scattered over her desk, and she was busily scratching out notes on a legal pad. Jenn cleared her throat twice before Jamie glanced up.

"Hey, Jenn," Jamie said, rubbing a hand over her eyes. She had spent the past few hours trying to get a grasp of the industry's trends so she could better predict the earning potential of a new Indian restaurant. She handed her assistant a stack of yellow pages filled with scrawled handwriting. "Can you type these up for me?"

Jenn didn't even reach for the papers. "No. It's time to go home now."

"Okay, tomorrow then," she said, not bothering to check her watch. She waved the notes until Jenn took them with a sigh.

Jenn flipped through the pages and squinted as she tried to read the hastily written words. "Why can't you type your notes like a normal twenty-first-century person?"

Jamie tapped her pen against her temple. "I can't type fast enough to keep up with this," she said, her attention wandering back to her work even as she spoke.

"Well, you apparently can't write fast enough either," Jenn commented with a frown.

"Just be grateful I double-check my own math and don't make you decipher the numbers," Jamie said. She flipped through a couple of pages in a journal before she registered the fact that Jenn was still standing by her desk. "You're still here."

"So are you. Why don't you go home to your family and finish this later?"

Jamie rolled her eyes at the overbearing tone Jenn always assumed when she was about to give a lecture. "I have to make up for the time I was out of the office this morning. I promise I'll leave in a few minutes. Now go home and enjoy your evening."

"A few minutes means a few hours once you lose track of time."

"Look, Jenn, I'll leave when I'm finished. I have to go watch a horse show this weekend, so I need to get through these journals in order to be ready for next week's meeting with Mr. Sanjiv. And why am I explaining myself to you?"

"A horse show," Jenn said with a smile, leaning her hip casually on Jamie's desk and ignoring Jamie's raised eyebrow at her insolence. "Sounds like fun."

"Not fun. Work."

"Another meeting with Ms. Brown, hmm? She certainly is beautiful and she seems confident enough not to take any crap from—"

"That's enough," Jamie said sharply, only making Jenn's smile broader. "Kate is a potential client, nothing more."

"Oh, *Kate* means nothing to you personally. Good to hear it," Jenn said with a laugh as she stood up.

Jamie sighed. "Can you get Elaine on the line before you go?" she asked.

"Call her yourself," Jenn said as she shut the door.

CHAPTER FOUR

Before sunrise Saturday morning, Kate stood on a step stool and swiped a wet sponge over her hunter's mane, preparing her for the show. The mare shook her head, annoyed by the water dripping down her neck, and Kate unsuccessfully tried to shield herself from the spray. She rubbed the cold water off her face with the sleeve of her sweatshirt and tossed the sponge into a bucket. She and her students were huddled along the edge of the temporary stabling, using its weak lighting as they braided their horses' manes in the predawn darkness. Mumbled conversations, the buzz of insects, and the occasional stomp of a horse's hoof were the only sounds Kate could hear. She loved the early-morning quiet of horse show days, even today with the threat of Jamie's attendance hanging over her. While her horses and students were calm and barely awake, and she only felt the chaos of the upcoming show as a hint of anticipation, Kate could almost block the sensation of Jamie's presence from her mind.

Almost. She separated a section of mane with cold-numbed fingers and plaited it tightly halfway down the hair before she added a piece of black yarn and finished the braid. She fought back the image of Jamie's finger trailing along the loosened strand of her own hair. Just five more braids and she would take a break for some coffee. She still couldn't believe she had asked Jamie to come today. She had gotten caught up in stories about her students, and the invitation had just popped out. She'd tried to take it back, to let

Jamie know the little show wasn't worth her time, but it had been too late. She glanced down the aisle at her young riders. They were calm and well behaved now, still groggy and sleep deprived, but their energy level would rise with the sun. She didn't know how she would be able to control them, ride her own horses, and still have time to impress Jamie.

She drained the last of her coffee and returned to braiding. The mare dozed while Kate tied the braids into small knots along the crest of the horse's neck. Kate was relieved she didn't have to do the same to Topper since his jumper classes were scored only on performance and not on appearance. He hated to stand still for long, and he would have frayed Kate's nerves more than they were already. She needed to convince Jamie she was good enough for the sponsorship, but more than that, she wanted to impress her for reasons that were entirely too personal. She had a quick vision of finishing a successful round on Topper and having Jamie congratulate her with a hug. Kate shook her head as vigorously as her mare had, trying to dislodge the image. She might need to dump the bucket of cold water over herself if she couldn't remove the distracting thoughts. She snipped the loose ends of yarn off the neat row of braids and returned the mare to her stall. Her priority was the sponsorship. Everyone and everything else had to take second place.

❖

"I'm sorry, but I thought I told you about this last week," Elaine said calmly as she wiped down the table after their Saturday breakfast. She tucked a wisp of gray hair back into her neat bun, refusing to meet Jamie's angry gaze, and carried the last of the serving dishes into the kitchen.

Jamie followed closely on her heels, a stack of syrupy plates in her hands. "And I told you I have to work today. Can't you change your plans?"

Elaine sighed as she started to rinse the dishes. "Usually I could, but my sister's been looking forward to my visit. She hasn't been well, you know."

"Exactly what's wrong with her?" Jamie asked skeptically.

"Gout," Elaine answered without hesitating.

"Liar," Jamie muttered under her breath, making Elaine turn away from the dishwasher she was loading and put her fists on her hips.

"I heard that," she said sternly. "Shall I get her doctor to write a note as proof?"

"Yes," Jamie said, leaning against the marble counter with her arms crossed over her chest. Elaine had moved in three years ago, soon after Anna had come there to live, and Jamie was grateful enough to have found her that she was willing to put up with Elaine's routine comments about her workaholic tendencies. But this obvious deception was pushing things too far, and Jamie didn't have time to deal with it today.

"Anna won't be a problem. She can bring some books and games with her. You won't even know she's in your office."

"You know damned well I won't be in the office today," Jamie said through gritted teeth, keeping her voice low in case Anna was in earshot. "I don't know when you and Jenn cooked this up, but I'm not going to put up with it today. You have to stay here with Anna."

"Or what? You'll fire me? Go ahead."

The two women stared at each other for several seconds. "Fuck," Jamie said finally, giving in. Elaine was trying to force her to take Anna to the horse show, and there wasn't anything she could do about it. Jamie needed her, and she knew it.

"I certainly hope you won't use that kind of language around Anna," Elaine remarked as Jamie stomped out of the kitchen.

❖

"Can we put the top down?" Anna asked once Jamie had buckled her into the backseat of the Mercedes.

"Maybe on the way home," Jamie said as she got in and fastened her own seat belt. "We're going to be on the freeway, and I don't want us to look too windblown when we get there."

Anna accepted Jamie's response with her usual stoicism, apparently too thrilled about the prospect of spending time with her aunt at a horse show to let one small disappointment ruin the day. Jamie started the engine and backed out of the driveway, glancing at her niece in the rearview mirror as they drove out of the condo's parking lot. Anna's strawberry-blond hair was a few shades lighter than Jamie's, and her eyes were as blue as her mother's had been. Today, they were lit up with excitement, and Jamie's heart constricted as she turned her gaze to the road ahead. What she wouldn't give to be driving Anna to a show so she could ride her own pony instead of having to watch from the sidelines.

She tried to come up with a way to strike up a conversation, but nothing came to mind, so she stayed quiet. Anna seemed fine with that, accustomed to the silence on the rare occasions she and Jamie were alone together. Elaine and Jenn might think Jamie should spend more time with Anna, but they didn't understand the pain she felt every time she looked at her niece. Grief when she saw the echo of her lost sister in Anna's eyes, guilt over the role she had played in Sara's accident, an infuriating inability to ever make things right for her niece. She paid for the best doctors, private schools, and presents for Anna, but those things could never ease her pain. She needed something more, but Jamie didn't have anything besides money to give. She felt her inadequacy in every interaction. Anna needed to spend less time with her, not more. She was better off in Elaine's comforting presence, no matter what the older woman believed.

Jamie easily found the show grounds, but it took a few minutes of driving among the horse trailers before she spotted a convenient parking space. By that time, Anna was almost bouncing on her seat in anticipation. When Jamie reached into the back to pick her up, she threw her arms around her aunt's neck in a rare show of affection.

"Thank you for bringing me here," she whispered, her voice filled with gratitude over the outing Jamie had spent the morning fighting to avoid. Jamie busied herself with the process of getting Anna settled in her wheelchair so she could hide the sudden sting of pain she felt at Anna's simple touch.

"Be careful on the gravel," she said roughly as she pushed Anna's chair along the rutted path. She hoped her niece would think it was just her customary gruffness, and not raw emotion, thickening her voice. As she had expected, the show grounds weren't designed to be convenient for a person in a wheelchair, and the constant maneuvering around piles of horse manure and thick tufts of grass was tricky.

They avoided most of the horse traffic and eventually found the show office. It was housed in a single-wide with wooden steps, so Jamie wheeled Anna to a shady spot and set her brake.

"I need to ask where my client's horses are stabled," she said. "You stay right here and wait for me, and then we can go watch the show."

Anna nodded at her then turned her attention back to the large animals and their well-dressed riders moving back and forth in the open area between the office and the rows of temporary stalls. Jamie glanced over her shoulder as she walked toward the trailer. Anna looked so small and helpless in her chair and her pink T-shirt with a picture of a horse nosing a striped cat. Jamie felt uncomfortable leaving her alone and she hurried up the steps to the office.

She was out again in a matter of seconds, with directions to Kate's location, but Anna had moved from her protected spot under the trees. She had apparently given in to the temptation of the beautiful animals and was wheeling her way across the gravel while Jamie jogged toward her. A gray horse shied away from the metal chair, nearly unseating his rider.

"Watch it, kid!" the girl shouted angrily, jerking on her reins and glaring at Anna. "Get that chair away from the horses."

Jamie could see Anna's face turn red with embarrassment as she tried to turn her wheelchair quickly on the loose gravel. The movement only brought her face to face with another horse that snorted in fear at the unaccustomed sight.

"Hey, you shouldn't be out here," a man said rudely, moving the nervous horse out of Anna's way.

Anna aimed toward the back of the stabling area, leaving Jamie to glower at the riders who had dared yell at her niece. "What the hell do you think you're doing, screaming at a little girl like that?"

"She's scaring the horses," the man said with a shrug, leading his horse in the opposite direction.

"And that gives you the right to yell at a child?" Jamie called after him. She wanted to go kick his scrawny ass, but she saw Anna turn the corner and head behind the last row of stalls, so she rushed after her. She came around the end of the barn and skidded to a halt. Anna was on a collision course with Kate, and Jamie pulled back into the shadows so she could watch and see what happened. She was so furious, she hoped Kate would say something rude to Anna so she could scream at her, tell her to take her million-dollar dream horse and go to hell.

Kate was holding Topper's reins as she tightened the girth on his saddle when she noticed the wheelchair heading her way. She held out a hand to stop the little girl.

"Whoa there," she said, squatting so they were at eye level. "Where are you off to in such a hurry?"

"I was in the way. My chair scared the horses."

"Well, some of these prissy show horses are scared of anything new," Kate said, keeping her voice steady when all she wanted to do was take her riding crop to the people who had made the girl cry. "I'm Kate. What's your name?"

"Anna."

Kate brought her horse a little closer. "Anna, do you want to meet Topper? He's not afraid of wheelchairs, but he might maul you looking for a treat."

She watched Anna's expression shift from wariness to delight as the gentle horse nuzzled her hands. Kate had seen similar transformations, hundreds of times, but she got choked up whenever she watched such a powerful reaction to a horse. She dug a sugar cube out of the pocket of her breeches and showed Anna how to hold it for Topper.

Jamie sagged against the stable wall as she listened to Anna's giggles ring out. She tried to get control of her response as she watched the elegant woman, with her beautifully fitted show clothes and her white-blond hair in a neat bun, kneel on the ground next to her niece. The two laughed together as Kate helped Anna feed Topper a lump of sugar.

"I love horses," Anna said in a normal voice as she stroked the bay's nose. "I wish I could ride one."

"Maybe you could someday," Kate started, making Jamie snap to attention and stride out of her hiding place. "I teach—"

"Anna," Jamie interrupted in a clipped voice. "Go back to the car and wait for me."

"But Aunt Jamie…"

"Now. Go." She waited until Anna had said good-bye to Kate and Topper in a low voice and wheeled herself down the aisle. "How dare you say something like that to her," she said in a dangerous tone. She watched Kate's mossy green eyes widen in concern.

"I didn't mean—"

"Didn't mean to tell her she might be able to ride a horse someday? Didn't mean to imply her spine might magically heal itself and she'll be able to use her legs again?"

"Jamie, please listen," Kate started, reaching toward her, but Jamie backed away in the direction Anna had taken.

"How dare you hurt her like that?" Jamie wanted to say more, wanted desperately to say something to make her anger disappear, to make Anna healthy again. But there were no words to do either one. She gestured helplessly with her hands and walked away from Kate.

The drive home seemed endless, and the lowered convertible top and a fast food burger and milkshake weren't enough to shake Anna's depressed mood. Jamie finally gave up, and they went home and to their separate rooms. There wasn't anything she could buy Anna that would make it better, and nothing she could say to herself would ease the disappointment of discovering Kate's insensitivity. She had been drawn to Kate against her better judgment and had foolishly moved close enough to get hurt.

Chapter Five

Jamie sat back in her chair and tried not to fidget while the nervous waiter moved dishes around to make room on her table. She had ordered everything on the menu at the Taj Mahal so she could better gauge the restaurant's chance of making it as a chain. The kid's hands were shaking so badly he nearly upended her water glass with a platter of chicken tikka masala. Jamie snatched the glass out of the way just in time.

"Why don't you bring the rest out later," Jamie said, working to keep her voice calm so she didn't snap at the young man. He nodded and left her with a table full of steaming food. When she'd told the owner she wanted to try a little of everything, she had assumed he would send out small samples of the various dishes. Instead, she had full-sized portions of each menu item. Jamie sighed and speared a piece of chicken, ignoring the curious stares of the other patrons. She still was too angry to have much appetite after the weekend's fiasco, and she should have had Jenn cancel this appointment. She had only come because she knew the owner had planned ahead to have her meal ready.

In truth, she admitted to herself, she'd needed to get out of her office. She had spent the morning pacing, for once not working or even thinking about work. Instead, her mind still fumed about Anna's experience at the horse show. All of Jamie's anger had focused on Kate Brown, and she wanted nothing more than to drive over to that woman's barn and personally deny her sponsorship application. But if she admitted her personal feelings were in control of her business decisions, then she would be letting Kate win. She'd send the application back to the PR department without a recommendation one way or the other. Someone else could handle it. Her lack of endorsement would be enough to guarantee its denial without making her appear responsible.

She tossed some rice onto her plate with more force than necessary, the loud clink of the serving spoon drawing everyone's eyes to her once again. She didn't need to take her frustration out on the restaurant's plates, so she took a deep breath and told herself to relax. She had finally been forced to leave her home last night since she couldn't stand Elaine's constant trips between Anna's room, where she tried to comfort the crying girl, and Jamie's den where she repeatedly apologized for her plot to send the two to the show together. After an awkward attempt by Jamie to talk to her niece, she gave up and headed into the city and the first bar she came across. She had spotted a likely candidate—dark hair, lovely olive skin, curvaceous figure—having a couple of drinks with co-workers, and she started her usual seduction routine. She initiated a physical connection, made eye contact, then walked away in order to let her target think she was making the first move. Jamie could sense the woman following her as she made her way through the crowd, but instead of slowing her stride to allow herself to be caught, she dropped her glass on a table and walked quickly out of the bar. She got in her car without a backward glance and sped off toward the freeway. She spent the next couple of hours driving aimlessly along Portland's highway system, her Mercedes obliging her need to push every turn faster than she should. The release from a casual sexual encounter would have been more satisfying, and probably safer, but Jamie realized she couldn't subject a stranger to the anger simmering just below her smooth surface.

The bells on the door jingled, breaking Jamie out of her trance, and she looked up to see Kate entering the restaurant. She forced aside the brief rush of pleasure at seeing Kate and refocused instead on her earlier anger. Jenn must have told her where Jamie was eating lunch—and probably drew her a goddamned map to the restaurant—

even after Jamie had explicitly told her she didn't want to see or talk to Kate today. Now she would have to fire the best assistant she had ever had.

"What the hell do you want?" Jamie asked coldly as Kate marched up to her and slammed a pamphlet down on the only patch of empty table she could find. Jamie refused to look at it, maintaining relentless eye contact with Kate. Her ivory skin looked more pale than normal and there were dark circles under her eyes. Jamie was irritated she even noticed those things, let alone that she felt a twinge of compassion for the woman.

"Read it," Kate demanded rather loudly, gesturing at the brochure. Jamie again detected a slight Southern drawl in the woman's angry voice. She opened her mouth to refuse, but Kate repeated herself more softly. "Please. Read it."

Jamie looked at the cover photo and then, after a quick glance at Kate, skimmed through the information about the North American Riding for the Handicapped Association. When she finished she ran a hand wearily over her eyes and swore under her breath.

"I run an accredited therapeutic riding program at my barn," Kate said. "When I told your niece she might be able to ride, that's what I meant."

"I thought..."

"I know," Kate said gently. "You were angry because Anna had been hurt by what those other riders said, and you took it out on me without giving me a chance to explain."

"Yes," Jamie admitted. "And I'm sorry."

"Well, good," Kate said, crossing her arms over her chest. She seemed unsure of what to do now that Jamie had apologized.

"Sit down." Kate hesitated, so Jamie stood and pulled out a chair for her. "You came all this way to yell at me, you might as well sit."

Kate dropped into the chair, keeping her back well away from Jamie's hands as she scooted closer to the table. Going from anger to guilt to a perverse relief that Kate wasn't the evil bitch she had thought was a bit much to process, so Jamie returned to her seat and just watched Kate for a moment while her mind struggled to catch up with her emotions. She was caught by surprise at how much she had really wanted there to be more to Kate than ambition and cold poise. She had felt betrayed when she thought the glimpse of warmth and kindness had been false, but now it seemed more dangerous to know that was the real Kate. How much harder would it be to ignore her attraction if she had to acknowledge it might be more than physical?

Jamie forced her mind away from those emotions, focusing instead on physical details while she struggled to control her thoughts. She observed Kate with an objective eye. Even though this wasn't a business meeting and Kate had obviously been upset by their encounter over the weekend, Jamie noted she was carefully dressed as if she were coming for an interview. The beige slacks and silky lilac shell made her look distant and professional even as her eyes flashed with heat that showed she obviously cared about the work she was doing. Jamie wondered if she would spend their entire professional relationship misreading this woman.

Jamie finally broke the silence, reaching for a piece of naan and gesturing for the waiter. "Have some food. There's plenty."

The waiter appeared with an empty plate which he simply handed to Kate since there wasn't room on the table. Jamie sighed and juggled the dishes, reorganizing the table so Kate wouldn't have to eat off her lap.

"This all smells good," Kate said politely as she took a small scoop of lentils.

Jamie laughed at her attempt to make the gluttonous lunch seem socially acceptable. "The owner wants us to invest in a second restaurant. I wanted to try his food."

"Oh, good," Kate said with apparent relief. "I didn't want to be rude. Couldn't he have just sent out a little bit of everything?"

"There's a thought," Jamie said sarcastically. She waved around the room at the other diners who were watching the pair surreptitiously. "But that would have lacked the entertainment value of this feast. Your little scene helped as well."

They ate quietly for a few minutes while Jamie tried to wrap her mind around the fact that just this morning she had wanted to kill Kate Brown, and now they were sitting down to lunch like old friends.

"Do you mind if I ask what happened to Anna?" Kate asked.

Jamie leaned back and folded her arms. "It was a few years ago," she began awkwardly. This wasn't something she discussed with people unconnected to Anna's medical team. "My sister took a turn too fast and ran her car into the median on the freeway. She was killed instantly, and Anna's lower spine was fractured. She spent the first year in and out of the hospital and she's had several surgeries."

Jamie left it at that, without filling in the rest of the gaps. Without saying Sara had come over asking Jamie for money again, using Anna as her pawn to make Jamie pay. Without saying she and Sara had gotten into a screaming fight, and that was why she had driven off in anger, too fast, out of control. Anna was only six, frail and helpless in her hospital bed, when Jamie had needed to step in as a mother. She had given up wondering why the universe kept forcing her into the role when she was such a failure at it.

"Has she lived with you since then?" Kate asked, her food untouched as she listened to Jamie.

"Yes. There wasn't a father in the picture. Actually, there were several candidates, but I don't think even Sara knew which one was really Anna's dad," Jamie said, her matter-of-fact tone glossing over the nights spent worrying about her sister, the failed attempts to talk her out of her wild ways and poor decisions. "I legally adopted Anna three years ago."

Kate seemed aware of Jamie's reluctance to continue the personal side of their discussion, as she turned the conversation back to the therapy program while she filled her plate with food. "Riding can be very beneficial for people with partial paralysis. The muscles used to stabilize the upper body while they're riding are similar to those used when we walk. Plus riding, just being around horses, is very…healing. The emotional breakthroughs are often greater than the physical ones."

Jamie moved the brochure around the table's edge with a fingertip. The thought of Anna on a horse without any control over her own body scared the shit out of her. She couldn't do much to help her niece, but at least she could keep her relatively safe in the confined world of her condo. "I'm sure it's helpful to some kids, but I'm not sure if it's a good idea for Anna. It doesn't sound very sensible."

"There's always some danger when it comes to horses and riding, I won't lie to you about that. But the rewards, the sense of freedom, are worth it," Kate said, in between bites of curried cauliflower. "All I'm asking is for you to think about it and talk to Anna's doctor. Just don't discount the idea right away. You saw how happy she was just to be around Topper."

"I promise I'll consider the idea," Jamie said. That was all she was prepared to offer.

"This guy really can cook," Kate observed, shifting the conversation as she took a second serving of tandoori chicken. Once again, she'd moved away from a subject Jamie deemed closed. Kate gestured toward another dish. "What's that one? Beef or lamb?"

"I have no idea," Jamie said, watching Kate lick sauce off her fingers. Her mouth suddenly felt dry and she took a drink of water. "When's the last time you ate?"

"Must have been early Saturday," Kate answered with a pointed look. "Something upset me and I lost my appetite."

"You seem to have found it again," Jamie observed. Now that her anger had blown over, Jamie moved on to the next pressing topic on her mind. "Since we're asking personal questions, what's the deal with you and Myra?"

Kate hesitated, her fork halfway to her mouth. "Myra? She's my best friend. Why do you ask?"

Jamie shrugged nonchalantly and busied herself by serving them each some fragrant potatoes. "I was just curious. She said you leaving town affected her as well, and I thought she might be going with you. As your lover?"

Kate choked on a bite of food and drank some water before she answered. "No. Myra and I met in high school when her softball team came to play and I was a cheerleader. We got caught kissing under the bleachers and the principal called in our parents. God, it was humiliating."

Jamie smiled. "Was that your first time being with another girl?"

"Yes. I guess I had known I liked girls for some time, but it was the first time I acted on my feelings. It was all over school by the next day. Not exactly how I would have planned on telling people."

"How did your parents react?"

Kate laughed and leaned back in her chair. "I remember sitting in the principal's office while he told them what happened. I could tell they were furious, and I thought it was because they had just found out their daughter was gay. It wasn't until the ride home that I learned they were angry because I was kissing someone from a public school whose parents didn't have any money or influence."

Jamie laughed out loud. "You're kidding."

"I'm serious. I remember Mom saying, 'I think the Wyckoffs' daughter is a lesbian. Why couldn't you date someone like her?'"

Kate's smile faded slightly. "The sad thing is, I did eventually date Judy Wyckoff. She was home from prep school for the summer and I managed to be everywhere she was. We inevitably hooked up. Myra and I stayed friends, at least, but never more than that."

"Do you always do what your parents want?"

Kate shrugged lightly, her expression indicating the subject should be closed. "I was young," she said simply. "And I liked Judy. It didn't seem wrong to spend time with her and get invited to be with the in-crowd. I don't use people like that anymore, of course."

"Now it's just horses. Topper is your new Myra, and the stallion is Judy Wyckoff," Jamie observed casually as she ate. She glanced up to see Kate looking at her with a shocked expression, and she hurried to apologize. "I'm sorry, that was rude. I have a habit of looking for patterns. It's not the same thing at all."

Kate accepted the apology with her usual grace, although Jamie's observation hurt. It echoed the guilty thoughts Kate had been having since she had made the decision to sell Topper and leave her farm. After a brief moment she closed off the emotions Jamie had obviously been able to read too clearly and returned to a light conversational tone. "What about you? That's the lesbian deal, isn't it? I share my first-time story and you share yours."

Jamie's gaze remained direct, but she shifted slightly in her chair and reached out to straighten her already perfectly parallel silverware. Kate recognized those subtle signs of discomfort, and under normal circumstances, she would have changed the subject of conversation. She chose to ignore Jamie's hints this time. She had been interrogated and scrutinized by Jamie throughout their short relationship, and turnabout was fair play. She enjoyed making Jamie as uncomfortable as she herself felt.

"I was twelve when my mom caught me playing a game of truth or dare with a neighbor girl," Jamie said. "We were just kids, so it was pretty innocent, but there was an obvious sexual element. She flipped and told my stepdad to punish me."

"What did he do?" Kate asked quietly, not sure she wanted to hear the answer. She had expected a Don Juan-type seduction story from Jamie. Not this.

Jamie only shrugged. "More than she had expected, I guess. It didn't work, though. I still like girls." She winked at Kate, her tone changing from intimate to casually flirting.

"Girlfriend?"

"I date…briefly," Jamie said.

"I see," Kate said with a slow nod. "Nothing serious, I take it. Has there ever been someone?" Jamie shifted more noticeably in her chair, but Kate didn't care if her question made Jamie squirm. For some reason, she wanted reassurance that Jamie was capable of being in love. For Anna's sake, Kate told herself. Not because Kate was beginning to feel like she was on a date with a very attractive woman. And talking about sex.

"I had been seeing someone for a few months, but it ended after Anna's accident. Theresa couldn't handle all the changes."

"Really?" Kate asked, surprised. "Anna seems so sweet. How could anyone look at that little girl and not care about her?"

"Well, they never actually met," Jamie said. "Anna was so vulnerable then, and I didn't want her to get close to someone since the relationship was bound to end anyway."

Kate didn't respond, reading between the lines of the story. She could only imagine the pain of losing a sister and watching Anna struggle through her recovery. Jamie had probably pushed her lover away to protect her own heart from the threat of further loss, not just Anna's.

Neither of them seemed interested in opening up any more conversational channels, so they finished their lunch without speaking. Kate eventually glanced at her watch and sighed. "I really should be going now. My parents are coming over this afternoon. Thank you for lunch. It was…nice."

Jamie stood when Kate did, as reluctant to see Kate leave as she had been angry when she walked in. "I'm glad we can put Saturday behind us. But I am wondering why you didn't mention the therapeutic program in your application."

"It's separate from my teaching business, and it's not a financially sound career move for me," Kate said as if the answer should have been obvious to Jamie. "The riders pay a small fee, and some insurance companies cover riding lessons, but the program barely breaks even."

Jamie was perplexed at the woman's inability to see how she could have used this program to her advantage. "But didn't it occur to you that running the program would be a good indication of character?" she asked as she walked to the front of the restaurant with Kate. "Or that it would help the PR angle if Davison and Burke sponsored you?"

Kate shook her head with a frown. "If I get the sponsorship, I'll spend most of my time traveling to horse shows. When I sell my barn, the therapeutic program might shut down. But there are others around Portland. If you do decide to let Anna try riding, there'll be places for her to go when I'm gone."

"We'll see," Jamie answered noncommittally, holding the door open for Kate. They shook hands and Jamie touched her briefly on the shoulder before she returned to her table. She couldn't eat another bite, but she wasn't quite ready to return to her office and the smug expression she knew would be on Jenn's face. Jamie sat alone, but her mind was crowded with the images Kate had forced her to remember. For a few moments she relived the darkness of the days after Sara died. She had been overwhelmed by grief and guilt over losing her sister and filled with doubts about her ability to take care of Anna. She could still hear the coldness in her voice when she told Theresa it was over between them, but she hadn't had a choice. Jamie couldn't risk relying on her, needing her, when she knew Theresa would probably leave her eventually. Jamie had survived on her own, but after her conversation with Kate, she started to wonder if mere survival was enough.

CHAPTER SIX

Kate was relieved to shed her business suit and slip back into worn Levi's and a T-shirt as soon as she got home. The weekend had been exhausting, even before the run-in with Jamie and her niece. She'd had five students in the show, as well as two of her own horses to ride, and she was up well before dawn each morning to braid horses' manes and muck stalls. Then that sweet little girl had wheeled into her barn aisle, tears streaming down a face Kate should have recognized as an innocent, youthful version of Jamie's. Kate had discovered firsthand why you shouldn't try to play with a cute bear cub. Mama Bear might be just around the corner, waiting to bite your head off.

Kate headed out to the barn to finish cleaning stalls before her parents arrived for tea. She usually got through all the barn chores well before noon, but today she had been too distracted to work until she could straighten things out with Jamie. She knew Saturday's argument had jeopardized her chances at the sponsorship, so she had forced herself to get dressed for business again and go into the city. Her anger at being so misjudged and her need to do anything she could to help Anna had helped bolster her confidence enough to face the rather terrifying Ms. Callahan.

She leaned against her pitchfork and let her mind wander back to their conversation. Since leaving the restaurant, she had run over her words so many times her head was starting to ache. She'd been so relieved to have fixed their misunderstanding, and so hungry after a rushed morning without breakfast, that she had let her guard down too much and talked to Jamie like a friend, or a date. Sharing intimate stories and asking personal questions were definitely taboo in a business relationship like theirs, and Kate flushed with embarrassment every time she recalled her freely offered commentary. Yet even in the midst of her shame, she had somehow enjoyed spending time with an intriguing woman like Jamie, and she tried in vain to stem her desire to learn more about her. She could tell there was much more to Jamie's life story than she had revealed, and the haunted look in Jamie's eyes had indicated not much of it was good. Kate tried to shrug off her curiosity and get back to cleaning. Jamie's personal life had nothing to do with her. She just needed the woman to make a decision about her sponsorship, and then they would be out of each other's lives.

Her unfocused thoughts made her late, and Kate was just sweeping out the barn aisle when she heard her parents' car drive in. "Damn," she muttered as she leaned the broom against a wall and ran toward the house. She slowed to a walk just as Don and Lily Brown were climbing out of their car.

"Mom, Dad, how nice to see you," she said a bit formally as she gave each of them a quick hug. "Come inside and I'll change before we have tea."

"Well, I certainly hope so, dear," her mom said, wrinkling her nose. "You smell like a horse."

Kate kept her polite smile pasted on her face as she led her parents into the house. She served them each a small glass of sherry before leaving them in the living room while she went into the back of the house to change. She shed her dutiful daughter persona along with her T-shirt as she rushed around her bedroom, flinging off her barn clothes and washing off as much dust and grime as she could. Less than five minutes later, she was back in the front room, wearing a flowery cotton top and khaki pants along with the appropriate smile.

"Finally," her mother said as she entered the room. Lily patted the couch and Kate sat next to her. "We have some exciting news. You'll never guess who we saw today!"

"Byron Hadley," her dad chimed in. Her parents grinned at each other happily while Kate tried to place the name.

"Do I know him?" she asked.

Her mother sighed. "Kaitlyn, he's the president of Hadley Accounting."

"They handle all the outside accounting for Davison and Burke," Don added helpfully when Kate still looked confused.

"Well, that's nice," she said.

"He's having a cocktail party at his house on Friday, and guess who's invited?"

"You?" Kate offered hopefully.

"No, silly. You are. We reminded Byron how close you and his daughter were in high school and how much you'd love to see her again, and he suggested you come to the party."

Kate swallowed some sherry, wishing it was straight bourbon. "I don't even remember her. What's her name?"

"That doesn't matter." Lily shrugged it off. "Most of the top executives from Davison and Burke will be there. It's a perfect opportunity for you to network and talk up your sponsorship."

Oh God. A happy reunion with a woman she didn't even remember, and yet another chance to socialize with Jamie Callahan.

Her parents were busy debating what outfit she should wear when her mother stopped and patted her knee. "Oh, Kaitlyn. This is what we worked so hard for all these years. This is why we left Kentucky to come here."

Lily paused and reached out to grasp the hand Don held out to her. "We did it all for you, to get you with the right sort of people. The kind of people who really matter in the world."

Kate would be able to buy the power and prestige her parents craved if she won the sponsorship. An opening to the right parties, the right connections. But she only saw more friendships with agendas, more pressure to conceal who she really was. She would have the excitement of riding a world-class stallion, but a million dollars couldn't buy what really mattered to her. Intimacy, belonging. She saw Jamie sitting in the restaurant, shifting in her chair as she told Kate details of her life she probably rarely shared. Kate had received her trust, for a brief moment, and it meant more to her than Jamie's approval of her sponsorship ever could.

Kate's dad nodded at her. "You've been right on the edge for so long, and this horse will take you even further than we imagined. Just think, no more cleaning stalls and messing around with these kids and their little horse shows. What would have happened if we had stayed on the farm in Kentucky? You wouldn't have had any of this."

Kate didn't say she enjoyed her barn and students. She didn't say she had loved Kentucky and had hated leaving. She had fond memories of laughter and love in their small bungalow, of riding ponies with the estate owner's kids. Her parents only remembered their work as a maid and stable hand on the big breeding farm where they met and fell in love. They hadn't wanted Kate to grow up and work in what they saw as servitude, and they had sacrificed so much to get her away from that. Now she had a chance to finally give them what they wanted for her. She knew she had the talent to ride an Olympic-level horse, so if she had the opportunity, did it really matter what she had to give up to make it happen?

She sat at the dining room table and ate fruit salad and finger sandwiches off china plates, pretending to have an interest in her parents' stories about people she barely knew. After lunch, her dad sat on the back porch and smoked while Kate and her mom planned her entire outfit for Friday's party. Although she would have preferred a cigarette to a fashion show, Kate was glad to see her mom so excited. She knew she had occasionally disappointed her parents with her lack of interest in social climbing, and now she had a chance to make them proud and to justify the sacrifices they had made. In her imagination, she pictured Jamie sitting on the couch observing them, adding her own name and LeeAnne Hadley's to the list of people Kate was willing to use to get what she wanted. Kate pushed the thought out of her mind. She made sure no one ever was hurt by her actions, so what did it matter if she took advantage of connections to move ahead in life? She only wished she could protect her own heart as easily.

Kate called Jamie's office as soon as her parents left and before she could change her mind. Jenn answered on the first ring and offered to put her through to Jamie, but Kate stopped her.

"No, please, I'd prefer to leave a message," she said, her words coming out in a rush. Her earlier conversation with Jamie had been about uncomfortable honesty, fleeting moments of openness. Kate had to be less than truthful in this call, and she didn't want to spoil her memory of their lunch together. "I'll be competing with the stallion at a show in Wilsonville in a few weeks and I wanted to invite Jamie…Ms. Callahan to come watch."

"I'm sure she'll be delighted to attend. I'll put it on her calendar," Jenn said.

Kate didn't think delighted was the word Jamie would have chosen. She gave Jenn the address and dates of the Country Classic while she mentally calculated the balance on her credit cards. "I'd like to reserve a hospitality tent at the show for the Davison and Burke employees and their guests," she said. A tent and refreshments at one of the most prestigious shows in the Northwest would cost more than she could afford. She was going far beyond buying a few new outfits in her attempt to get this horse, and not all of her sacrifices were financial. Before Jenn could respond, Kate pushed on. "And I hope I'll have a chance to see Ms. Callahan at Byron Hadley's party on Friday."

"Why yes, she'll be there. I called to accept the invitation for her this morning."

"Wonderful," Kate said, hoping her sigh wasn't audible over the phone. When she hung up, she wiped her sweaty palms and told herself the little lies didn't matter. And it was worth it to spend money she didn't have in order to get the money she needed. It was all part of the game.

❖

Jamie hung up the phone after talking to one of Anna's physical therapists and turned her office chair so she faced the Willamette River. She sighed wearily and let her mind wander as she watched the Hawthorne Bridge rise to let a tall sailboat pass underneath. Within seconds, traffic had stacked up on either side as the concrete deck slowly rose in the air. This was why she usually kept her back to the window. She could watch the activities along the river for hours, but she rarely allowed the sight of them to distract her from work.

Today was different, though. Even after she had returned from lunch with Kate, their misunderstanding from Saturday resolved, she still couldn't shake the woman from her mind. At every turn there seemed to be something new to learn about her, some odd aspect of her character that managed to escape her tightly reined-in public persona. Jamie could imagine her in high school, trying hard to fit in a social group and learning at a too-young age how to use people to her advantage. But Kate was compassionate by nature, and she couldn't hide the guilt she felt about benefitting from someone else. Jamie knew she'd hit a sore spot when she had carelessly compared Kate's sale of Topper to her betrayal of Myra. As an outsider, Jamie had a less emotional response to Kate's childhood actions, and she was certain Kate could easily have fit in any crowd without even trying. Kate was beautiful as a woman and had probably been very pretty as a teen. Add her easy charm and kindness, and Judy Wyckoff most likely would have jumped at the chance to date her no matter her motives. Jamie knew she would have, if there had been time for things like girlfriends during her high school years.

Jamie was simply too interested in Kate, and the feeling was frightening because it was so rare. Usually her interest in a woman didn't go further than her behavior between the sheets, but with Kate she wanted to know more. To ask more questions, to simply listen to her talk. And not just about the big issues, like her parents and her childhood, but about simple things like movies and food and music. When she started to picture herself and Kate walking along the riverfront holding hands, she abruptly swiveled her chair away from the window, swearing out loud as she banged her knee on the heavy desk.

In an attempt to resolve her obsession with Kate, Jamie had followed through on her promise to call Anna's doctor and ask about the possibility of letting her ride. Jamie had expected him to side with her and quickly dismiss the idea as ridiculous, and she had been surprised at his immediate and wholehearted endorsement of it. He enthused about how helpful therapeutic riding could be for Anna, not only for the physical reasons Kate had listed, but mainly for the psychological benefits. Jamie, still unconvinced, had called every other medical professional who had seen Anna in the past couple of years, hoping to find one who would agree with her that riding was unsafe. Not only did they all encourage her to give it a try, but they repeatedly spoke about horses lifting Anna's mood and being good for her mental well-being. Jamie did her best to care for Anna, but apparently everyone thought her niece had unmet emotional needs.

As call after call forced her to confront the issue, Jamie had to admit she had been so wrapped up in her own grief and guilt, and so concerned about protecting Anna, that she might actually be harming her niece.

Jenn tapped on the office door and Jamie felt a sense of relief when she entered. She needed the distraction of a work-related issue to get her mind off her personal problems.

"Kate Brown just called," Jenn said, dashing Jamie's hopes for some sort of pressing investment crisis. "She wants to reserve a tent at the next show for the bank to use."

"To sleep in?" Jamie asked with a confused frown.

Jenn laughed. "God, no. A hospitality tent. Food, drink, shade, that sort of thing."

"Sounds nice," Jamie said warily. "Can you find out how much it will cost?"

"Already did," Jenn said as she dropped a slip of paper on the desk in front of Jamie. She had itemized the cost of the tent, as well as catering and serving staff. Jamie raised her eyebrows in surprise as she read the total cost.

"She can't afford this. I'll get Dave to sign off on the expense, so make the reservations and charge it to the company."

"Already did," Jenn said as she turned to leave. She stopped halfway to the door. "Oh, and Ms. Brown said she'll be attending Byron Hadley's cocktail party on Friday and she hopes you'll be there as well. I said you would and I called the Hadleys to change your RSVP from no to yes."

"Do you even need me to be here?" Jamie asked, trying in vain to hide her smile.

"I'd prefer it if you telecommuted," Jenn said.

"Aw, you'd miss me," Jamie said to the closing door. Jamie turned back toward the river. She hated these networking parties and had stopped attending them as soon as she was successful enough to avoid work-related socializing. Still, she would probably see some acquaintances there, and it might be fun to catch up. She wondered what Kate would choose to wear to a party, and the vista in front of her faded into the background as she let her imagination wander to other forms of natural beauty.

CHAPTER SEVEN

For once in her life, Kate appreciated the extensive notes her parents had made her keep during her school years. She had lists of her friends, including details about the way they dressed, what hobbies they had, how their parents were connected. Throughout Kate's youth, those notes had dictated what clubs she joined, what movies she saw, even what food was in her family's fridge. They had encouraged her to add to them every night, with a diligence most parents reserved for homework. She found them tucked in her yearbook and was able to piece together a clear picture of LeeAnne Hadley before Friday's cocktail party.

Kate wondered what her friends would have written about her if they had been asked, but she figured they would only have been able to repeat the vague half-truths her family encouraged others to believe. That her wealthy parents worked in law and finance. That they were from a well-respected Kentucky family and that she had flown back there for her coming-out party. Not out of shame, but for her parents' sakes, she never revealed the truth. That her dad worked for a landscaping company that mowed lawns outside of banks, and her mom cleaned law offices at night. That they had gone to Kentucky to visit old friends and not for a debutante ball, thank God. She supposed the main goal in her life was to be accepted enough so other people took notes about her, so they'd be able to fit in *her* circle. Since few people ever saw past the façade she had erected, those notes would never capture the real her. She had always suspected there was so much more to her friends' lives as well, things that never were seen and never found their way into her notebook.

Kate left her Lexus with the valet and walked up the steps toward the Hadleys' brightly lit house. The Lexus had been another gift from her parents that they couldn't afford since they hated having people see her drive her beloved GMC pickup truck. She lingered in the shadows on the massive staircase and prepared herself for a night of playacting. Flirt with LeeAnne, be gracious with her hosts, and chat with every member of Davison and Burke she could find. Those were the easy ones. Being civil to Jamie Callahan and avoiding any physical contact or controversial conversation with her would be more difficult. Kate could still feel Jamie's hand resting on her shoulder when she'd left the restaurant after their lunch together. Such a simple touch, but it made Kate long for more. Kate added a mental warning to avoid too much alcohol as she put on a confident smile and walked toward the front door.

Kate's hosts were standing just inside the foyer, greeting their guests as they came through the door. Some instinct drew her eyes to the room behind them where she easily picked Jamie out of the crowd. She was deep in a conversation with two men, gesturing broadly as if trying to prove a point, so Kate felt safe to let her gaze rest on her for a few moments. Jamie was wearing a sleeveless gold top that brought out the same tones in her hair. The front of the blouse draped in a loose V, and Kate caught herself following it down toward Jamie's chest. She blinked to refocus her thoughts and stepped forward to meet the Hadleys. She introduced herself and Byron beckoned for his daughter to join them. Kate brushed off her sense of shame at using a weak connection just to be invited here. Jamie looked so confident, so natural among these people, and Kate felt like a fraud in comparison. She wanted to simply walk away from it all, but then LeeAnne came toward her with a welcoming grin. Kate ran a hand over her dress, smoothing the silky fabric against her thigh. She fit in here. She dressed the part, knew the right words to say. She started walking and met LeeAnne halfway across the foyer.

"LeeAnne, how good to see you again," Kate said with a big smile as she gave her former classmate a light kiss on the cheek. "I was thinking of you just the other day because *South Pacific* was on television. Do you remember when our high school drama club put it on?"

LeeAnne laughed with delight, placing her arm companionably over Kate's shoulder as she led her to the bar. "I haven't thought of that in ages," she said. "Didn't Jimmy what's-his-name knock over one of the palm trees during a love scene?"

"Yes," Kate said, joining in the laughter. She found herself drawn in by LeeAnne's wide smile, and she started to remember her as a person instead of just a sketched-out list of qualities. Judging by her skintight dress, LeeAnne apparently hadn't outgrown her love of red clothes. With her bright red hair the dress should have been a disaster, but LeeAnne had always been able to pull it off. "I hope you'll be revisiting your success with a rendition of 'Bali Ha'i' for this evening's entertainment?"

"Get me drunk enough and you never know what I'll do," LeeAnne said suggestively, leaning toward Kate and giving the impression she was already well on the way. "Speaking of which, what would you like?"

"Knob Creek Manhattan, easy on the vermouth," Kate told the tuxedoed bartender. She stepped just out of LeeAnne's reach and leaned an elbow on the bar, refusing to glance toward Jamie again. She kept her tone light since she was only interested in the kind of flirting that would end when the party did. "So, what have you been up to since high school?"

❖

Jamie stood across the room drinking a thirty-year-old Macallan and watched Kate's grand entrance to the party. When she had first come to work for Davison and Burke, she had dutifully attended the many social functions like this one and hated every moment of every one. She told herself the twinge of excitement she had felt about this party was due to her host's excellent taste in scotch and definitely not because Jenn had told her Kaitlyn Brown would be attending. Tonight Kate was playing wealthy socialite, Jamie noticed. She was wearing a halter dress in some sort of shiny, pale-gray material. The skirt was just short enough, and the back low enough, to be sexy but not slutty. The strappy high heels and tasteful emeralds that glinted at her throat and earlobes were the perfect accessories. She looked gorgeous, and apparently the red-haired LeeAnne Hadley thought so as well. For every inch Kate put between them, LeeAnne moved two toward her. Jamie decided it would be interesting to watch from a distance and see how Kate handled herself in this type of situation. She managed to observe their interaction for about five seconds before she strolled over to the bar and slid her arm around Kate's waist.

"You look beautiful tonight," she said, giving her a quick kiss on the temple. Kate looked as if she couldn't decide between fainting dead away at Jamie's greeting or laughing hysterically.

"Ms. Callahan, how nice to see you again," she said, hiding her amused smile by taking a sip of her drink. "You know our hostess, LeeAnne Hadley?"

Jamie reached out to shake the woman's hand. "Nice to meet you," she said, her left arm not leaving Kate's slender waist. "And how do the two of you know each other?"

"We went to the same schools in Wilsonville," LeeAnne answered. "And you two are..."

"Business associates," Kate said quickly, pulling away gently. Jamie let her arm fall away, but she stayed close to Kate. She tried not to ask herself what her possessive response meant.

"Well, I'll let the two of you discuss your...business. I have guests to greet, but I hope to have a chance to talk more before you leave." This last was obviously directed at Kate.

"Good friends?" Jamie asked, moving away now that the threat had gone.

"Good enough," Kate answered with a shrug. Jamie watched her take another drink out of her frosty glass. She raised her eyebrows in question and Kate continued. "Good enough to get me invited to this party. So I could see you."

Jamie swallowed some scotch, enjoying its smooth burn down the back of her throat. She had a feeling that flirting was simply part of Kate's party persona, so she tried not to take it seriously. Still, the shy smile and steady gaze made it difficult to care whether the suggestive undertones were real or designed to weaken Jamie's defenses and make her do Kate's bidding.

"You know," she breathed into Kate's ear, enjoying the delicate hint of Chanel as she leaned close, "it's going to take more than a few compliments to make me endorse your application."

"Exactly what will it take, Ms. Callahan?" Kate asked softly.

Sex, Jamie wanted to say. It suddenly seemed so simple. She was attracted to Kate, and that infatuation was making it difficult for her to concentrate at work, at home, everywhere. The easiest way to take care of it was just to sleep with her, get Kate out of her system, and then she would be back to her normal controlled self. It wouldn't be her most ethical business decision, but it also wasn't expressly against the rules. Since her attraction was only physical, having sex with Kate shouldn't have any bearing on her decision-making abilities. She tried to conveniently forget that her every reaction to Kate, since the woman had first walked into her office, had been emotional and not professional.

Jamie caught Kate watching her with those earthy green eyes that made such a startling contrast with her sophisticated outfit. Those same eyes flitted occasionally to the drape of gold material covering Jamie's breasts, and Jamie silently vowed to give Jenn a bonus for buying the top for her and insisting she wear it to the party. She stepped even closer, so her thigh brushed Kate's, and wondered why it was suddenly so difficult to find the right words to say. *Let me take you home so I can rip that dress off you.* Jamie could truthfully include propositioning women as one of her skills on a resume, but for some reason this felt different, and all of her usual lines were too awkward. She was about to just blurt something out when Kate's expression shifted in an instant, and Jamie straightened up and looked over her shoulder.

"Dave, good to see you," she said, her tone all business as she shook her boss's hand. "David Randall, I'd like you to meet Kaitlyn Brown."

"Ah, the girl who wants to buy a pony," he said. Jamie and Kate both laughed along with his joke.

"It's every girl's dream, isn't it?" Kate said with an innocent smile, all traces of her flirtatious side gone. *Damn*, thought Jamie, *she's good.*

They moved naturally from a conversation with Dave to one with a group of LeeAnne's college friends. Jamie stuck close to Kate's side as they mingled with various people, aware she was giving the impression they were there as a couple. They hadn't touched one another since leaving the bar, but the warmth between them was so palpable Jamie figured everyone could sense it. She let Kate do most of the talking, while she quietly wondered at her relief that they had been interrupted before she had managed to bring up her brilliant idea of sex. *How about I take you out to my Mercedes so I can make you come?*

She tried to distract herself by observing Kate's interactions with the other guests, and soon she became so interested in what she saw that she almost forgot about her plan to seduce Kate so she could move on with her life. She watched and eavesdropped in amazement as Kate changed her tone, expressions, and language like a chameleon, depending on who was nearby. It was subtle and masterful, Jamie decided. Kate never pretended to be someone else, but she would draw out specific aspects of herself to fit her company. She could move from flirtatious to intelligent to deferential in a heartbeat. Eventually Jamie got tired from simply watching the transformations and she had a feeling Kate must be exhausted.

She finally pulled Kate aside and took the empty Manhattan glass from her hand. "I need to talk to you," she said in a low voice, indicating a quiet corner. "I'll get us refills. Meet me over there." Kate agreed. If she was surprised or confused by the request, her perfectly composed expression didn't betray her.

"You really want this, don't you?" Jamie asked as she handed Kate her fresh drink and watched her expression shift to blank weariness once they were alone. "You just impressed the hell out of everyone in the room."

"I know I can do this. I have the talent, I just need the money." Kate's words were sincere and simple, but Jamie knew they were intended to meet her own expectations of forthrightness and honesty. "You'll come to the show and actually watch me ride this time? I'll show you what I can do."

Jamie ignored the suggestive nature of that statement. Kate was only talking about riding, nothing more personal. "Jenn already reserved the hospitality tent," she said.

Kate whipped her head toward Jamie in surprise. "I was supposed to do that. It was my suggestion, so I should pay."

Jamie shook her head. "It'll help me make a decision if I can watch you ride and see the horse in person, so to speak. The company is taking care of the tent and catering."

"I should, well…thank you," Kate said. Jamie didn't need the intimate knowledge she had of Kate's finances to interpret the relief evident on her face.

"You're welcome," Jamie said as she rested her shoulder against the wall near Kate. "So, I talked to Anna's doctor, and he said it might be okay for her to try lessons."

Kate's face lit up in the first real smile Jamie had seen all evening. "That's wonderful. She must be thrilled."

"I haven't told her yet," Jamie said with a shake of her head. "She'd be too excited to sleep, so Elaine and I decided to wait until we're sure before we tell her."

"Elaine?" Kate asked too casually, taking a sip of her drink.

"Her nanny," Jamie said, her eyes leaving Kate's and roaming around the room to make sure they weren't about to be interrupted. "One of those sexy au pairs from Europe," she said, then laughed at Kate's shocked expression. "Elaine is seventy-one and she's from Vancouver, Washington. She takes care of Anna and does the housekeeping as well."

Kate joined in her laughter. “I suppose you make her wear one of those French maid uniforms while she’s dusting?”

“Of course. And a bikini when she’s washing the windows.”

Kate shook her head. “I hope you pay her extra for that. So, can you bring Anna on Tuesday at six thirty?”

“I don’t know if we’d be ready to start this week,” Jamie said with a frown. Although she liked the thought of seeing Kate again, she wasn’t sure she could bear to watch Anna riding around on some huge horse. The doctors’ unanimous concerns about Anna’s emotional health had been enough to make Jamie reluctantly okay the lessons, but even the thought of watching her ride made Jamie’s heart rate rise. “I was just thinking that sometime in the future she could maybe try it.”

Kate watched her with an understanding expression. “It’s all right to be nervous,” she said.

Jamie gave a short laugh that didn’t sound convincing. “Why would I be nervous? I’m not the one getting on the horse.”

“Why don’t you bring Anna over Monday afternoon about four? She can meet the horses, and if it goes well we can let her take a short ride.”

Jamie ran a hand through her hair and sighed. “Fine, I’ll do it. But if I think Anna is in danger at any point, I’m pulling her off and taking her home.”

“I think you’ll be surprised at how well she does,” Kate said softly, laying her hand on Jamie’s arm. “Just wait until you see her face light up.” She pulled her hand away before Jamie could reach out to grab hold of it.

After a healthy dose of Manhattan her Southern accent was showing itself again, and Jamie wondered what other activities might make Kate’s composure slip enough to really bring out that drawl. *Let’s go fuck in the bathroom.* She cleared her throat and attempted to find a neutral conversation topic. “You’re very good at all of this,” she said, gesturing around the room with her scotch. At Kate’s questioning look, she elaborated. “Mingling, talking, being what people want.”

"Years of practice," Kate said with a frown. "And you're very good at not caring whether any of them really like you or not. That makes them scared of you."

"Either way, it's a question of power."

"I wish I could just be myself and…" Kate started.

"Bullshit," Jamie said, earning her a startled look from Kate, her mouth open in a gasp of surprise that brought life to her usually controlled expressions. Sexy. Like her smile when she was riding Topper or her flash of anger when she confronted Jamie in the restaurant, the involuntary reaction transformed her face from porcelain to flesh. Jamie wanted more. She put her hand next to Kate's head and leaned closer, the intensity of her gaze pushing Kate against the wall. "Don't try to tell me you aren't enjoying this because I see it in your eyes. You like having this control over other people, the ability to make them like you, the strength you get from keeping part of yourself secret. Like I said, it's all about power, and you like having it."

Kate opened and closed her mouth a couple of times as if searching for something to say, but Jamie pushed on before she could speak. "You don't want to stop playing the game, but you make so much of an effort to see people and figure out what they really want. You just want someone to do the same for you."

Jamie watched the pained expression flash over Kate's face, and she knew she had struck deep with her words. She decided she should pull back a little and lighten the mood. This kind of intensity led women to expect a relationship, not the type of casual sex she had in mind. "You're good at playing the game, but we're just the farm team here. If you get the sponsorship, you're headed to the major leagues."

Jamie eased away from Kate, releasing the pressure that had kept her pinned against the wall like a butterfly specimen. "We can help you finance this horse, but once you have him it'll take more than schmoozing at parties to get the corporate endorsements you'll need to back a training barn and the steady stream of Olympic-quality horses that will keep you in the spotlight. The big-name sponsors will recognize a novice in a heartbeat."

Kate sighed, seeming weary at the thought, but she accepted the change in tone with relief evident in her voice. "I suppose you have some words of advice for me?"

Jamie shrugged, a smile playing over her face. "Are you asking me to be your mentor? You should know I demand strict obedience from all of my disciples."

"Whatever you say, guru. I'm here to learn."

Jamie let the tempting implications of that slide and she glanced around the room. "First, you need to identify the big names and find ways to connect with them outside the workplace. They don't want to feel like you're always pushing business talk with them. Dave Randall collects modern art and he travels to Seattle for most Mariners' home games. See the man who just came in? That's Carl Burke, as in Davison and Burke. He's a golfer and he loves cigars. When I was first hired, I found these things out and made sure I just happened to have similar hobbies."

"You smoke?" Kate asked in surprise.

"Ugh, no. But I now have a six handicap."

"What else?" Kate asked.

"When I told you Jenn had reserved the hospitality tent at the show, you were too grateful. If you expect us to give you one and a half million, you should definitely feel entitled to a few thousand for a tent and some booze."

"So I should have said thank you and left it at that?" Kate asked.

"Yes," Jamie said, getting lost in Kate's eyes that watched her so intently. "Or better yet, you should have reserved the tent and sent us the bill."

Kate seemed about to answer when she glanced past Jamie's shoulder and suddenly raised her voice. "I'm afraid I have to disagree with you, Jamie. I enjoy a maduro more than a claro."

Jamie frowned, trying to figure out the shift in conversation when a male voice interrupted them.

"I hate to eavesdrop, but are the two of you talking about cigars?"

Jamie turned to face the newcomer. "Hello, Carl. Actually we were just…"

"Maybe you can settle an argument," Kate spoke over her with a charming smile and a pronounced drawl. "Your Ms. Callahan was just saying how much she loves a lighter cigar that won't overpower her scotch, but I find them too understated for my taste. I much prefer something like a sweeter, more full-bodied Ashton to complement my bourbon."

"Much as I hate to disagree with such a lovely young woman, I'm afraid I have to toe the company line on this and side with Ms. Callahan. I can't believe you've hidden your taste for cigars from me all these years, Jamie. And who is your delightful friend?"

It took an effort, but Jamie managed to keep from rolling her eyes in annoyance as she made the introductions. She almost called Kate "Scarlett," but she didn't think Carl would understand her humor.

"Ah, the horsewoman," Carl Burke said, shaking Kate's hand. Jamie was relieved he didn't try to kiss it. "I'm looking forward to watching you ride at the Country Classic. I have a granddaughter showing there as well. I trust Jamie has been doing her usual bang-up job with your application?"

"Yes," Kate said with a grin. "She's been most…thorough."

"Wonderful. I'd better get back to my wife, but Jamie, I'm going to have her invite you to dinner soon. I have an old Talisker and some Fuente Gran Reservas that pair excellently. I hope you'll bring Ms. Brown along, and perhaps we can convince her to join our side."

Jamie kept a smile on her face until her boss had moved away. "You little Southern bitch," she said in a teasing tone to hide a curious wave of disappointment. Not at the disgusting prospect of smoking a cigar with Carl, but at the realization that Kate would probably be gone by then, and she wouldn't be able to invite her even if she wanted to.

Kate just laughed. "You might want to learn how to cut and light a cigar before then. Smokers can recognize a novice in a heartbeat."

❖

Jamie was almost relieved when she and Kate were eventually pulled in separate directions by LeeAnne and Dave. She stood with the group from her office and managed to keep her focus on the conversation rather than on Kate. She was rapidly reevaluating the bright idea of moving their relationship to a more physical level after spending the evening talking and laughing with her. Usually the more time she spent with a woman, the less she wanted her sexually. Being with Kate only made Jamie want her *more* and that was unacceptable. Still, the second-guessing didn't stop her from excusing herself and following when she noticed Kate slip out to the patio. Jamie found Kate sitting in the shadows, on a low bench next to a built-in barbecue.

"You're following me?" Kate asked as Jamie sat down near her.

"You're hiding?" Jamie asked in turn, resting her arm along the back of the bench.

"LeeAnne was getting a little too friendly, and I thought it would be better to disappear than to throw a drink in her face."

"Good choice," Jamie said with a nod, resisting the urge to go back in and take care of the drink throwing.

They sat in silence while all of Jamie's resolve to avoid contact melted away. "I forgot to give you my most important piece of networking advice," she said as she moved her arm forward so it rested along Kate's shoulders. Her thumb gently traced the strap of Kate's dress.

"What's that?" Kate whispered, her eyes slipping closed as Jamie's fingers moved into her hair.

Jamie inched closer and let her free hand rest on Kate's thigh. "You should identify the one person who can help you the most and focus all of your attention there."

Kate opened her eyes and turned her head to face Jamie. "Why, I suppose that would be you," she observed.

Jamie smiled and tightened her fingers in Kate's hair, urging her closer until their lips met. The first light brush of Kate's lips hit her like a fist in the stomach. Kate gave a small gasp of surprise, and Jamie took advantage of the opportunity to slip her tongue in

Kate's mouth. Instead of resisting, Kate leaned into her and met every thrust of Jamie's tongue with one of her own. Her hand slid up to the drape of fabric between Jamie's breasts. Jamie had expected that, since Kate's eyes had traveled there enough times that evening, but she was completely unprepared for the physical jolt she felt at Kate's light touch.

Jamie moved her right hand up Kate's thigh and under the hem of her dress. A few more inches, and she knew she would find Kate to be as wet as she was. One tug on her thigh, and Kate would be straddling her lap, grinding her hips into Jamie's. Any one of Jamie's ridiculous pick-up lines, and Kate would be hers for the night.

And then what? Every inch of Jamie screamed out at the thought of walking away from Kate right now. How much harder would it be to leave after touching her, tasting her? Jamie slipped out of Kate's grasp and stood up shakily. It was time to run.

"I am very sorry," she said, enunciating each word carefully to keep her voice controlled. Her words sounded cold even to her own ears. "That was completely unprofessional. I must have had too much to drink."

"Me too," Kate agreed, even though they each had stopped after two drinks. "I'm tired and I…"

Jamie held up a hand to stop her. "No need to apologize. I'm the one who initiated…this. It won't ever happen again."

She turned to leave, but stopped again. "This won't affect my ability to make an unbiased decision about your proposal, but if you'd prefer I can ask Dave to assign…"

"No," Kate interrupted in turn. "We got carried away, but it didn't mean anything. There's no reason for our business association to change."

Jamie nodded and left, moving quickly through the house to avoid talking to anyone. She sat in her car for a long time, hoping irrationally that Kate would follow her out and insist she finish what she had started. Finally, Jamie started the car and drove home, ignoring the nagging thought that Kate might turn to the willing LeeAnne instead.

❖

Kate managed to get inside and lock herself in a bathroom before her composure slipped completely. She sagged against the door, sliding down until she was sitting on her heels. Dear God, what had she done? The more important question was, what had she been about to do? And she knew exactly what the answer to that was since the mere thought of it made her wet. She wanted Jamie Callahan, and it had nothing to do with the small amount of liquor she had consumed.

Kate ran through the evening's events, trying to pinpoint precisely when she had lost her mind. Maybe it was when Jamie's strong hand cradled her neck so gently. Or when she proved her ability to see past Kate's masks to the vulnerability that lay beneath them. Or was it when Jamie had first approached her at the party, wrapping an arm around her waist and shooting that fiercely possessive look in LeeAnne's direction? Whatever the cause, Kate hated herself for allowing her defenses to come down. Her actions were unprofessional and inappropriate, and she knew her parents would have been ashamed of her for throwing away her chances at the sponsorship. At the same time, a small, mean part of her mind thought they wouldn't care if she had slept with Jamie, as long as it guaranteed her endorsement of Kate's cause.

Kate replayed the scene in her mind, still feeling her body's response to Jamie's touch. Jamie's fingers brushing her shoulder, tangled in her hair, sliding up her thigh. Even after Jamie's rejection, Kate ached to hear a knock at the door, to hear Jamie's voice calling her, to hear her own cry out in release. Kate had been weak, too willing to be seduced, but Jamie had turned her down. It must have been yet another test in a lifelong series of them. And she had failed. She had proved without a doubt she would do whatever it took to seal the business deal, and Jamie had been more interested in that information than in Kate herself. What Jamie didn't realize was Kate hadn't even spared a thought for horses or Olympic dreams when she was in her arms. All she had wanted was Jamie.

She eventually got off the floor, said her good-byes, and drove home. She lay across the bed, not caring about the wrinkles she was making in her expensive dress. She would be very surprised if she saw Jamie at her barn on Monday. Instead, she would expect a politely worded note from her efficient assistant, denying Kate's application. The only bright spot Kate could possibly find was that Jamie hadn't yet told Anna about the lessons. She would have hated it if her foolish actions had been the cause of the little girl's disappointment.

Chapter Eight

Kate raised the jump another six inches and turned back to the stallion that stood in a corner of the arena, watching her every move. She waved her arms and shooed him into a canter, but he didn't need much encouragement to aim toward the jump she had set and sail over it. Her breath caught every time she watched him jump. His muscles bunched and propelled him off the ground in a perfect arc, with perfect form. He snorted and danced in place as she raised the jump a little more.

He cleared the fence easily as Kate shifted her weight, rising up on her toes as if she were jumping with him. Soon she would be, and the idea was as exciting as it was intimidating. She had never ridden a horse with such power, but she couldn't wait to give it a try. Kate had welcomed his arrival yesterday, hoping he would be enough of a distraction to make her forget about the disastrous Hadley party. To make her forget Jamie. He had done his best to keep her mind occupied, with his incessant neighs and his determined attempts to destroy his paddock, but Kate couldn't stop reliving Friday night. Sometimes she focused on her shame after Jamie's rejection, but other times, especially at night, she imagined herself back on the patio with Jamie's hands on her. And with a much more satisfying ending.

Kate whistled and the stallion trotted over to her. His coat was dry and he looked as if he could have jumped for hours, but Kate didn't want to overdo it on his first workout. She buckled his halter in place and led him back to his stall. Tomorrow she would ride him for the first time. Maybe it would keep her from worrying whether Jamie would decide to show up for Anna's ride. She hadn't called to cancel yet, and Kate debated how she should handle their meeting if Jamie did show. Cool indifference? Meek apology? She didn't have a precedent for this type of social situation and she felt lost without a clear part to play.

Jamie glanced in the rearview mirror as she drove Anna to Kate's barn on Monday afternoon. She had expected her niece to be wildly excited about the prospect of being near a horse, but instead she was very subdued. That wrenched at Jamie's heart more than anything. She knew Anna had been deeply hurt by her experience at the horse show, and she was probably preparing to be disappointed yet again.

Jamie had nearly decided to skip the appointment. She wasn't looking forward to being around Kate, and try as she might to convince herself that her interest in Kate was only physical, she knew it was much deeper and far more dangerous than that. She had only felt this kind of attraction, one that threatened the fine balance she had achieved in her life, a few times before, but it had always been easy enough to restore her equilibrium. Either she ignored the feelings until they disappeared, or she engaged in a quick affair to ease the tension so it didn't affect her daily life. Thoughts of Kate had become too persistent to ignore, however, and although Jamie had spent the evenings in her usual bars, she had chosen to leave on her own each time. After Friday's kiss, it was clear that getting Kate out of her system with a casual fling was out of the question. The only recourse she could think of was to summon all of her self-discipline and simply fight her attraction with brute mental strength.

Jamie could find only one positive, but uncomfortable, side effect of her obsession with Kate. Long, sleepless nights had given her time for some soul searching, and memories of those early years after her mother had left, when she had first left home with Sara haunted her. She had worked harder than a girl of fifteen should have needed to in order to provide a home and safety for her sister, but she had given her little else. Jamie's very survival had depended on her ability to ignore the pain and anger—and the nightmares—which followed from her stepfather's home to her new apartment. She had shut down so much that now she wasn't able to give Anna any of the love and nurturing she needed. Her detachment and self-control had made her successful in her career, but she wanted more for Anna.

With her customary drive and logic, Jamie had created an action plan to meet Anna's emotional needs, and riding horses seemed to be an ideal part of that plan. It would give Anna a chance to connect with the animals she loved while acting as a form of physical therapy. As difficult as it would be to face Kate again, she had to do it for Anna's sake. Jamie had been the one to make the first move on Kate. It simply wouldn't happen again.

She parked the Mercedes on a paved area near the barn and saw Kate heading out to meet them. "Stay here a second, okay?" she said to Anna before she got out of the car.

She met Kate halfway across the parking lot. "I didn't think you'd come," Kate spoke first. "I'm glad you did…for Anna, I mean."

Jamie took a step closer, wanting to erase the awkward blush that colored Kate's cheeks. She took the initiative so they could move past the uncomfortable memory of their kiss. "I need to apologize for what happened at the party," she said bluntly. "My behavior was unacceptable given our business association." She stopped and ran a hand through her hair. "I don't have any excuse for the kiss. I find you very attractive, but I was out of line."

Kate waved her hand in dismissal, seemingly relieved to have the topic out in the open. "I had as much a part in it as you did. We're not the first two people to ever make a mistake like that after having too much to drink. At least it didn't go past a simple kiss."

A simple kiss? Jamie had experienced plenty of those, and what she and Kate had done at the Hadleys' went well beyond that. At least it had seemed so to Jamie, but apparently it had mattered more to her than to Kate. The thought aroused an irrational anger in her, and instead of letting the matter drop, she pushed on. "For the record, I never meant to imply that any sexual favors would guarantee…"

Kate stepped closer, her green eyes darkening with anger at Jamie's coolly spoken words. "Are you suggesting I would have had sex with you to get the sponsorship?" she hissed, standing toe-to-toe with Jamie. "For God's sake, we were just joking around and it got out of hand. I want your company's money, but I wouldn't prostitute myself to get it."

Jamie stood her ground as Kate glared at her angrily, fighting the urge to grab her and finish their kiss. At least she had managed to coerce some sort of emotional response from the controlled Kate. Her overheated emotions made her pursue the matter, as if she wanted Kate to lash out at her. "I should let you know that if you decide to sue for sexual harassment I wouldn't fight it, and you'd have the money for your horse."

"Do you want me to sign a fucking waiver to prove I won't sue? If I had thought for a second you were sexually harassing me, I would have been back inside filing a complaint with those idiots from your legal department. Jesus, it was nothing. I kissed LeeAnne at the party as well, and she's not panicking about a lawsuit."

Jamie took a step back, her face turning to stone. A slap would have been more welcome than Kate's words. She had pictured Kate turning to LeeAnne for comfort, and it seemed she was right. "As long as we understand each other," she said coldly.

"Perfectly," Kate said with equal coolness. "We're both adult enough to overlook a small indiscretion and not let it affect our business relationship or Anna's day."

At the mention of Anna, Jamie quickly turned and walked back to the car where her niece was sitting quietly and playing with a plastic model horse. She went to the trunk and pulled out Anna's wheelchair while Kate leaned into the car to greet her.

"I'm so glad you could make it today, Anna," Kate said in a bright voice. "I know Topper is looking forward to seeing you again."

Kate's running commentary about the horses, so at odds with their prior conversation, helped put Anna at ease and restore Jamie's sense of priorities. Seeing the shy smile on her niece's face, Jamie decided to take Kate's cue and concentrate on giving Anna a special day. If Kate could so easily dismiss their argument and the kiss, she certainly could as well. It was almost a relief to tamp down the disappointment and jealousy she had been feeling and return to her stoic self. She managed to convince herself that just picturing Kate and LeeAnne together would effectively block out any attraction Jamie felt toward her.

Kate took charge of Anna's chair and wheeled her into the lounge. Although she hadn't noticed it on her first visit, Jamie was glad to see Kate's barn was set up to accommodate a wheelchair. The doorways were wide with smooth sills, and there were asphalt paths leading to the arena and the parking area. Even the lounge furniture was arranged so Anna could easily maneuver.

She hadn't been expecting other people to be around though, and she wasn't pleased to see Myra sitting on the couch talking to a young man.

"Anna, these are my friends, Myra and Chris. Jamie, you remember Myra?" Kate smoothly made the introductions. Jamie shook hands with Chris, a young man whose cowboy hat and boots made an odd juxtaposition with his long hair and tie-dyed shirt. He looked a bit lost between generations. Jamie nodded at Myra who gave her a knowing wink before turning to Anna with a friendly grin. Jamie had no doubt Kate had told her about their encounter, but everyone seemed willing to pretend things were okay for Anna's sake. Just ignore the feelings and they'll go away. It had always worked for her in the past.

Kate knelt by Anna's side. "I need to show your aunt something," she said. "Do you mind if Chris and Myra take you out to meet the horses for a few minutes?"

Jamie was about to protest when Myra chimed in. "C'mon, Anna, let's stop by the pop machine first."

Anna smiled in agreement. Jamie watched Chris push Anna's chair along while Myra talked easily with the little girl. She didn't register Kate's hand on her forearm until she gave a small squeeze.

"She'll be fine," Kate assured her. "They won't go too close to the horses until we're back."

Jamie nodded, not sure if the horses were the cause of her sudden anxiety. She turned and followed Kate outside, surprised she was willing to be around Jamie without chaperones. They walked over to the small barn in silence, and Kate climbed up on the fence around the stallion's paddock. Jamie followed her lead and leaned on the top plank, close enough for her bare forearm to brush against Kate's. The innocent touch brought Jamie back to Friday night, to the feel of Kate, tense with passion, in her arms. The memory alone was nearly enough to break Jamie's determination to wrestle her attraction into submission.

"He's here," Kate said unnecessarily as the large chestnut burst out of his stall at the sound of Kate's voice. He snorted loudly and came toward them in a high-stepping trot.

"Jesus Christ," Jamie said. The horse's coat, the rusty color of drying blood, was covered in a light sheen of sweat. It slid over muscles more clearly defined than Jamie would have expected after his weeks of inactivity. She hadn't been sure what to expect in over a million dollars' worth of horseflesh, but this animal looked ready to prove his worth. His attitude practically dared her to say he was worth less than his ridiculous price tag.

Kate acknowledged her exclamation with a wry smile. "Impressive, isn't he?" she asked, her eyes never leaving the horse. She leaned back when the horse trotted past them again, her forearm muscles flexing against Jamie's arm. So strong for a woman, but so weak compared to the giant of a horse. Jamie scooted closer, ready to grab Kate off the fence if the horse came at them. "He got here Saturday morning," Kate said.

"Have you ridden him yet?" Jamie asked as the horse circled the paddock with his tail in the air. He squealed and lashed out with his hind legs, contacting the fence and making it rattle.

"This morning," Kate said. "I gave him a couple of days to settle in, but he really needs the exercise."

"Looks like it," Jamie said, gesturing with her head at a section of the new fence that already showed signs of being patched up. She fought down a wave of nausea at the thought of Kate on top of this stick of dynamite. “How is he to ride?”

Kate hesitated. “Powerful,” she finally said.

Jamie pulled her eyes off the magnificent horse. “This is your dream horse. I would expect a little more gushing than that.”

“We just need more time together,” Kate said, meeting her gaze with a confident look. “He’s been stuck on a plane and in a quarantine stall for a few weeks. We’ll figure each other out.”

Jamie looked at the horse again. He had the same look in his eyes she usually did when she went to the negotiation table. And she never walked away the loser. “You’re sure this is a good idea?”

“Of course. By the time you see us in the Country Classic, we’ll be working as a team.”

They slid off the fence and returned to the main barn. Jamie tried to ignore the ringing crash as the stallion connected with the fence again. At least it didn’t sound as if he had broken through this time.

“I free jumped him yesterday,” Kate told her as they walked. “That means I turned him loose in the arena and let him go over some jumps without a rider,” she explained. “He’s as good as Marty said. He’s definitely got the talent to make it to the Olympics.”

“And you want to be on him when he does?”

“Of course,” Kate replied in a confident voice as she led Jamie into the barn. Jamie halted, shaken by a vision of Kate trying to control the stallion, and even more by her sudden realization. She wished Kate had said no.

Kate turned back and saw Jamie watching her with a frown. “Are you coming?” she asked. Jamie only nodded and followed her to the crossties where Myra was grooming a small horse while Chris and Anna watched. The animal was a nondescript-looking chestnut-and-white pinto with a Roman nose and large ears. Kate adored the shaggy beast, but she had to admit he was nothing much to look at, especially after witnessing the impressive Guns Blazing.

“Wow, he’s really…Ouch!” Jamie said when Kate pinched her arm midsentence. She could comment on the pinto’s looks, but she wouldn’t let Jamie insult him.

"Don't you dare call Spot ugly around me or anyone else here," Kate threatened in a low voice.

"Spot?" Jamie repeated with a strangled laugh. "God, you're kidding, aren't you?"

"I am not. He's one of my best horses, and I wouldn't trade him for a million dollars," Kate said. She flushed a bright red when she realized she was trying to do exactly that, with Jamie's help. "Oops, I shouldn't have said that."

Jamie laughed, and Anna looked over with a surprised expression at the sound. Kate hadn't heard Jamie laugh much in the short time she had known her, and she doubted Anna did either. Jamie walked over to her niece and ruffled her hair. "Hey, kid," she said, winking at Kate, "let's go meet Spot, prince among horses."

Kate stood back as Jamie lifted Anna and took her over to the horse. Kate noticed a slight hesitation before every move Jamie made, as if the touching, the closeness were new to her. Anna wrapped one arm tightly around Jamie's neck while she shyly patted the horse with the other, and Spot stood with his eyes half-closed while she fussed over him. Myra stepped closer and handed Anna a soft brush, showing her how to use it to groom Spot's coat, then she held her arms out and Anna moved willingly to her. Jamie looked lost as she stepped away. Kate wanted to touch her, to reassure her, but she only moved so she was standing close to Jamie.

"I didn't expect anyone else to be here," Jamie said quietly while Anna's attention was on her task.

"It takes three volunteers for most of our riders," Kate said, following Jamie's gaze to Chris. "Two sidewalkers and one person to lead the horse."

"I could have…" Jamie started, but Kate held up her hand.

"I don't like to have family members supporting the riders, especially at first. They tend to be more protective and can even do more harm than good if they panic and try to pull the child off the horse."

"I don't panic," Jamie informed her icily.

"Funny," Kate said, "I remember at the party you threatened to take Anna off if you even had a hint something was wrong." She winced at her unintended reference to Friday night.

"I remember a few things from that party," Jamie said, leaning close to Kate's ear. "But not that."

Kate cleared her throat, wishing she could as easily clear her mind of images of her and Jamie together. She changed the subject back to riding to conceal her awkward emotions. She explained how they would support Anna's legs but not actually hold on to her, so she would need to use her own muscles to support herself.

"We'll drape an arm across her thigh but not grip her legs at all so we won't accidentally pull her off balance," she continued.

Jamie watched Chris and Myra as they laughed along with something Anna said. She fought the tension between her rising panic and the pleasure of seeing Anna smiling and happy. Myra quickly saddled the patient pinto, and the group headed over to the arena where Chris brought out a couple of riding helmets for Anna to try on. The helmet made the dangers real. Jamie decided she couldn't go through with it, and she took hold of Kate's arm, leading her away from the others.

"Look," she said when they were out of earshot. "I don't know if it's a good idea to have Anna ride today."

"Anna seems relaxed around the horses," Kate said gently. "What's wrong?"

"It's just that she isn't used to being around strangers, especially men. I don't know how she'll react to having Chris holding her like you said."

Kate glanced over to where Chris was kneeling, talking to Anna. She was giggling as he put his too-large cowboy hat on her head.

"I've known him a long time," Kate said. "I'd trust him with my own child without hesitating." She looked back at Jamie, her eyes concerned, and Jamie met Kate's gaze, carefully keeping her expression shuttered. She wouldn't back down on this.

Kate must have recognized that because she suggested a compromise. "Maybe Anna would be more comfortable if Myra and I were her sidewalkers. Chris can lead Spot."

Jamie let herself get lost in Kate's eyes for a moment as she struggled with her trepidation. She had finally gotten accustomed to trusting Anna's doctors and physical therapists and now she had a whole new set of people to allow close to her niece. Kate seemed to sense her agitation, and she lifted a hand and gently threaded her fingers through the bangs that fell over Jamie's forehead. "She'll be safe," Kate said quietly. "You're right here."

Jamie felt her breath catch at Kate's simple touch, and she nodded silently before stepping away to check on Anna one last time. The little girl was wearing a safety helmet with a Mickey Mouse sticker on it and Jamie squatted next to her wheelchair.

"You nervous, kid?" she asked in a whisper. Anna nodded, her blue eyes wide.

"Me too," Jamie admitted. "I think we'll deserve a double-scoop hot fudge sundae after this ride."

"With whipped cream?" Anna asked as Chris led Spot toward them.

"Of course." Jamie locked eyes with Kate as she came to wheel Anna up the ramp. She put on her best boardroom glare so Kate would know she had better take good care of her niece.

"Come on, Anna," Kate said, tossing a smile over her shoulder at Jamie. "I think your aunt is scared of this sweet little horse. Let's show her there's nothing to worry about."

Kate forced aside the fleeting glimpse of vulnerability she had seen in Jamie's eyes so she could concentrate instead on getting Anna safely into the saddle. Jamie had been so cold when she arrived, so at odds with the passionate woman from Friday who had ripped aside every barrier Kate had erected around herself. She had apparently been untouched by the kiss that had battered Kate's defenses, but it seemed she wasn't immune to jealousy. Kate guiltily knew the peck on the cheek she had given LeeAnne at the beginning of the evening wasn't a kiss in the same sense as what happened between her and Jamie, but she had been glad to see some spark of emotion in Jamie's eyes when she mentioned it. Except for her brief laughter over poor Spot's name, Jamie had seemed her usual arrogant self, intent on making Kate realize how little she cared about anything. Until she admitted her concern about Chris.

One of the main reasons Kate didn't let parents work with their own children was they often transmitted their fears to the child. Unlike her complicated aunt, Anna was easy enough for Kate to read, and all she saw in her was the expected anxiety as she faced a new experience. She hadn't shown any nervousness around Chris or Myra, and like many of the handicapped kids Kate dealt with, she was accustomed to the assistance and touch of others. Kate guessed Jamie had her own reasons for her concern. She suspected it might be connected to the difficult childhood Jamie had hinted at in the restaurant, but Kate stopped herself there. The idea was too painful to consider right now, when she had to focus on Anna's safety and well-being.

She pushed Anna up a ramp leading to a large mounting platform with steps going down the other side. Spot stood quietly next to it, with Chris holding him in place and Myra standing on a block of wood on his off side. Kate easily picked Anna up in her arms and set her on top of the patient horse, all the while explaining what she was doing in a loud enough voice for Jamie to hear, too. She draped her forearm over Anna's lifeless thigh and gripped the saddle's flap. Once Myra was in the same position on the opposite side, Kate told Chris to start walking Spot.

Anna gave a little shriek as the unaccustomed movement made her lurch a little, but Kate resisted the urge to try to help her balance. Instead she told her to hold on to the curved bar that had been specially made for her therapy saddle and shot a warning look at Jamie who had come close and looked ready to snatch her niece to safety.

They walked slowly around the rail of the indoor arena while Anna kept a death grip on the saddle and Jamie circled nearby, a stern expression on her face, looking dangerous in her black jeans and tight T-shirt. Myra hummed the theme from *Jaws* under her breath, reminding Kate of her reference to sharks after her first meeting with Jamie. Kate fought an urge to giggle and instead raised her voice as she talked to Anna, trying to drown out her friend's laughter. She kept up with the latest television shows and the teen pop stars her students liked, so she brought up a few until she heard a spark of interest in Anna's stiff responses. She latched on to the topic of a recent *Animal Planet* special and soon Anna was relaxed enough to join in the conversation.

A couple more turns around the arena, and Anna was comfortable enough to let go of the saddle and wave at her aunt. Kate took advantage of Anna's increasing relaxation and encouraged the girl to pat Spot in various places. As she leaned over to rub his shoulder or scratch behind the saddle, she gradually grew more confident in her ability to move and balance. Jamie, in turn, had finally stopped her stealthy prowl and instead paced in and out of the arena door. Kate was relieved to see such small accomplishments, and soon she had Chris stop Spot near the door while she called out for Jamie to bring Anna's chair over to them. The ride had only lasted ten minutes, but Kate knew Anna would feel the effects of the new exercise and she didn't want to overdo it on the first try. She also had an intuitive sense that Jamie's nerves were frayed enough for one day. Kate had only seen a cold businesswoman when she'd first met Jamie. But after watching her with Anna and getting glimpses into her past, Kate could see a hint of the insecurities and fears, the love and compassion, that burned behind Jamie's controlled expression.

She carefully took Anna off Spot and returned her to the safety of her chair before bending down to return the little girl's hug. When she stood, Jamie surprised her by stepping forward and wrapping Kate in her arms. Kate returned the embrace, her hands sliding over the muscles under Jamie's fitted shirt and her whole body responding to the warmth and strength she felt. Resisting her sudden rush of desire, Kate stiffened to keep from melting into Jamie's arms. A whispered thank you was breathed on her neck, followed by a gentle kiss, before Jamie stepped away.

They left Chris and Myra to care for Spot and walked to Jamie's car. Kate wavered between the urge to apologize yet again for her behavior on Friday and the more insistent wish to forget the whole night.

"Thanks for spending so much time with us today," Jamie said.

"Thank you," Anna echoed.

Kate gave Anna's shoulder a squeeze. "It was my pleasure." Kate straightened and looked at Jamie. "I hope you'll come tomorrow," she said.

Jamie smiled. "That would be *my* pleasure."

"To the therapy lesson," Kate added. She and Jamie always seemed to be carrying on two conversations at once. One on the surface, and a second disconcerting one of subtext.

Jamie lifted Anna out of her chair. "We'll be here," she said over her shoulder. "Won't we, kid?"

It was with a sense of relief that Kate watched Jamie finally get in the driver's seat and start the car. Kate's main intention today had been to bring a smile to Anna's face, but she had also seen the afternoon as an opportunity to repair some of the damage she had done by letting herself slip out of control with Jamie at the party. She was too tangled up with her. Their relationship should have been so simple, with clearly defined rules they both accepted and understood. Instead, they seemed to clash somehow, as if they had separate agendas, while still being drawn together by some unknown force. Even Kate's personal relationships rarely seemed this *personal*. Most of Kate's students and their parents hugged her after the therapy lessons, reaching out in gratitude or for reassurance or sympathy. But Jamie's embrace was different, and she still felt the imprint of Jamie's body pressed against her own. Jamie had trusted Kate with her secrets, her fear. And Kate had let Jamie see her without her socialite clothes and mask in place. There were layers of fabric between them, people around them, but Kate felt they were both naked, raw, when Jamie held her.

She waved good-bye to Anna as Jamie's Mercedes slowly made its way down her driveway. She decided she must be insane, because as glad as she was to have Jamie off her property, she was already looking forward to seeing her at Anna's lesson the next day. Kate's regular teaching had always been a great networking tool. Her rates were steep enough so she attracted a high-end clientele, and her students won enough to keep their wealthy parents happy. She had hoped she could work the same magic today, impressing Jamie and helping Anna in one swoop. Instead, she had gotten snared in their complex relationship, and she found herself wanting to know more about Jamie and the reasons behind her fears. Her rational side knew delving into someone's personal life rarely was a good business decision, but for once, other parts of her were shouting down rationality. She turned back to the barn. Maybe cleaning some stalls would help her come to her senses.

Chapter Nine

Jamie drove a much happier Anna to her first official lesson the next afternoon, relieved that this time she didn't have to bother examining her motives to figure out why she was looking forward to seeing Kate again. She needed to meet the other volunteers before she'd be willing to step back and let Elaine take Anna to the barn. She met personally with every one of the constant stream of doctors and physical therapists who worked with her niece. Jamie had no qualms about walking out of an appointment if either she or Anna felt uncomfortable, and she would do it again today if necessary. After yesterday's trial ride, however, she felt more at ease with thc prospect of a group lesson than she had expected. She was a little uncomfortable with the suspicion that Kate had read too much into her hesitation about Chris yesterday, but at the same time she was relieved to be understood. Anna needed touch, from her doctors and therapists and Elaine, but Jamie had to protect her, even if it meant she had to let Kate close enough to see her worries, closer than anyone had ever been. The vulnerability she felt was worthwhile since she had no doubt Kate would be careful about who worked with Anna.

"Hi, Anna," Kate called out. "Come meet the other riders in your lesson."

Jamie pushed Anna's chair over to the arena. "This is Anna, and her aunt Jamie," Kate said. "And this is Alex, his mom Bev, and Gwen."

"Hello, Alex," Jamie said even though he didn't seem aware of her presence. She shook hands with Bev and Gwen.

"C'mon Anna, let's get ready for the lesson." Kate took charge of Anna's chair, leaving Jamie with Alex's mom.

"Is this Anna's first ride?" Bev asked while the students were being fitted with helmets.

"She was on for a few minutes yesterday," Jamie said, watching Kate as she knelt by Anna's chair and checked the straps of her safety helmet. Seeing the two of them talking and laughing like old friends made Jamie's throat tighten. Kate had gotten closer to Anna in a couple of days than Jamie had in nine years. She thought she should be jealous, but she felt proud. To see Anna trying a new and exciting activity. To see Kate making a difference in her students' lives. And she felt proud to be here with them.

"Alex has been coming here for just over a year," Bev continued, her tired eyes following her son. "He's autistic. When he first started, he wasn't verbal at all, but now he says a few words."

Jamie could hear the pride and awe in Bev's voice. Such a simple accomplishment in some ways, but to this woman it was like a miracle. "Kate's wonderful with the kids," Bev continued. "I'm sure Anna will love riding as well."

Jamie could only nod as Kate joined them again. "You okay?" she asked quietly, her hand on Jamie's arm as she looked into her eyes with concern.

"I'm fine," Jamie assured her, squeezing Kate's hand briefly. The small touch, the simple understanding, shook Jamie more intimately than sex ever had. She quickly pulled her hand away out of habit and was surprised by the desire to reach out to Kate again.

Kate nodded. "You'll be walking with Chris and Alex, and Bev and Myra will be with Anna."

Jamie watched Bev walk over to check on her son before the ride. This was a new experience for her, and she felt overwhelmed at the sudden responsibility she would have for this woman's child. She would protect him, and in turn she had to trust Bev to take care of her own niece.

"It's better this way," Kate said. "Really, it is."

Jamie met her beautiful eyes and smiled. "I'm beginning to understand that," she said. Kate looked like she wanted to say something more, but Chris came over to them, and the moment was lost.

"Hey, dude, Alex is riding Frosty. C'mon over and I'll show you what to do." He headed toward a roan mare.

"Did he just call me…?" Jamie started to ask.

"Everyone's dude to Chris," Kate interrupted, laughing at Jamie's expression. "Don't worry, you don't look like one at all." Her gaze briefly traveled over the front of the purple tank top Jamie wore with her jeans.

Jamie felt as if Kate had fondled her in front of everyone. "Careful," Jamie muttered, not really sure which one of them she was warning.

Although Chris looked a little flaky to Jamie, he was serious when it came to her role in the lesson. He carefully explained how she was to support Alex, and ran through some examples of things that could possibly go wrong and how she should handle them. That part made Jamie feel a little sick, but she ignored the feeling and focused like a good student. Chris untied Frosty and led her over to the mounting block, telling Jamie to wait until they had Alex on and away from the ramp before she came over and took Kate's place at his side.

Jamie waved at Anna, who was waiting her turn near the ramp, and then stepped in and slipped her arm under Kate's where it rested on Alex's thigh. She had to be close to Kate so Alex was never left without support, and she let her free hand briefly rest on Kate's hip. Her fingers flexed against the soft denim, and the casual contact left Jamie wanting more. A dangerous addiction. She thought Kate leaned into her touch for a second, but she figured it was just her imagination. Once she was in place, the teenaged girl who was leading Frosty, one of Kate's students, started walking around the arena.

It felt awkward at first for Jamie to be around the little boy. Besides Anna, she rarely was around children unless a client brought one along to a meeting, and even then she only interacted enough to be polite. She let Chris handle the talking and she simply walked alongside, but occasionally he would switch to a low tone and explain something to her. She grew more comfortable with the situation as she understood more about Alex's needs. Chris told her they tried to keep the external stimuli simple for an autistic child like Alex, so he could find one thing to focus on and not get overwhelmed. She eventually joined in as they took turns running Alex's hands over Frosty's neck or mane, and she cheered along with her little group the one time he seemed aware of the mare enough to say horsie.

Once Kate had the three students mounted, she spent the lesson moving among them. They had such different needs, and Jamie watched in amazement as Kate changed every time she moved to a new group. Her years of training as a social chameleon worked for her as she adapted her teaching to fit the students, changing her tone and teaching methods for each of them. At the same time, there was never a hint that she wasn't genuinely interested in each one of them. With Alex, she concentrated on simple objects and textures, handing him soft toys and repeating their names to try to get him to echo her words. Gwen was able to ride on her own, and it looked to Jamie like Kate was acting as a friend as well as instructor. She led Gwen through some stretching exercises, but much of the time she walked by her side and listened intently to her. With Anna, the games were more complex since she could pick up objects and throw balls through hoops. Jamie had been to enough therapy sessions to recognize that Kate had her niece bending and moving in ways that would stretch her muscles and challenge her balance.

By the end of the lesson, Jamie had grown quite impressed with Kate's skills. Yesterday's ride had been simply a fun experience for Anna, but today was so much more. Kate's ability to adapt in order to best communicate with her riders reminded Jamie of Kate's smooth transitions at the Hadleys' party. Most of all, though, Kate was so compassionate and encouraging that Jamie could sense the students' and volunteers' desire to please her. She felt a sense of pride as she watched her teach, and she insisted to herself it was only because she felt good about bringing Anna here. It had nothing at all to do with her own feelings for Kate.

❖

Kate walked alongside Gwen and listened as she described the ways she'd managed her MS during the past week. She fought to ignore Jamie, who had watched her with those sharp eyes during the whole lesson, and she came up with a few exercises to help Gwen with the stiffness she had been experiencing lately. While Gwen used the stirrups to help stretch her muscles, Kate quickly glanced around the ring to make sure everyone else was okay. Jamie met her gaze and gave her a wink before turning her attention back to Alex. Kate rolled her eyes and turned back to Gwen. They chatted about Gwen's daughter for several minutes, and then it was time to move on to Anna.

Kate had stashed a few stuffed animals around the ring and she led Anna on a scavenger hunt to find them. She started with some that were easy to reach, but as Anna started to figure out how to adjust her weight as she moved in the saddle, Kate had the girl stretching high and low to get them. She knew Jamie was taking good care of Alex, but she had no doubt Jamie was also aware of everything that was going on with Anna. And with Kate. She felt Jamie's attention with a prickly awareness that was both exciting and confusing. And very distracting.

Kate finally moved back to Alex and spent some time handing him rings that were easy to grab. While she encouraged the distracted boy to notice them long enough to take a grip and hold them, she could see how much Jamie had figured out about the process. She had expected her to remain aloof, doing her job and not getting involved, but Jamie clearly could recognize the small increments of Alex's progress. When he finally closed his fingers over the ring long enough to keep it in his grasp, she slid those long fingers of hers over his and praised him in a warm voice. Kate was so surprised she almost tripped over a jump, and Jamie's free arm reached out to grab her.

"You can let go now," Kate murmured in a low voice when Jamie kept her free hand lightly on Kate's waist as they walked. Jamie pulled her closer, steering her around another jump, and Kate felt her arm brush against Jamie's breast. The light contact traveled straight to her groin.

"You seem to trip a lot," Jamie observed, withdrawing her arm.

Kate felt a blush creep over her face as she moved out of Jamie's reach. It was a common joke at these lessons that she often got so distracted with her students she would stumble over poles and even other horses while teaching. Jamie had rescued her several times already during the lesson, and Kate was still reeling from having Jamie's hands on her so often. The realization that she could have simply approached Alex from Chris's side instead of Jamie's made her face grow hotter. She walked to the center of the ring, out of reach.

"Remember, I'll be at a show next week, so we won't have a lesson until a week from next Tuesday," Kate announced as the riders finished their class. She was almost glad to see the lesson come to an end. It was exhausting to try to keep track of three students with such different needs while trying so desperately to ignore Jamie's observant gaze. The almost playful touching every time they were near each other had frayed Kate's nerves. Her body responded so intensely to Jamie's touch she felt as drained as she would after an afternoon of sex.

Kate trailed behind the group as the volunteers led the horses back to the barn. Either she gave in to her desire to get closer to Jamie, or she made the effort to bring their relationship back to a professional level. While the first choice had immediate appeal, the second was the only one that made sense for her. A lifetime of dreaming for a chance like the stallion couldn't be thrown away on what would probably be a short-lived, difficult affair, if Jamie let her close enough even for that much. It was time for a little damage control and a whole lot of distance.

"Hey, Kate," Myra called as Kate slowly caught up to the others. "Did you ask Jamie if she'd check out your grant proposal?"

"No," Kate answered shortly. And she wasn't about to. She wouldn't be able to relax until she got Jamie off her property and out of arm's reach. "I'm sure she has better—"

Jamie held up her hand to stop Kate's sentence. "What grant proposal?" she asked Myra.

"Well, when Kate moves back east, I'd like to keep her therapy program going," Myra said, oblivious to Kate's attempts to shut her up. "At least what I can manage outside of my regular teaching at the high school. I'll be starting from scratch, though, so I'll need some cash to get it going. Kate drew up a grant application, but I thought you could take a look at it and make sure it's all in order."

"I'd be glad to," Jamie said before turning to Kate. "Why are you waving your arms like that?"

Kate sighed, shooting an irritated glare at Myra. "We don't want to waste your time—" she started before Jamie broke in.

"Nonsense, I'm happy to do it."

"Great," said Myra, pushing Kate toward her house. "Go get the proposal and we'll meet you in the lounge. Chris, you can finish up out here, can't you?"

❖

Jamie was sitting on the lounge sofa drinking a Coke with Myra and Anna when Kate returned with a thick binder and her laptop. Kate handed the binder to Jamie and set her computer on a table near the door.

"I thought Anna and I could play on the computer while you two chat," Kate said before sitting with her back to Jamie.

Jamie opened the binder and started to read, trying to keep her eyes from wandering to the white-blond ponytail that hung down Kate's back. Her fingers almost twitched in their desire to rub Kate's shoulders, to knead away the tension Jamie saw there. She knew the short hour of riding time had been draining on Kate as she struggled to give each rider such complete attention.

"Hey, Kate," she called, drawing her attention away from the computer. "I don't want to tell you how to do your job, but wouldn't it be easier to have a lesson made up of students with similar needs?"

Kate sighed. "I'd love that," she admitted. "So kids like Anna could play games together. And Gwen would enjoy a lesson with other adults who have MS so it could be more of a support group than just an exercise session. But I can't afford time away from my regular students for so many lessons, plus I'd need more horses and some paid staff instead of relying on volunteers."

Kate pointed at the binder Jamie held. "I go into that in the proposal as well. I've had a lot of ideas about how I could make the lessons more effective with the extra funding."

Jamie nodded and turned back to the grant. She read through the detailed plans that would take Kate's part-time program and turn it into a serious business.

"Are you up for this?" she asked Myra cautiously. She didn't want to insult her, but what Kate was proposing went beyond a simple after-work project. She kept her voice pitched low so she wouldn't interrupt Kate and Anna, who seemed intent on their computer program.

Myra shook her head. "That's why I wanted you to see the proposal. I could handle the program the way it's run now, just a few hours a week. But I'm worried she's turning it into something bigger, and I can't quit my job to do this."

Jamie ripped a clean sheet of paper out of the back of the notebook and started jotting down page numbers. "You'll need to get her to change these sections," she said, showing Myra the areas where Kate had gotten carried away with her own vision of expansion. "And this whole part needs to go, unless you're planning to buy a barn and implement these improvements."

"No, I'd have to board the horses somewhere." Myra leaned over Jamie's shoulder and read her notes. "I'll never be as good at this as she is, but I'd hate to see the program end when she moves."

Jamie finished her page of recommended changes to the proposal, and then she took a fresh sheet of paper and quickly jotted estimates of the dollar amounts Myra would need for each facet of the program.

"Here's a more reasonable estimate of the allocation of funds. I'm just guessing with these numbers, of course, since I'm still not overly familiar with the horse business. I'm sure you and Kate can be more specific."

Myra read over her list and gave a low whistle. "For someone who's new to the horse world, you certainly catch on quickly. I appreciate your help with this."

"My pleasure," Jamie said, tucking her notes into the binder and handing it to Myra. "When it's anything to do with numbers, I tend to pick it up fast."

"Is that why you got into banking? Or is it just the money?"

Myra seemed honestly interested, her earlier sarcasm vanishing as Jamie helped her sort through the intricacies of the grant process, so Jamie tried to answer truthfully.

"I'm good at math, and I am pretty fond of money as well, but it's more than that. I've just always liked banks, I suppose. They give you security, and not just financially. You can keep documents there, or money, and they'll guarantee it's safe," she said with a shrug. "I worked my way through college and my MBA as a teller, and when I started looking for a job as an investment analyst, I focused on the banking industry because I knew it so well."

"I would have thought you'd have to move to New York or Chicago to really make a fortune at your job."

Jamie shrugged again. "I would be able to make more in a bigger market, but Portland is home. I do well enough here."

Anna's laugh over something on the computer made Jamie turn her attention back to her niece and Kate as they intently discussed whatever was on the laptop's screen. She didn't elaborate to Myra, but Anna was the main reason Jamie had remained in Oregon. She had originally considered the idea of moving east after Sara left home, but once Anna was born she quickly gave up that plan. She would never have sacrificed either the rare occasions she was allowed to see her niece while Sara was alive, or the unending hope she still might be able to make a difference in Sara's life. She hadn't done a good job parenting either Sara or Anna, but she had been the only one around to try. Since the accident, she'd worked hard to surround Anna with a supportive and competent medical staff, and she wouldn't simply uproot her. Her employers knew she wasn't planning to leave Portland, but they were also well aware she had the skills needed to be successful on a bigger scale than Davison and

Burke. They made the effort to keep her happy at her job, and she had never regretted staying.

"What are they doing?" she asked in order to change the subject, raising her voice enough to get Kate's attention.

"It's some sort of simulated horse farm," Myra answered with a shake of her head. "She spends all day taking care of horses and cleaning stalls. God knows why she feels the urge to create a fantasy barn after all that."

"Sounds crazy," Jamie agreed with a laugh, although she certainly could understand loving your job so much it felt like a hobby.

"Aunt Jamie can't play computer games," Anna informed Kate, her voice serious.

"Aunt Jamie doesn't like to play computer games," she told her niece firmly. "There's a difference."

Kate threw a glance over her shoulder at Jamie and then whispered something that made Anna giggle.

"If you're going to encourage insubordination, I think it's time for us to go," Jamie said with mock seriousness.

Myra stood up when she did. "I'll go make sure Chris is okay with the horses, so you can walk them out, Kate," she said, smiling at her friend's glaring expression. "Thanks for your help, Jamie."

"Anytime," she answered, pushing Anna's chair out of the door Kate held open for them. They walked silently to the car and she carefully buckled Anna inside.

"I'm impressed with the work you're doing here," she admitted to Kate as they stood facing each other in the driveway. "Thanks for opening this up for Anna, for us."

Kate just nodded, as if not trusting herself to speak, and Jamie took that opportunity to step closer. She raised her hand and traced the faint stain of red that colored Kate's cheeks every time she came near. Jamie was turned on by the visible evidence of Kate's awareness, her arousal, and she wanted to explore a little deeper and find out what other responses Kate might be hiding.

"You're not thinking of LeeAnne right now, are you?" Jamie couldn't help asking.

Kate frowned. "No. That wasn't…I might have exaggerated…" She broke off in confusion, and Jamie felt a slow smile spread over her face. It suddenly seemed so natural to bend down and give her a kiss good-bye, to give in to the urge to slide her hands along Kate's jaw and into her hair. She finally forced herself to release Kate's lips, staying close and resting her forehead against Kate's.

"We've got to stop doing this," she observed calmly, as if that simple, chaste kiss hadn't just raised her blood pressure dangerously high.

"Seems to me you're the one who always starts it," Kate said. Jamie smiled and backed toward her car door.

"I haven't heard a no yet," she said.

Chapter Ten

The city was still colored in the muted grays of predawn when Jamie lowered her light scull into the Willamette River. She slipped off the dock and settled onto the narrow seat without jostling the boat, her movements precise and economical after years of practice. She pushed away from the dock at an angle, her sigh echoing the light splash of water against the bow as the narrow scull nosed into the current. She rowed with the river's flow for a few hundred yards as a warm-up before she turned to head downstream.

Portland had yet to fully wake to the new business day, but a few early risers shared the river with Jamie. Some jogged or biked along the paved path in the riverfront park next to the Willamette, and there were a couple of scullers upstream, but still Jamie felt the relaxed isolation of a solitary rower. She had rowed on an eight-crew sweep during college, and she enjoyed the exercise and camaraderie she experienced as a member of the team. But it was only on her solo trips that she felt such peace and strength in moving through the water on only her own power.

This morning, the sense of peace took longer than usual to set in. The puddles made by her oars were uneven and choppy, and twice she rapped the knuckles of her right hand smartly with the left oar, something she hadn't done since her first lessons. She kept going, using her back and legs to push the scull against the current, fighting to tire her body enough so it would take over and force her mind to be silent.

Her thoughts kept returning to the day before. Anna had spent the whole car ride home chattering happily about Kate and Spot. Jamie, luckily not expected to do more than listen, found she was fascinated by Anna's perception of the ride. To the wheelchair-bound girl, the horse's slow gait had seemed fast and powerful, and she had enjoyed being taller than everyone else for once. Now that her niece had safely returned to the ground, Jamie could relax and appreciate how much the experience had meant to her. Still, she had never expected to be so glad to see Anna *in* her chair as she was after the short ride.

She was willing to let Anna continue with lessons, but from now on Elaine would be the one to drive her there. Jamie trusted her, and she found she was trusting Kate, with the most precious thing in her life. The worrisome part was she was tempted to trust Kate with herself. With her memories and stories, with her failures and the despair that she could ever atone for them. That was a risk Jamie couldn't take, one she hadn't dared take since she was a child, and she knew it would be better to avoid seeing Kate in a social setting. She would keep their interactions professional from now on. She had told Elaine exactly that the night before, hinting that her participation in Anna's lessons would be inappropriate given her business relationship with Kate. She hadn't mentioned that every time they were near each other, she wanted to throw all of her professional ideals aside and simply take Kate in her arms.

Two more weeks. Jamie chanted in her mind in time to the dip of her oars. Kate's million-dollar horse had finally arrived and she would have a week and a half to get him settled and accustomed to her before the big show. Then a weekend of lounging in the hospitality tent, watching Kate ride, and Jamie would need to make her final decision. Two more weeks, and they would be free of each other. And if Kate got her money, she would be out of the state and Jamie could find a new place for Anna to ride. Someplace where she could be sure Anna, and her own heart, would be safe.

By the time Jamie's scull shot past her imaginary finish line, her rhythm had settled down to the beat of *two more weeks*. The twin ripples left by the blades of her oars were symmetrical and tight, and the boat moved straight and steady through the water. Jamie had pushed herself to competition speed in order to tame her mind, and she felt the effects of the workout in her aching shoulders and lower back. She turned downstream toward the dock and let the little scull drift in the current while she caught her breath. Her thinking had calmed, but not by much, and she knew she'd have to row the entire length of Oregon if she wanted to drive thoughts of Kate fully from her mind.

❖

Jamie's determination to stay away from Kate lasted all the way until Friday morning. A consortium of local lawyers she had been courting for several months finally signed on with Davison and Burke, and she had spent nearly every waking hour over the previous three days analyzing their existing investment portfolio and detailing the changes she wanted to make. She worked with a fevered intensity in an attempt to distract herself from thoughts of Kate. Although she enjoyed the smaller projects she did for Dave Randall, she was relieved to be out of the depressing, and inevitable, lull between large jobs.

By Friday, however, she had the bulk of work completed and only needed a few hours to tidy up the presentation for Monday's meeting. She gathered her papers and locked her office, telling Jenn to take the rest of the day off. She left the building with a big smile, amazed she had finally managed to turn her assistant speechless. It felt good to get past her without a snide remark for once.

Jamie sat in her car and debated whether she should go home or not, since she knew Anna was at school, but she quickly gave up the pretense and decided to call Kate. It had been a productive, satisfying week at work, and she told herself there was nothing unusual about wanting to share that feeling with someone. Still, she couldn't admit any of that to Kate because it sounded too much like a friendship, so while she dialed her phone she searched instead for a business-related excuse to see her.

❖

"Cedar Grove." Kate answered her phone as she stretched across the tailgate of her pickup truck and tugged on the corner of a bag of grain.

"Kate?"

"Yeah," Kate said. She slid the grain across the bed of the truck and dropped her phone as she tried to pick up the heavy bag with one hand. "Damn. Hello?"

"Kate, it's Jamie." Kate stopped fumbling with the feed and focused on the call. "If you're not busy, I'd like to come watch you ride the stallion. Then I can determine how much progress you make by the show."

Kate looked at the truck full of fifty-pound sacks of feed. "No, I'm not busy," she said. "When did you want to come?"

"I'll be there in fifteen minutes."

Kate shoved the phone in her pocket and sagged against the truck. Perfect. Leave it to Jamie to pick the worst possible time to visit. A shrill whinny from the stallion's paddock jolted her back to life. She mentally listed the hour's worth of jobs she needed to cram into fifteen minutes.

Clothes first. Kate jogged to her house and sifted through the closet, grabbing the cleanest pair of breeches she could find. She pulled them on and picked out a matching shirt. She seemed to spend a lot of time dressing for Jamie. Trying to impress her. Kate couldn't deny her interest in Jamie and her obvious attraction to her, but those feelings didn't belong in their relationship. Jamie had control of her future. She could call and announce her arrival as if she was visiting royalty, and Kate had to drop everything and perform on demand.

Kate hurried back to the barn. She had groomed the stallion earlier, so she could leave him for last. She hung her shirt in the tack room to keep it clean and started putting away the feed wearing only a sports bra with her breeches. The bags left streaks of dust on her arms as she hoisted them on her shoulder one by one and hauled them into the barn without stopping to catch her breath. She would ache tomorrow, thanks to Jamie and her spot inspection. Kate's anger grew with every heavy sack. She had thought they were growing closer during the therapy rides, but Jamie was back to business today. Kate dropped the final bag and used an old towel to wipe sweat and dust off her arms and chest. She buttoned her shirt and masked her emotions. She could be professional as well.

❖

"He's not as well-behaved as Spot," Jamie observed as she walked down the barn aisle toward the crossties. The large chestnut danced back and forth in the confined space, neighing occasionally in a loud, ringing voice. Kate easily stepped out of his way, seeming to anticipate his moves. Her movements were calm, but her face was flushed with annoyance. Jamie wasn't sure if she or the stallion was the most irritating to Kate at the moment, but she was glad to at least have some competition in that battle.

"One of my mares is in heat," Kate said, slipping a bridle over the stallion's ears. "They've been calling to each other all day."

She took a firm hold on the reins and led the stallion toward her outdoor arena. He jigged behind her, tossing his head in impatience. Jamie remained where she was standing in the barn.

"Are you coming, or do you plan to watch from up here?" Kate snapped over her shoulder.

Jamie ignored her angry tone, blaming it on the stallion that was nipping testily at Kate's arm. "Look, I really don't need to watch you ride. I don't want you to get hurt because I made you do this."

"I was planning to school him this morning anyway, so don't think I'm out here because of you. He'll be fine once I get in the saddle. Besides, I can use your help setting jumps."

Jamie followed reluctantly. This had seemed like a convenient excuse for her visit, but now she regretted being the reason Kate was going to ride. Jamie wasn't pleased with the prospect of watching a rodeo event, but she couldn't leave Kate out there alone. Kate closed the arena's gate behind them and tightened the stallion's girth before turning back to Jamie.

"Can you give me a leg up?" she asked. Jamie went over and took hold of Kate's bent knee, then dropped it again.

"Are you sure about this?" she asked, standing close behind Kate.

"Just put me on the damned horse," Kate said. She bent her knee again and this time Jamie lifted her easily into the saddle. She let her palm rest on Kate's leg as her thumb idly wiped at a smudge of dirt on Kate's beige breeches. The stallion shifted his hooves and Kate's thigh tightened. Jamie felt a matching tension in her stomach and she wanted to rub, to explore the muscles under her hand. She let Kate go and stepped back. Their lives were intersecting for a short time, and then she and Kate would go in separate directions. She had no right to feel protective of Kate or to feel a desire that threatened to outlast sex.

She sat on the rail of a low jump and watched as Kate started to move the horse around the ring. Surprisingly, he settled right to work as Kate quietly trotted him in figure eights and serpentines. Jamie was just starting to relax when Kate asked the horse to canter and he reared so he was nearly vertical to the ground. Jamie heard the thud of her heart as her body tensed, ready to run toward Kate. And do what? Before she could react, the stallion's front hooves returned to earth. Kate seemed unfazed, and she quickly controlled the animal before sending him forward in a smooth canter. Jamie took deep breaths to counteract the surge of adrenaline. The horse had acted so quickly. He was all grace and power, and the stunt would have been beautiful to watch on a nature show about wild horses. In the ring with Kate on his back, it was closer to terrifying.

Kate finished her warm-up and came over to tell Jamie how to set the jumps. "Does he always do that?" Jamie asked as she lowered the rails on a few of the fences.

"Rear? No not much. Only a couple of times," Kate amended. "I'm starting to feel when he's about to try something, so I can usually prepare for it. He's a little distracted right now because of the mare, but he needs to get used to it. There'll be plenty of them at the shows."

"Great," Jamie said with an attempt at a smile. "If he gets this excited over one, what will he do with a whole harem?"

Kate just laughed and trotted away, her spirits seeming to lift as she spent more time in the saddle. She jumped the stallion over the low fences and gradually had Jamie raise them until the poles reached the tops of the standards. Jamie had to admit the horse looked talented. He cleared the high obstacles by several inches, making everything seem effortless. Jamie could tell Kate was working harder than she had done on Topper, as if it took all of her strength and concentration to coax the stallion into a smooth performance. When she finally brought the horse to a halt and dismounted, she was breathing hard, but the stallion looked as fresh as he had at the beginning of the ride.

They were quiet on the walk back to the barn. "What did you think?" Kate eventually asked.

"I'm not an expert, but he sure is something to watch," Jamie said. "He's very…explosive off the ground."

"You should try sitting on him," Kate said with a grin. Jamie could tell Kate meant that in a positive way, but there was no way in hell Jamie would want to be up there. It had been bad enough just to watch.

Jamie stood by while Kate untacked and groomed the horse. They walked him over to the small barn together, and Jamie expected the horse to take off like a shot once he was turned loose in his paddock. Instead, he wandered over to a pile of hay and started eating calmly. His unpredictability bothered Jamie more than constant wildness would have done, and she tried to shake off her uneasy feelings about the horse. Kate would be riding the stallion even if Davison and Burke weren't considering a sponsorship, but Jamie felt an uncomfortable sense of responsibility. Nothing to do with a personal concern for Kate's safety, of course. She trailed behind Kate in silence until they returned to the main barn where she took Kate's saddle out of her arms and carried it into the tack room for her. Kate hung her bridle on a hook near the sink and

Jamie came closer and captured her hand. She stroked the calluses on Kate's palm and traced the edges of her fingers. Kate's hand was slender and beautiful, rough from work and the outdoors. Capable. Jamie's touch was sensitive enough she could feel when a shiver ran through Kate.

"You're shaking," she said accusingly, holding Kate's hand lightly between her own.

Kate laughed and pulled her hand away. "I'm not scared, I'm just hungry. I haven't eaten yet today."

"It's almost eleven," Jamie said, glancing at her watch. Kate just shrugged and started to clean her bridle with saddle soap. Jamie took the wet sponge away and tossed it in the sink. She grabbed a rag off the counter and wiped soapy residue off her hands before reaching for Kate's and doing the same, trying not to linger this time. "Leave that, and let's go get lunch."

She tugged a protesting Kate out to her car. "I can't, Jamie. I have to clean my tack and I have lessons this afternoon."

"What time do you teach?"

"Four," Kate admitted. "But I really should—"

"Eat," Jamie suggested. She hoped her expression made it an order.

Kate shook her head but stopped arguing. "You're annoying. Let me change first, at least. No, you wait here," she added when Jamie started to follow her to the house. "I'll be right out."

Jamie pulled her car into the driveway by the house, and Kate was quickly back outside, wearing jeans and a polo shirt instead of her breeches. Her blond hair hung loose around her shoulders. She stepped into the low car, and Jamie caught a glimpse of the crotch of Kate's jeans where the seams had frayed, probably from hours of rubbing against a saddle and those suede chaps. Then Kate slid her other leg in and blocked Jamie's view.

"Ooh, nice," Kate said, snuggling into the comfortable leather seat next to Jamie. "Where are we going?"

"It's a surprise," Jamie said, feeling oddly lighthearted with Kate so close. She fought the temptation to hold her hand, figuring she just might get slapped if she tried. What she really wanted to do was reach between Kate's legs and play with the loose threads on her jeans. She drove slowly through the residential streets of Wilsonville and pulled into the drive-through of a Mexican fast-food restaurant near the freeway.

"This is the surprise?" Kate asked with a grin. "Really, you'll spoil me."

"I'd like to," Jamie said. "Now, what do you want?"

She tossed their bag of food in the backseat and got onto I-5 heading north. She accelerated up to speed quickly, slipping the Mercedes through the traffic until she was in the fast lane even though she would only be on the freeway for a few miles. She noticed Kate had her hand braced against the dashboard.

"What's wrong?" she asked in concern, glancing over at Kate who looked a shade paler than normal.

"My God, do you always drive like this?" Kate gasped, her eyes never leaving the road.

"Like what? We're on the freeway, so how do you expect me to drive?"

"At the speed limit?" Kate suggested. "Or at least reasonably close to it?"

Jamie rolled her eyes. "What's the point in having a car like this if I'm going to putter along in the slow lane?" She patted the car's dash. "This baby's built for speed."

Kate slapped at her arm. "Keep both hands on the wheel, please," she said.

"It only feels like we're going fast because we're so much closer to the ground than you are in that big truck you drive," Jamie informed her. "Oops, there's our exit."

She confidently eased the car between two trucks as she took the exit to Highway 205 and headed for the fast lane again. She took corners and made lane changes more abruptly than usual, enjoying the little squeaks and gasps from Kate at each turn. Kate had scared the hell out of her on that horse, and Jamie didn't mind getting a taste of revenge. Besides, she liked hearing the sounds Kate made. Jamie took the exit for Lake Oswego and braked quickly at a stoplight. She laughed and reached over to pry Kate's hand off her dash. "Honestly, you just spent the morning galloping around on Man o' War, and a couple of fast turns in a car freak you out?"

Kate relaxed somewhat as Jamie drove more carefully through the town of Lake Oswego, another affluent suburb of Portland. Jamie parked in the lot of a waterfront park and grabbed their sack of food.

"Are we having a picnic?" Kate asked as she climbed out of the car, relieved to be out of Jamie's deathtrap.

"Sort of," Jamie said. "It's part of the surprise."

"I thought the NASCAR routine was enough excitement for one day," Kate muttered as she and Jamie walked along a paved path that led through the park's gardens. The air was moist from the lake and the dense foliage, and Kate took a deep breath, glad to be near the water after a day spent sweating in her barn and dusty arena. When they reached the Lake Oswego Rowing Club, Jamie unlocked the metal gate and led the way down a narrow ramp to the boathouse.

"Hey, Rusty," Jamie called out to a man who was varnishing an old wooden scull. The slender boat was propped on a couple of sawhorses on a small patch of lawn at the bottom of the ramp.

"Hey, Jamie, how you doin'?"

"Not bad. Mind if I take the rowboat out for a couple of hours?"

"Go right ahead," he waved them on and returned to his work.

Kate followed Jamie onto the dock and around the blue boathouse. When Kate realized they were going boating, she expected Jamie to choose a fancy yacht or sleek black speedboat. Not the small fiberglass rowboat that drifted lazily on the lake. Jamie leaned over to set their food on the center seat and then reached back to help Kate into the boat.

"Don't tell me you're afraid of the water, too?" Jamie asked when Kate hesitated.

"No, I'm not. I just didn't expect this…from you."

"What do you mean by that?" Jamie asked, her hands on her hips.

"It's just…kind of romantic," Kate said. And sexy, as Jamie stood with one foot in the old boat and one on the dock, straddling the narrow strip of water between them.

"I'll be sure to dump you in the lake after we eat. Would that be more what you expect from me?"

Kate took Jamie's hand and gingerly climbed into the rocking boat. Jamie loosened the rope from the cleat and pushed away from the dock, rowing them toward the center of the lake.

"Oh my, I seem to have forgotten my parasol," Kate said with a heavy drawl, trailing her fingers in the water. Jamie sliced an oar through the water and splashed her.

"Bitch," Kate said with a laugh.

"Oh, very ladylike."

Once they were well away from the dock, Jamie secured the oars and let the craft drift, keeping an eye out for other boaters. Kate handed her a taco and they sat facing each other while they ate.

"Do you do this a lot?" Kate asked around a mouthful of burrito.

"Take beautiful women a-courting on the lake?"

"I meant boating in general." Kate had never imagined Jamie with a hobby, but this clearly was a beloved one. Jamie's mouth rested in a half smile, and the frown line between her brows disappeared.

"I learned to row at the club here, on an eight-crew sweep like the one hanging on the side of the boathouse. Rusty was one of my coaches when I was in college. Now I keep my scull on the Willamette so it's closer to work and I can get on the water most mornings."

"I'll bet you're good at it," Kate said.

Jamie laughed. "I am, but you somehow made that sound like an insult."

Kate gave her a guilty smile of acknowledgment. "It's just that you seem to do everything well," she admitted. Like kissing. Kate's body still got warm at just the memory of their kiss. "Most of us have to work hard to succeed."

"Believe me, I know what hard work is," Jamie informed her. "And rowing is like math. There are ratios and angles and you train until you're as close to the ideal as possible. I can do that. When it comes to things that don't have absolute values, it seems to get harder for me."

"Like Anna?" Kate asked.

Jamie hesitated. She meant her feelings for Kate, her desire for something she couldn't yet articulate and knew she couldn't have. Because Kate was going away. "Yes," she said. "Like Anna."

As if in silent agreement, and much to Jamie's relief, they dropped the serious subjects. Jamie lounged easily in the boat, occasionally paddling a little to get out of someone's path. Kate propped her bare feet on the seat beside Jamie, eventually relaxing enough that her complexion smoothed, the lines of tension gone. They talked about inconsequential things, and Jamie tried to remember the last time she had left work early for something other than an emergency or one of Anna's medical appointments. She soon abandoned that line of thought, since nothing came to mind. She had originally come up with this spur-of-the-moment idea at the barn in an attempt to do something nice for Kate. She wanted to show her appreciation for Kate's help with Anna, and getting her away from the barn, the horse, and stress about the sponsorship seemed better than having Jenn send flowers or a card. The afternoon had turned out to be more special to Jamie than she had expected, though. Lying back in the boat with the sound of water dripping off her raised oar, she felt more at peace than she had in years. She tried to convince herself it had more to do with being on the lake after a week of satisfyingly hard work than anything to do with the woman sitting across from her.

Nevertheless, she did take a chance and reached for Kate's hand during the drive home. She was surprised Kate didn't protest, although she nearly squeezed Jamie's fingers off during a rather sharp turn. Jamie dropped her off next to her house and left with a quick good-bye, no kissing this time, and a familiar wave of sadness replaced the temporary peace she had been feeling. Their excursion had been a captured day, a little relief from work and stress for both of them, but certainly not something that could become a habit. Jamie drove away wondering why she already felt a sense of mourning after such a perfect afternoon.

Kate watched Jamie's car disappear around the corner before she went into her house. Her shoulders ached from the day's heavy lifting and her ride on the stallion. She had been more upset by the horse's rear than she had let on. She had lost focus, her mind on Jamie's hand covering her thigh, the caress of Jamie's thumb. Kate swallowed some aspirin for her sore muscles. Jamie was too much of a distraction, and Kate could get hurt if she wasn't more careful. Physically, if her mind wasn't on her riding, or worse, emotionally, if she started to care for Jamie too much.

CHAPTER ELEVEN

Jamie piled a plate with sandwiches and cookies, balanced it on top of two plastic cups of lemonade, and brought the stack over to the corner of the hospitality tent where Anna and Elaine were sitting. She was glad to have a shady spot for them since it was over ninety degrees and the horse show was being held on a large open field. The surrounding hillsides were forested and looked lush and cool, but the grounds themselves were bare and grassy with every inch devoted to some aspect of the competition. The show was bigger than Jamie had expected, with four rings for judged events and two warm-up areas that were full of horses and looked like chaos to her. The Davison and Burke tent was situated on the adjoining corner of the two largest rings, so they had a great view of most of the competition.

The well-maintained grounds were definitely more wheelchair friendly than the other show Jamie and Anna had attended. The grass was trimmed short, and wide tanbark paths crisscrossed the show so the snack bar, barns, and parking lot were easily accessible. Low white chains clearly marked the designated pedestrian areas, and short picket fences controlled the horse traffic, so Jamie could relax and not worry about a repeat of their first disastrous show experience. Anna had already discovered the trailer a local tack shop sent to the show, and she had a box with a brand-new riding helmet sitting next to her chair.

Jamie handed sandwiches around before taking one for herself and settling on a folding chair next to Anna. Although she considered this a workday, she had made an effort to spend time with her niece, and even Elaine was smiling at her for a change. The tent had proved to be a brilliant idea, and during a brief talk with Dave Randall at the coffee urn, the two had decided to make it an annual tradition and to possibly sponsor a class the following year. Many of their clients had some connection to the horse world, and there had been a constant parade of children and grandchildren in fancy riding outfits through their buffet line. It was a comfortable way for Jamie and her coworkers to mingle socially with their investors, and Jamie had even made a few promising new contacts. It would have been an ideal day if Jamie hadn't spent most of it watching for some sign of Kate.

"So, why are the jumps so much brighter in this ring?" Jamie asked her niece around a mouthful of ham sandwich. She waved toward the right where the poles were painted in vibrant whites and primary colors. The arena on the left had a course of jumps that were natural earth tones, some of them filled with fir boughs. The two smaller rings across from their tent were filled with similarly brown- and green-toned jumps. She realized she hadn't been paying much attention to the show itself, since she had been focused on networking.

"That's the jumper ring," Anna said with confident authority, pointing at the brighter jumps. Kate had loaned her a few books on the subject, and Jamie was proud to see how quickly Anna had absorbed the new knowledge. "They jump higher fences, and they're judged quanta…on how many poles they knock down and how long they take to finish the course."

"Quantitatively," Jamie offered.

"That's what I said." Anna rolled her eyes at Jamie's correction, and Jamie had to raise her hand to her mouth to cover a smile. Anna's expression looked so *normal*, so typical for a long-suffering preteen. She had always been so quiet, so careful in Jamie's presence, and Jamie was happy to see Anna growing more comfortable with her. Jamie felt herself relaxing as she listened to Anna talk. "The other ring is for hunters, and the fences are supposed to look like the ones you'd see on a foxhunt. The horses are judged on how pretty they look and how well the person rides."

"Subjectively?" Jamie suggested. She much preferred the first option. Better to be judged on some measurable factor instead of being subject to the judge's whims. "So, Kate will be in the jumper ring. Those fences don't look *too* high."

"That's 'cause they're set for beginners now, so they aren't even three feet high. Everyone's put in classes by how old they are or how experienced, and the better riders jump higher," Anna said, tapping a page in her program with an impatient gesture, as if Jamie should have been able to figure it out on her own. "See, in Kate's class they'll be over four feet."

Jamie, suddenly not as hungry, set down the unfinished half of her sandwich. She was going to need something stronger than lemonade to help her through this day.

"Look," Anna patted her arm and pointed across the ring. "There she is."

Jamie followed her gesture and immediately spotted Kate in shirtsleeves and tan breeches, her silvery blond hair caught in a high ponytail. She was standing next to two girls on ponies, pointing at the fences in one of the distant hunter rings as she talked to them. The jumps in the far two arenas were noticeably smaller than the ones near Jamie's tent.

"I should go say hello," Jamie said, getting to her feet quickly.

"Maybe you could ask her to come see me?" Anna suggested shyly.

"I will," Jamie assured her, giving Anna's thin shoulder a quick squeeze. It was much easier to be comfortable around her niece when they had a conversation subject so close at hand. Yet one more reason to appreciate both this day and Kate's influence on them. Kate had become a common thread between Jamie and Anna, between Jamie's work and home lives. Jamie had always fought to maintain separation, and she was surprised to find she liked the connections.

She left the tent and stepped over the white picket fence that marked the boundary of the closest warm-up arena. As she made her way over to Kate in the smaller ring, she stayed close to the temporary fencing that bordered the riding areas so she wouldn't be trampled by the horses of all sizes as they moved around in some pattern only they could discern. She finally made it to the second warm-up ring, only to find that Kate was now standing next to a small white jump in the middle of the crowded area. Jamie dodged among the horses and ponies until she reached the center of the ring where Kate's students trotted back and forth over a cross rail while she called out a series of instructions to them.

"He's still brown, Bethany," Kate yelled as one of the girls awkwardly popped over the jump.

"Is that code?" Jamie asked quietly, standing close. Kate started at the sound of her voice.

"It's supposed to be a joke," she said with a nervous-looking smile, meeting Jamie's eyes briefly before she turned her focus back to the girls. "Bethany stares down at his neck instead of looking where she's going."

"Ah, very funny," Jamie said before her smile was replaced by a concerned frown. She reached out and cupped Kate's chin, running her thumb along the tense jawline. "God, you look exhausted."

Kate stepped back and out of reach. Tired lines were etched on her pale features and her green eyes had shadows underneath them. "It's been a long week," she admitted. "But we've come a long way since you saw us last. I'm sure you'll be impressed with Blaze's performance."

"Blaze, Spot…you don't come up with the most original names," Jamie observed as Kate raised the jump so it was a single rail, about two feet off the ground.

"Both of them came pre-named, so don't blame me," Kate said, more sharply than the little joke warranted. She raised her voice and snapped out her next instruction. "Girls, canter this vertical a couple of times."

Far from being upset by Kate's tone, Jamie saw it as a sign of real exhaustion that Kate let her cool façade slip in front of Jamie and her students. Jamie worried about Kate riding the stallion without the energy and focus she needed to stay in control of him.

To stay safe. "I'll let you get back to work," she said quietly. "Come by the tent when you get a chance. Anna wants to see you, and you can get some lunch."

"After this class," Kate said before turning back to her students. Jamie waited for a break in the sea of riders, feeling like a pedestrian on the autobahn, and jogged out of the warm-up ring.

❖

Kate attempted to refocus her attention to her riders, and off Jamie. Somehow the woman had an annoying ability to reach past whatever mask Kate had on and reveal what she was really feeling. And today what she felt was tired and out of sorts. Jamie had appeared looking so clean and at ease, with a crisp white shirt worn loosely over a white tank top and those sexy designer jeans she had worn on her first visit to Kate's barn. Kate, on the other hand, felt dusty and grimy after a morning in the dirt arenas with the sun beating down on her, and worn-out after a week babysitting the high-maintenance stallion that seemed intent on tearing down her barn board by board. Whatever he couldn't kick to picces he tried to chew. After a few days of steady exercise his attitude was improving, but Kate could sense he would be a horse that would constantly be testing his boundaries. She was in awe of his talent, though, and exhausted as she was, it had been worth it for the thrill of riding such an animal. Unfortunately, his talent seemed to attract too much attention, and Kate's normally quiet barn had been disrupted all week by friends and local trainers who wanted to see the horse. The focus her riders needed before a big show had been dispersed in too many directions for Kate's comfort.

Even Kate's parents had wanted to come out and watch her ride the horse that would launch their daughter's career. Kate had been in pigtails and short stirrups the last time they had shown any interest in watching her ride. They had approved of her hobby, were thrilled to see so many children of the social elite in Kate's lessons, and had worked long hours to buy her the best clothes and tack. Kate would have gladly ridden in rags if she could have had her parents at the shows to congratulate her after a good ride, or console her after a bad one.

Kate dusted off her students' tall black boots and gave them some last-minute instructions and encouragement as they waited to compete. She knew their parents were in the stands ready to cheer them on, and she had been planning to ask her own to come to a show for once in her career. She had quickly dismissed the idea after they came to watch her ride the stallion. Her mare had just come in heat and the stallion was a terror. After a sweaty hour in the arena, he and Kate were working as a team for the first time since he had arrived, and she had triumphantly dismounted and waited for her parents' praise. Her mom's only comment was that it was a shame the stallion wasn't black, which would show Kate's fair coloring off better on a magazine cover. Kate had been exhausted when they finally left.

Jamie's unexpected visit the day after her parents' should have left her equally drained, and she was still surprised it had turned out to be such an enjoyable afternoon. *Not* because Jamie was there. Because she had a decent schooling session with Blaze, except for his spectacular rear, and a rare two hours away from the barn and on the water. Kate rubbed her hands down her breeches, trying to erase the sensation of Jamie holding them, caressing each finger with such intent concentration until Kate had trembled with arousal.

Kate shook off the distracting memory as she watched Bethany and Danielle jump the course one at a time, and she leaned forward on every takeoff as if she were in the ring herself. Bethany rode in with an expression of doom but came out with a smile after a safe but unspectacular round. Kate counted that as a success for the girl's first show. Danielle was more experienced, and as Kate was applauding the smooth round, she caught herself making plans for Danielle to move to a more advanced level in the next show season. Kate reminded herself she wouldn't be around for the next season. Her students would move on to a new teacher, a new barn, and Kate would leave.

Kate waited until her students collected their ribbons, a second-place red for Danielle and a fifth-place pink for Bethany, before she headed to the hospitality tent. Although Jamie had been joking at the Hadleys' party, she was correct in saying Kate would be moving to the big leagues once she started her Olympic quest. Her time at shows would no longer be just for her and her students, and she would have to get used to the social responsibility. For a start, that meant putting more effort into being civil to Jamie Callahan.

She came to a halt at the entrance of the shady tent, caught by the picture of Jamie kneeling next to Anna's chair and listening to something the little girl said. Kate was struck by the difference between this show and the last one Jamie and Anna had attended. Kate remembered Anna's face streaked with tears when she came around the corner of the barn, and Jamie's expression stiff with anger and pain as she fought to protect her niece. Now Anna was talking and gesturing with animation. And there was such an awkward tenderness in Jamie's expression as she listened. Kate stood still for a moment, not wanting to interrupt the intimate family scene, but then Jamie glanced up and met her eyes, and the same tenderness briefly focused on her before Kate blinked and broke eye contact. Jamie stood and quickly made her way to Kate's side.

"Come and sit down for a few minutes," she said, putting an arm across Kate's shoulders and insistently guiding her to the quiet corner of the tent.

"Jamie," Kate pulled her to a halt before they reached Anna. "I'm sorry I snapped at you back there. I shouldn't have."

"No big deal." Jamie waved off her apology and continued on her way. "You have a lot on your mind today," she tossed over her shoulder.

Kate followed her and bent to give Anna a hug before Jamie introduced her to Elaine. Kate remembered Jamie's jokes about Elaine's housecleaning uniforms. She pictured the plump woman in a bikini, washing windows, and she hoped her sudden urge to laugh only looked like a friendly smile. Jamie gently pushed Kate into an empty chair. "Have you eaten today?"

"I had breakfast," Kate said, not sure if coffee and a maple bar at four thirty really qualified. "But some lemonade sounds good."

"Are you enjoying the show, Anna?" Kate asked once Jamie left to get her drink.

"Yes. But it makes me miss riding."

"I know what you mean," Kate said, smiling at Anna. "I like to watch my students, but sometimes it makes me itch to get on a horse myself. I'm sorry I had to cancel the therapy lesson this week so you have to wait so long between rides, but I've been here since Tuesday morning."

"I'll be bringing Anna to the next lesson," Elaine said. "So I'll finally get to see what all the fuss is about."

Kate felt a wave of emptiness and she saw a similar emotion on Anna's face. "I guess I assumed Jamie would bring her again," she said. Kate attributed her reaction to sheer exhaustion. After tomorrow's Grand Prix class, Jamie would have all the information she needed to make her decision. There really was no reason for Kate to expect to see her after that.

"Oh, Jamie takes Anna to all of her new appointments, but once she approves of the person involved, then I get to take over," Elaine said, her shrewd glance seeming to take in both Kate and Anna's fleeting expressions of disappointment. "But I can't wait to meet this handsome Spot fellow I've been hearing so much about."

Kate seized on that topic and started to describe her other lesson horses to Elaine, when Jamie reappeared by her side with a plate laden with food. She handed it to Kate before sitting on the grass next to her.

"I'm really not hungry," Kate started to protest.

"I brought a little of everything, so just eat what you want," Jamie said with a shrug. She set a glass of lemonade on the ground next to Kate. "So Anna might get to ride other horses?"

Kate took a small bite of icy watermelon that soothed her parched throat. She continued her monologue about the horses, urged on by Anna's rapt expression and Jamie's typically insightful questions. After a few minutes she realized she had eaten most of the food on her plate.

"It's a good thing I have a few hours before I ride," she said with an accusing glance at Jamie. "I can't go out there on a full stomach."

"This woman needs a nanny to keep her fed," Jamie informed Elaine. "Maybe you should moonlight with her on the weekends."

Kate joined in their laughter, feeling at ease for the first time that day. "I really should get back to the barn, or my students will come looking for me." She gave Jamie's shoulder a quick nudge with her knee before she stood up. "I'll see you after I ride this afternoon."

Kate left feeling surprisingly refreshed. She had been dreading the required visit to the bank's tent, but it had been easier than she had expected to spend time around Jamie. Because it felt like having a picnic lunch with family. She came to a sudden halt at that thought and was nearly run down by a trotting horse. She moved on quickly, waving an apology to the rider as she pushed aside that ridiculous notion. It was dangerous to think of Jamie as anything but a business associate. This stupid longing for more would only break her concentration and make her do something foolish that could cause her to lose the sponsorship, the one thing she really wanted. She hurried back to the stabling area, determined to refocus and hoping her stallion hadn't torn down his stall while she'd been gone.

Chapter Twelve

Kate's jumper class was one of the last of the afternoon. By that time, Jamie's patience had worn a little thin after hours of watching hundreds of horses jump over some variation of the same course. The riders were dressed conservatively in dark jackets and tan breeches and the horses were mostly shades of brown or gray, so they all started to blend. Their tent had cleared out after the lunch crowd, and even Anna's enthusiasm was starting to wane. She had spent the past half hour reading a book about dragons while Elaine did a crossword puzzle.

Jamie stretched out in her chair, her long legs propped on an ice chest while she watched the jump crew raise the fences yet *again* before Kate's class. They were nearing five feet, and Jamie did her best to forget that for tomorrow's Grand Prix they would be even higher. From their seats, they had a clear view of a red-and-white monstrosity that looked wide enough to fit a couple of horses between its rails. Jamie tried to ignore it as she turned her attention back to the warm-up ring where Kate and Blaze had been trotting around for fifteen minutes. Jamie could tell even from a distance that Kate was the center of attention among all the riders out there. No surprise, since she was riding such an impressive horse, but Kate would draw admiring looks even if she were out there on Spot. Jamie saw in Kate the beauty of an athlete. Supple but strong, relaxed but responsive. The dichotomies suited her. And Kate inspired dual responses in Jamie. She was proud of Kate's abilities and talent, but she wanted to drag her off the horse like a Neanderthal. She wanted to see Kate succeed but didn't want to see her go. Jamie turned back toward the red-and-white jump when the class was about to begin.

She had learned enough during the day to follow the rules of the class. Each rider would make an attempt at the course, and they received faults for knocking down poles, refusing to jump, or going over the time allowed to complete the round. Anyone without faults would return for a timed jump-off over a shortened course, and the horse and rider with the fewest faults and the shortest time would win. Since this was only a warm-up before tomorrow's big class, and it was Blaze's first show in the States, Kate had told Jamie she wasn't planning to push him too hard or too fast. Jamie hoped that translated to safe.

The first horse finally came into the ring, and Anna put her book aside to watch. Jamie stayed in her relaxed position, refusing to let any of her anxiety show. She had no reason to care whether or not Kate did well here. On the contrary, it would make Jamie's job easier if she failed this weekend. After years of investment analysis, Jamie knew the worst thing she could do was to get too emotionally attached to the outcome of any venture. A cool head helped her make the right decisions or remedy any possible mistakes.

After five horses had completed the course, two of them with clear rounds, Kate moved into position at the back gate. Jamie sat up, her elbows resting on her knees in what she hoped was a nonchalant pose. As long as she didn't have to shake hands with anyone, she decided she could pull it off.

"Oh my," Elaine said in an awed voice. "That is one impressive animal."

"No shit," Jamie muttered quietly, earning her a disapproving frown from Elaine. Anna was so intent on watching, Jamie doubted she'd noticed the quiet curse.

Kate and Blaze sailed around the course at a noticeably faster pace than the other entrants. For a horse built like a tank, he had a surprising lightness about him when he jumped, drawing his knees up tightly and making it look effortless. Kate, on the other hand, had a look of fierce concentration on her face. When she rode close to the tent, Jamie could see lines of tension around her mouth and a tautness in her forearms that were the only indications she was working hard to control the strong horse. She had the same grace about her Jamie had seen when she'd first watched her ride Topper, but some of the joy was missing. Still, Kate had been riding her own horse for five years and this one for only a week. Jamie hoped time would help Kate find that connection again.

Kate left the ring to a loud round of applause, and Jamie realized she had been holding her breath the whole ride. To prove she really didn't care about the outcome of the class, Jamie stood up and wandered to the back of the tent. She found Dave talking to one of the junior associates, and she joined them in conversation, only occasionally glancing back at the arena. The three of them walked back toward the ring together when the jump-off started.

The audience gasped in unison as the first rider in the jump-off pulled his horse into an impossibly tight turn in order to save time between fences. The horse's front hoof nicked the rail, and it teetered but didn't fall. The second to go managed to beat his time, but at the expense of knocking down two poles and ending up with eight jumping faults.

"I have to admit, that woman has guts," Dave said appreciatively as Kate trotted back into the ring to start her jump-off round.

Jamie didn't answer, her attention focused on Kate who looked so small on the massive stallion. She was relieved to see them take the fences at about the same speed as their initial round.

"Hmm, look at her time," the associate said, gesturing at the electronic timer. "It'll be easy to beat."

"She wasn't trying to win this class," Jamie told him. "They competed mainly to give the horse experience in the ring before tomorrow."

"So we'll see her really go for it in the Grand Prix?"

"She'd better, if she wants Davison and Burke's money," Dave said with a laugh as the two of them walked away. Jamie knew he was right. Tomorrow would be Kate's final chance to prove herself to Jamie and the rest of the company. She wouldn't hold anything back.

Still in the ring, Kate struggled to convince the stallion to stop after he sailed over the last fence with room to spare. She had to circle him twice at a fast canter before she could slow him enough to leave the ring safely. In her rides at home, and in this jump-off, she hadn't pushed him for speed, and she hoped she'd be able to control him when she finally did unleash the power she could feel building inside him.

Kate glanced at the hospitality tent as she trotted from the ring. She could see Jamie standing in the shadows, watching her. Kate felt as if she was sitting on dynamite these days. The stallion, the sponsorship, the impending upheaval of her life. And her feelings for Jamie. Kate only hoped she would survive the inevitable explosions with her heart intact.

❖

Jamie helped Elaine get a very weary Anna into Elaine's minivan. She promised she would be following them home soon, and she made her way back through the emptying parking lot to the field behind the show rings where the exhibitors' party was being held. A band was playing country music, and strings of lights illuminated the tables full of barbecue. Jamie grabbed a bottle of beer and wandered through the crowd in search of Kate. She spotted her in the food line, surrounded by a group of her students.

Jamie put some chicken and coleslaw on her plate and stood off to the side, watching Kate interact with her kids. They clamored for her attention, and Jamie could tell she made an effort to talk to each one individually.

"So, what did you think?" Myra asked as she came up behind Jamie.

"She rode well. I'm interested to see how they do when she really is trying to win," Jamie lied. "You've been around her this week, is having this horse everything she expected?"

Myra shrugged. "He's pushy, arrogant, and overbearing, but nothing she hasn't dealt with before. I told her she should change his name from Blaze to Jamie."

Jamie laughed. “Are you saying I helped prepare her to handle him?”

“Compared to you, he’s a cinch,” Myra said. She started to walk away and then stopped. “Don’t you dare break her heart.”

Jamie wasn’t sure how Myra meant that, but she chose to interpret it in a purely professional sense. “You know I can’t make a decision until I’ve seen what they can really do together.”

Myra gave her a half smile. “I’ve never known her to back down from a challenge. Keep that in mind.”

Jamie took a long drink of her beer and looked back in Kate’s direction. She had separated from her group and was heading for a trash can. Jamie walked over and intercepted her.

“Congratulations,” she said, taking Kate’s plate and throwing it away with her own. “Third place seemed okay for today.”

“Thank you,” Kate accepted with a smile. To Jamie’s eyes, she was already looking more relaxed than she had all day. “He got to see the fences and get a feel for the footing in the ring. That’s all I wanted.”

Jamie glanced over to the dance floor where couples were swaying to a slow song. Since the Hadley party, she had only had small tastes of Kate. A kiss, isolated touches. Jamie wanted her arms around Kate, Kate’s body pressed against hers. A public dance would be safe. Jamie could hold Kate and still keep control. She had noticed several same-sex partners dancing, so she decided to give it a shot.

“Would you like to dance?”

Kate nodded, and Jamie placed a hand on her lower back as they walked, unsure whether Kate had agreed because she had been caught off guard or because she knew she was in the final push for Jamie’s approval and was trying to be amenable.

Whatever the reason, Jamie was happy to have Kate safely in her arms for a little while. Kate had changed from riding clothes to jeans, and Jamie settled her hands on Kate’s hips, catching her thumbs in the belt loops to keep her hands from wandering to the ass she had been admiring all day. Kate rested her hands on top of Jamie’s shoulders, her arms a little stiff as if making sure the two of them stayed separated.

Jamie couldn't remember the last time she had danced with another woman. She'd expected to have some awkward steps, but the two of them moved together smoothly. She felt Kate's stiffness ease a little, and she took that chance to tug gently on Kate's hips and fit them more snugly against her own. She pulled her as close as she dared with Kate's students around, and lowered her cheek to Kate's hair.

Jamie expected to feel a physical jolt when she touched Kate, like she had on the Hadleys' patio, but this time their coming together was more like a sigh, as soft as Kate's breath on her neck. Her thumbs escaped the belt loops and gently traced the top of Kate's hip bones. She was overwhelmed by the wave of protectiveness she felt. While she was in Jamie's arms, Kate couldn't be hurt, and Jamie realized with a wave of apprehension how much that was starting to mean to her. She couldn't want that because Kate would eventually leave her arms and ride that blasted stallion again, moving back east and leaving her old life behind.

"You don't have to go through with it, you know," Jamie said, leaning toward Kate's ear.

"With what?" Kate asked. She leaned back to meet Jamie's eyes and the movement made her hips push forward. Jamie slipped her hands into Kate's back pockets. She pressed harder, feeling soft flesh over firm muscle, and pulled Kate's pelvis against her own. The contact was a powerful distraction and she spoke her thoughts out loud before she could stop herself.

"Tomorrow. You don't have to ride him in the class tomorrow."

Kate stopped swaying to the music but she didn't make any move to pull away. "Why would I want to quit?"

"Let someone else buy him, and stay here. Stay with your students, with your therapy program." Jamie couldn't ask Kate to stay for her, when all she could offer was a brief fling, a few weeks of passionate sex. How long would it be before Kate realized she had given up her dream for an illusion of a relationship? But Kate's work gave her life meaning, purpose. Jamie could ask her to stay for that.

"I'm not afraid," Kate said with a frown, her green eyes turning to jade.

"I didn't say you were. But can you honestly tell me you were having fun out there?"

Kate pulled away, but she remained close enough to speak without being overheard. "This is my career we're talking about, not some silly hobby. It might not buy me a fancy sports car or a live-in nanny so I don't have to spend time with my own family, but to me it's just as important as your job. It might not always be fun, and it'll take a lot of hard work, but I am not a quitter."

"Then I wish you luck tomorrow," Jamie said coldly. "I hope you get everything you want."

Jamie walked away. She headed to the dark parking lot to find her fancy sports car, so she could drive home where Anna's nanny would have bathed her and put her to bed. She feared Kate was heading toward a similarly empty life. She had seen the light on her face when she talked to her students or rode her own horse, even when she joked around with Myra. No Olympic medal could replace what Kate was leaving behind. Even if Kate couldn't appreciate the connections in her life, Jamie could. But she could no more change the course of Kate's life than she could change her own at this stage. Jamie had put up too many barriers to be able to develop the kinds of relationships Kate was about to throw away. They had already made their decisions, and in Jamie's opinion they'd both lost.

CHAPTER THIRTEEN

Sunday's sky was covered with a marine layer Jamie knew would burn off in a few hours, leaving them sweltering in the sun yet again. She drove through a misty drizzle that wasn't wet enough to require windshield wipers, but enough to have left a moist sheen on her hair when she walked to her car. The gray skies suited her mood, although she tried to tell herself to be relieved that this day would prove to be her last interaction with Kate.

As Jamie left the city streets and freeway traffic, she felt some of the depression that lingered after last night's interaction with Kate ease slightly. The farm hosting the competition was in the midst of Wilsonville's agricultural region, and the road was lined with nurseries, large stables, and dense hazelnut groves. Jamie's silver car slipped quietly along the winding road until she saw, looming in the mist, the bronze statue of a mare and foal that stood at the entrance to the show grounds.

Anna and Elaine would be following along later, but Jamie had an early-morning meeting with a potential client she had met the day before. She was one of a group of business owners, connected by their Stanford sorority, who were interested in forming an investment club. Since they lived along the West Coast, the project would offer Jamie plenty of opportunity for travel, as well as a potentially hefty commission. She had worked into the small hours of the morning preparing a sample portfolio for the last-minute meeting, and she welcomed the overriding sense of tiredness she felt after intense work and too little sleep.

It was comforting to be back to her old self, with one exception: her future plans would include Anna—and Elaine—in her travels. If she scheduled her trips for late in the week, they could join her for weekends in Disneyland or Seattle. She knew she had Kate to thank for her changing relationship with Anna. She had forced Jamie to confront the lack of connection in her life, and Jamie vowed she would at least give Anna a chance to be a loving, normal human being. Watching Anna ride had also proved to Jamie that her niece was capable of so many more activities than she had realized, and the idea of taking family trips was suddenly a possibility.

Jamie slowed her car and pulled into the driveway that led past the empty arenas and to the parking lot behind the temporary stabling. Each barn tried to outdo the others with elaborately decorated stalls, and Jamie quickly spotted the green and gold curtains that marked Cedar Grove's barn area. She parked nearby, grabbed her worn briefcase, and took a stroll through Kate's section of the barn before heading to the hospitality tent. Matching tack trunks sat near each of the ten stalls, and polished nameplates and halters hung neatly by every horse. A long string of the ribbons Kate and her students had won so far fluttered gently near a now-empty sitting area with canvas chairs and potted plants. Jamie casually glanced around the rest of the grounds when she came to the end of the aisle. Even though the show hadn't started yet, quite a few riders were already out, exercising ghost horses in the fog. She thought she saw Kate and Blaze at the far end of the open field where she had danced with Kate just last night. Jamie turned away. Last night's dance—the confession it pulled out of Jamie and the wrenching way it ended—no longer mattered. The only thing that mattered was Kate's performance in this afternoon's class.

When Jamie got to the hospitality tent, she arranged her notes on one of the folding tables. She hadn't expected there to be coffee yet, so she had stopped by a small espresso stand for lattes and scones. She shrugged out of her black leather jacket and ran her hands through still-damp hair. Her black jeans and teal, patterned button-down shirt had a professional look, even though they were still appropriate for a day at a horse show. Her potential client was at the show to watch her two daughters compete, so she wouldn't be dressed for the office. Jamie didn't want to look as if she was trying too hard to impress.

Brenda Colton arrived precisely on time, and Jamie stood up to greet her. The woman was wearing dark jeans and a red fleece pullover, her light-brown hair cut in a classic chin-length bob. They shook hands and Brenda sat down with a shiver.

"It's colder than I expected this morning," she said with a laugh as she burrowed deeper into her sweater. Jamie handed her a latte and she accepted it gratefully. "I guess I should enjoy it while it's here. By about noon I'll be complaining about the heat."

Jamie asked about her daughters' classes for the day, and the two spent a few minutes on small talk about horses and the Colton's family farm in Bend, a city in eastern Oregon. Jamie was grateful she had learned enough over the past couple of weeks to carry on a fairly knowledgeable conversation about the sport. She was about to start her business proposal when Brenda gestured toward the field. Jamie looked up in time to see Kate riding past the tent on her way back toward the stabling area.

"Have you seen that stallion, Guns Blazing?" Brenda asked.

"Yes," Jamie said simply, her eyes on Kate. She sat tall and relaxed in the saddle, wearing those brown ass-hugging chaps that could make Jamie forget her own name. Blaze walked easily on a loose rein, looking as calm as his rider. Apparently their early-morning exercise had been beneficial, Jamie thought with relief. She pulled her attention away from the pair with effort.

"He's all my girls have been talking about," Brenda said, shaking her head. "You'd think the latest teen idol was here, to hear them talk."

"It'll be interesting to watch him in today's Grand Prix," Jamie said, turning back to the papers in front of her. Yet another point in favor of endorsing Kate. Jamie's business sense kicked in, and she could see mentioning Davison and Burke's sponsorship of the pair would probably help her convince Brenda to sign with them, but she couldn't ethically exploit that PR angle unless it was official. "I've drawn up a couple of possible investment strategies given your group's long-term goals. This first one is more aggressive, but it has a high earning potential," Jamie said as she flipped open a leather folio and brought out several charts.

By the time their lattes and scones were finished, Jamie felt confident in her chances with Brenda's group. They wanted to work with a woman, and Jamie had struggled against the opposite sentiment enough times in her career to appreciate a little reverse discrimination. Brenda seemed impressed with her thorough presentation, and they arranged for a conference call with the other investors later in the week. Jamie tossed her briefcase in the trunk of her Mercedes, along with her jacket since the day was already heating up, and she returned to the tent in time for yet more coffee. So far, a good day. If she could just get Kate safely over those huge fences and out of her life, it would be perfect.

❖

Kate slammed her tack trunk lid shut loudly enough to bring Blaze's head out of his stall. The big horse chewed his mouthful of hay and watched her as she dropped onto the trunk and sat there with her head in her hands. *Damn that Jamie*, she thought for probably the hundredth time in two weeks. Last night she had held Kate so gently, almost urging her to stay in Oregon, planting doubts in Kate's mind about her decision to leave. And now, less than twelve hours later, she was having breakfast with some beautiful, rich-looking woman right there in the Davison and Burke tent. At least Kate hadn't paid for the damned thing.

Blaze lost interest and returned to his breakfast as Kate sighed and arched her back, stretching sore muscles. She had been awake since three, braiding manes and tails for the show and making sure her students' tack was clean and in order. They were ultimately responsible for their own equipment, but the championship classes on the final day of such a big show were too important for her to be comfortable leaving the details to a bunch of teenagers' haphazard organizational skills. She had finally left the barn behind, taking Blaze out for an early-morning gallop to settle his mind. After about ten minutes of bucking, the stallion gave up his attempts to unseat her and settled into his work. She was riding him back to the barn, aware that she had succeeded in tiring herself out more than the horse, when she had spotted Jamie and her new friend having their cozy breakfast.

She stood up and carried her saddle into the stall they were using as a tack room, setting it on a metal stand and carefully wiping away the dirt that had splattered on it during her ride. Logically, she knew Jamie had every right to breakfast or lunch or whatever with another woman. But she still could feel Jamie's hands on her while they danced, pulling her close until their hips ground together. The thought of those hands on someone else made Kate want to throw something. Hard. At Jamie.

Kate's anger was part jealousy and part weariness. If she was being truthful, Jamie hadn't actually planted doubts in Kate's mind about the choice she was making. The doubts had been there, ever more insistent over the past week, and Jamie had simply, and continually, made her acknowledge them. In the foggy early morning, alone in the quiet, Kate could let herself admit she resented what this horse represented. She resented the hours spent exercising him, hours that would have been fun and challenging enough on Topper or her younger jumper. She resented missing a student's ride yesterday because Blaze needed an hour of warm-up before his class. She especially resented having to cancel her therapy classes because she just didn't have time to spend helping kids like Anna who so desperately needed her. And how much more would she resent it when these things, instead of being pushed aside momentarily, were out of her life completely? Of course she knew she could replace them with other students or horses or chances to volunteer when she moved, but the ones she loved were right here. Her parents had left Kentucky in search of better opportunities although she had been happy where she was. Now, she would repeat the pattern and give up what she had in search of something else, something *other* people considered better.

But Kate had started on this path, had been on it since she moved to Oregon, and she wasn't going to quit now. Jamie was only questioning her commitment to this dream, not expressing any affection for her, when she'd asked if Kate really wanted this sponsorship. It was business to her, even though she'd asked her questions in that soft voice while she was holding Kate so intimately. Kate knew she'd be foolish to think Jamie really cared.

Girlish voices and laughter, and the answering whinny of a pony, alerted Kate to the arrival of some of her students. She put a cover on her saddle and hung it up on a rack, heading out of the stall to greet the kids and nearly turning back again when she saw Jamie wandering behind them.

After a quick wave, Jamie went over to the stallion's stall and leaned on his door, seemingly watching him eat while Kate went over the day's schedule with her students. Once she had set them to work grooming their horses, she reluctantly joined Jamie.

"I saw you out riding this morning," Jamie commented, her eyes never leaving the horse. "The two of you looked more relaxed together."

"We're getting along just fine," Kate said in a cool voice. She was relieved Jamie had apparently only caught the end of her ride, and not the bucking spree at the beginning. Kate opened the door and went into the stall where she busied herself by running a brush over Blaze's already-shiny chestnut coat.

"Mr. Burke asked me to invite you to lunch today. I know your class won't be until around two, so is eleven thirty okay?"

Kate turned to see that Jamie had come in the stall behind her. Jamie approached the stallion quietly and ran a hand along his neck. He nuzzled her leg briefly and returned to eating. Kate's irritation grew as she watched Jamie petting the big horse. Just two weeks ago, she had looked like a complete novice around the animals, and now she seemed comfortable in a stall next to the huge stallion. Was there anything that didn't come easily for her?

"I can't promise anything," Kate said. Jamie turned away from the horse and met her eyes. "If one of my students is in a class…"

"Kate," Jamie's voice was dangerously low. "Unless you're the one riding in a class, you need to be there."

Kate stepped forward at the mildly threatening tone she heard. "You can't tell me what to do."

"Actually, I can," Jamie said with a shrug. "If we give you the money, the contract will contain PR obligations we'll expect you to fulfill. This is one of them."

"Okay, I'll be there," Kate said, angry to admit Jamie was right in this case. Of course lunch with her primary sponsor was something she had to do, like it or not. Still, having to acknowledge it, even to herself, made Kate feel unaccountably angry and she looked for a way to lash out. "I suppose your new girlfriend will be there, too? Or do your relationships ever last for breakfast *and* lunch?"

"My girlfriend?" Jamie repeated, her forehead creased in confusion before her expression cleared. "Oh, you saw us this morning."

Kate turned to leave, but Jamie moved faster and had her pinned in the corner of the stall before Kate could reach for the door's latch.

"*That* was a business meeting," she said, her face inches from Kate's. "But I'm touched that you care."

"I don't—" Kate started, but Jamie lowered her mouth to capture Kate's, silencing her protests. She fought her response to Jamie's kiss for a few seconds, wishing Blaze would come over and take a chomp out of her, but then she had to give in to her own desire. That giving in was so complete it took her breath away as she snaked her arms around Jamie's neck and pulled her close. Jamie made a surprised noise as Kate changed into such a willing participant, but she recovered quickly and pressed Kate harder against the stall's wall. Her hands slid under the loose sweats Kate wore to protect her breeches, cupping Kate's rear as her thigh moved between Kate's.

The barn and horses faded into the background until Kate was only aware of the woodsy, clean smell of Jamie's skin and the unmistakable scent of her own instantaneous arousal. Kate was lost in the sensations as Jamie pulled her hips forward, dragging her across a strong thigh and bringing her dangerously close to an orgasm from just that simple move. Vague words flashed across her mind as she sucked Jamie's tongue into her mouth. *Barn... students...show.* As if she had spoken them out loud, Jamie moved her lips away even as Kate started to break off their kiss.

"Yes, you do care," Jamie said softly, still leaning close as her fingers traced over Kate's face with a gentleness that was as powerful as her kiss had been. "And clearly, so do I. This isn't good for either of us, Kate. Maybe it's for the best that after today—"

"Kate? I can't find my martingale." A voice from a few stalls down interrupted Jamie.

Kate ducked under Jamie's arm and started for the door. "You're right. After today…" Kate shrugged as if the kiss hadn't set her body on fire, as if Jamie's words hadn't seared her heart. She left the stall as calmly as she could and headed to the tack room. She had spent a lifetime searching for a woman who could break past the barriers she so carefully erected and truly touch her to the core. Jamie had crashed through her walls all right, and then she'd walked away. Leaving Kate alone, exposed, and desperate to fit her mask back in place.

❖

When Anna and Elaine finally arrived, with renewed interest in the show after a good night's sleep, Jamie was lounging in the tent and chatting with Dave about his beloved Seattle Mariners. She brought coffee for herself and Elaine, and cocoa for Anna, over to their corner of the tent and listened to Anna's lengthy explanations about the day ahead. She could feel the added excitement as the show started, and Anna told her about the various special classes held on the final day. The stakes were higher in both the hunter and jumper arenas as horses vied for championship ribbons in their various divisions. The morning started with medal classes, where the riders competed for a chance to qualify for finals held later in the year, some at other shows around the country.

Jamie stared out at the ring in front of her, but all she saw was Kate. Kate's pale skin flushed with desire after their kiss, her normally tidy ponytail slightly askew, those gray sweats that hovered just above her hips and practically begged to be ripped off. Jamie bit her lip to keep from groaning out loud at the memory of Kate's warmth sliding along her thigh. She always was the one in control when it came to sex, but after a glimpse of the fire burning just under Kate's carefully controlled surface, Jamie knew she'd be willing to let go for once and go anywhere Kate led her.

She must have checked her watch a thousand times before eleven thirty finally came. Kate was right on time, her lunch-with-a-wealthy-sponsor persona firmly in place and no sign of the irritation she had shown earlier with Jamie. There was no sign of passion.

"Jamie, how nice to see you again," Kate said, greeting her with a friendly handshake. Jamie was relieved, not hurt, by her indifferent expression. Kate's response to her kiss had been real, powerful, and if Kate could cover her passion so smoothly, then her control was firmly in place. And that control would keep her safe today as she rode the stallion and as she fought to win her sponsorship.

"Hello, Kate," Jamie said in an equally neutral tone. She wondered if she was hiding her own emotions as well as Kate was. It was all she could do to keep her hands and mouth to herself. "You remember Carl Burke?"

"Of course. I'd never forget a fellow cigar aficionado." Jamie smiled as Kate ramped up her Southern accent while she and Carl talked about cigars. She had been concerned that Kate might back out of this lunch, and Jamie knew how important Carl Burke's endorsement was for her sponsorship. A good word from him could even override Jamie's judgment, and Kate would have been foolish to let this chance slip away.

Jamie and Dave joined the two of them for lunch at a table in the back of the tent, and she managed to seat herself next to Kate. At first she took charge of the conversation and led the group through some safe topics, but once it was clear Kate could handle it on her own, she relaxed and ate quietly. She shifted in her chair so her thigh gently touched Kate's until she felt the heel of a leather riding boot kick her ankle hard.

"Ouch," she said loudly enough to draw the eyes of everyone in the tent.

"Oh, I'm sorry," Kate said with concern. "Was that you? I felt something crawling on my leg and thought it was a bug."

Carl peered under the table, but Dave met Jamie's eyes with a smirk. "Maybe it was a rat?" he suggested to Kate.

"Could be," she answered seriously. "I've seen one creeping around this weekend."

"Shall we move to another table?" Carl suggested gallantly, but Kate assured him she was fine.

"Besides," she added, with a glance at Jamie, "it would probably just follow us anyway."

Jamie shook her head and continued eating, resisting the urge to throw some food at Dave who was chuckling happily. When Kate excused herself to go prepare for her class, Jamie walked her to the edge of the tent.

"See? It follows wherever I go," she said to Jamie with a frown.

"Amusing. And such a wise idea to imply that the person deciding your fate is vermin."

"I have no doubt you'll be able to separate business from pleasure," Kate said as she started to walk away. Jamie stopped her with a firm grip on her upper arm.

"Believe it or not, I want you to succeed," she said, softening her hold when Kate stopped. "Good luck today. Be safe."

Jamie was lost in the indefinable emotion she saw on Kate's face, but she couldn't begin to read Kate's thoughts when her own were so jumbled. "Thank you," Kate said simply before she walked away.

Jamie returned to her niece, aware that she really did want Kate to prove herself worthy of this sponsorship. Partly because she worked hard and deserved success, but mainly because Jamie knew her heart would only be safe when Kate was out of reach.

Chapter Fourteen

Kate was in a corner of the big field, riding the stallion through a series of exercises, when she saw Myra approaching. She trotted over and gratefully accepted a bottle of water from her friend.

"Peter won his medal class," Myra informed her as Kate thirstily drank the cold water. "Danielle got Reserve Champion in her division and Jennifer got a third in the adult medal."

Kate shook her head and handed the empty bottle to Myra. "I hate missing everything," she said as she shifted her black safety helmet in a futile attempt to find a cooling breeze. She was proud of the good ribbons her students had won, but part of her wondered if they would have done a little better with her there to encourage and advise them.

"It's just one day," Myra said. "So, how's the big guy doing?"

"Great. I think we're really starting to click," Kate said, wiping a hand across her sweaty forehead. It was well over ninety degrees, and she had already been riding for almost an hour. The stallion needed the flat work to get him focused and somewhat compliant before they started jumping.

Myra looked at her friend with the annoyingly knowing gaze Kate had seen too often. "Save the PR crap for Callahan. Your class is starting in fifteen minutes and you're twelfth to go. We really should get over to the warm-up ring."

Kate nodded and turned Blaze back toward the crowded show area. "I thought the other three rings were supposed to be finished by the time the Grand Prix started." Both of the warm-up arenas were still full of horses and ponies, and she hoped Blaze wouldn't take an interest in any of the mares.

"There've been gate holds on both hunter rings all day," Myra said in annoyance. "Lots of lost shoes because the footing's been so bad, and that led to conflicts between the rings. Everything's running behind schedule."

When they got closer, Kate picked up her reins and swung Blaze into a trot. She circled the warm-up ring a few times, dodging in and out of the other horses' paths, and she was relieved to feel him relatively calm under her. She aimed him at the small jump Myra had set, and he cleared it easily.

It took a few feet of added height before the stallion started to pay attention to the jumps. He was so athletic he got bored quickly with the little fences. By the time she was called on deck, Kate felt they were working as a team.

"How does he look?" she asked unnecessarily when she jumped off him near the back gate and pulled on her navy hunt coat. She hadn't worn it while schooling since the wool blend was too hot to be comfortable.

Myra readjusted her saddle and gave her a leg up. "Amazing. His form is perfect, so just get out there and have fun. The class is yours to win."

Fun, right. Riding the stallion was thrilling. Important. Scary. Not fun. Blaze stood quietly at the gate as they waited their turn, and Kate let her attention wander briefly to the Davison and Burke tent. She could see Anna sitting close to the railing, but there was no sign of Jamie near her. Kate thought she could see a slender figure pacing back and forth behind the little girl, but the shadows made it hard to identify anyone. She refocused on the jumps in front of her. Those obstacles required no less than her full attention. This was one class where a wandering mind could be dangerous. And in any case, letting her thoughts stray to Jamie was always a dangerous proposition.

Kate's name was finally called, and she trotted into the ring on the big stallion. She could feel the attention of the spectators and the growing excitement of the horse beneath her. She saluted the judge and the horse leapt into a canter, as if he were planning to go ahead and finish the course whether or not she was coming, too. She quickly rebalanced and got his stride under control before she headed for the first jump.

Although they were in a different order, the jumps were basically the same as those from Saturday's class. The added height and width were enough to force Blaze to be more careful than he had been over the lower ones, and Kate felt a little more in control this time. He allowed her to rate his stride so they met the fences at a good distance, and he was even sort of responsive to her aids in the corners. Even so, by the time she finished the clear round, she was dripping with sweat and her hands were blistered despite her leather gloves.

She walked Blaze through the crowd to a somewhat quiet corner, smiling her thanks at all the words of congratulation coming her way. It wasn't until she dismounted, sliding to the ground and leaning wearily against her horse, that she let her façade slip a little.

She accepted the bottle of water that was pushed into her hands. "I think I'm going to throw up."

"I'll try not to take that personally," Jamie said wryly.

Kate's eyes flew open. "I didn't mean—" she started, but Jamie shushed her.

"You're not being judged out here," she said, casually moving her arm around Kate to give her more support. "Save your energy for the jump-off."

Kate wanted to argue. To say she was *always* being judged. Especially now when so much was at stake, especially here where so many people were watching. But she was too exhausted to fight or to act. She leaned back and let Jamie's arms support her.

❖

Kate's nausea seemed to be contagious, because Jamie felt it herself. She had watched Kate walking the course with the other competitors before the Grand Prix started, and that's when she considered going home and letting someone phone her with the results. Anna had explained that the riders were allowed to go into the ring on foot so they could check distances between fences and determine the route they wanted to take. While it was a logically sound idea, the sight of Kate standing next to fences she couldn't see over made Jamie very uncomfortable. Watching her jump over them on that beast of a stallion made her physically ill. Jamie spent her workdays watching people take chances with their money, their lives, and she had always kept a distance from both the pain of loss and the thrill of success. But she couldn't separate herself from Kate anymore. She could read Kate's tiredness, the tightness of her muscles, the stress of concentration. And Jamie felt it all with her.

She had felt so relieved to see Kate make it safely through the first round that she had given in to the temptation to go find her. The driving need to have any sort of physical contact was overwhelming, and Jamie took a chance she wouldn't upset Kate too much by seeking her out. Surprisingly, Kate hadn't resisted her touch, and she let Jamie's arm remain around her while the rest of the class finished.

Kate would be last to ride in the jump-off, after six other riders who had also had clear rounds, and the crowd around the arena was growing as almost everyone at the show came to watch what promised to be an exciting finale. By the time the jump crew entered to adjust the course, Kate looked revived. The water and rest seemed to have restored her energy, and she stepped away from Jamie so she could quickly check the new course before she mounted the chestnut.

Jamie stood off to the side, careful not to be in the way of the horses milling around, and watched Kate do a quick warm-up. They were calling her as next to go when she turned for one final practice jump.

Jamie saw the girl ride her buckskin pony across the ring, and directly into Kate's path, only seconds before she heard Myra and Kate shout, "Heads up!" in unison. The girl walked on, oblivious to them, and Jamie had a sudden vision of Kate and Blaze landing on top of them. Instead, Kate pulled her right rein hard only a stride before her take-off, and Blaze propped with stiff forelegs before ducking out to the side. Propelled by inertia, Kate sailed straight over his shoulder and into the rails of the simple fence.

As they were designed to do, the plain white poles collapsed to the ground, and Kate went with them. Jamie was at her side in a heartbeat.

"Kate, baby, are you okay?" she murmured, half expecting to be cradling a lifeless body in her arms.

"I'm fine," Kate said, wincing as she slid off the pole that was under her hip. "Really, Jamie, I'm all right. Let me up."

Jamie kept her grip tight on Kate's shoulders as she looked around for one of the medics who were on hand throughout the show. "Don't move," she ordered. "We need to get you checked by a doctor."

As Jamie sat with Kate, she was dimly aware of people shouting, "Whoa!" as they tried to catch Blaze. She could hear him snorting as he trotted around the ring, and she kept her body in front of Kate's to shield her in case he tried to trample them. Kate struggled against the strong hands holding her on the ground.

"Jamie, let me up!" she said again as she gave a strong push and broke free. Myra came over with Blaze, who had finally let someone catch him, and Kate reached for the stirrup that had been flung over his neck during his run.

"What the hell are you doing?" Jamie asked, pulling Kate back as she prepared to mount.

"Jamie, listen to me," she said in clipped tones. "I am getting on this horse and finishing the class. Now, back off."

"Can't you stop her?" Jamie asked Myra in frustration.

"I'm not stupid enough to try," Myra said with a shrug as she helped Kate into the saddle.

Jamie raised her hands in a gesture of frustration as Kate walked over to the back gate where they were calling her name. Jamie headed out of the warm-up ring, determined not to watch what she considered to be a suicidal ride, but she made it only a few steps before she felt compelled to turn back. She stood next to Myra, fuming.

"This is insane," Jamie said angrily.

"It's part of riding. Sometimes you fall and…"

Jamie glared until Myra stopped talking. She could see that the stallion was more excitable after his romp in the warm-up ring, and Kate's forearm muscles were contracted with the effort of keeping him under control. Her face was set in determination, though, and once the signal to start was given, she sent the horse toward the first fence at a fast gallop. Two jumps later, she braced a hand on Blaze's neck and pulled the horse into a tight turn to the third obstacle, making up time by cutting the corner sharply. They met the next few jumps with barely a break in stride, and Jamie gasped with the audience as Kate turned the horse in the air as they were soaring over the next-to-last jump. He cleared the last fence with a foot to spare and then sailed through the timer three seconds ahead of the closest competitor.

❖

Kate gradually slowed the stallion's ground-eating gallop. One Grand Prix down. How many to go? She didn't need her time or the shouts of the audience to confirm she had won the class. The moment she had asked the stallion for speed and he had responded without hesitation, she had been confident they would win. She had done her part, had done all Jamie and her company could expect.

Kate spotted Jamie at the gate. She was standing still, not applauding with everyone else. Kate trotted toward her, needing the strength Jamie had offered when Kate was resting between rounds, when she was lying on the ground after her fall. But before Kate and the stallion left the ring, Jamie turned and walked away.

Jamie left the arena behind as the audience cheered and clapped. She was too relieved to have Kate safely finished with her class to have any control over how she might react when Kate was close enough to touch. She took the long way back to the Davison and Burke tent so she had time to compose herself. When she arrived, the atmosphere in the tent was festive, and everyone congratulated her as if she had ridden the damned stallion herself. To make things worse, she was forced to recount the story of Kate's fall several times since the tent didn't offer a good view of the warm-up arena.

Just when she thought she might explode, Elaine came over and rescued her, saying Anna needed her. They packed up their belongings and took them to Elaine's van before giving in to Anna's request to congratulate Kate. Jamie went with the two of them, but once they reached the end of Kate's barn aisle she held back and let Elaine and Anna go on without her.

Kate was untacking the stallion and chatting with the people around them. Her face was bright with the excitement of riding well and winning such an important class, but she immediately stopped to give Anna her attention. She handed Blaze's lead rope to Myra and knelt to talk to Anna. Jamie stuck her hands in her pockets and watched as one of Kate's students, a teenaged girl who had been at Anna's lesson, called out to her niece and took her over to see one of the ponies.

Jamie felt a strange sense of loss as she watched Anna laughing with a new friend and Kate smiling as she accepted yet another offer of congratulations from someone in the crowd around her. Jamie knew she had been wrong last night when she'd suggested Kate give up her dreams, just as she had been wrong to hold Anna back from trying to have a normal life. A wave of loneliness washed over her as she observed the festive group, and she wasn't sure if even work could manage to fill the void these two were leaving in her. Kate glanced over and gave her a brief smile tinged with weariness, before Jamie watched her turn back to her horse.

Chapter Fifteen

Jamie walked around the edges of Kate's barn aisle, struggling to regain her composure, after Anna and Elaine went home.

The day had been exhausting for Jamie, with the fall, the jumping classes, and the knowledge that Kate had proven herself worthy of the sponsorship all combining to leave her raw. She had spent so many years fighting any emotional entanglement with even those closest to her, and suddenly Kate had opened up too many channels of feelings. Jamie had to fall back on her last defense and simply pretend nothing mattered.

She got back to the stalls, determined to at least act distant and professional even if she felt nothing of the sort, and she simply sketched a quick wave at Kate who was busy dismantling her stabling area and loading horses and equipment into her large van. Kate's efforts were hampered by all the people who stopped by to congratulate her and to get a look at the big stallion, and Jamie didn't want to interrupt her time in the spotlight. Myra was trying to take on most of the work so Kate could talk to the well-wishers, and Jamie pitched in to help. She was happy to have the physical labor to keep her from dwelling too much on her reaction to Kate's fall. She knew Myra was right when she said it was part of riding and that every sport had its risks, but what had truly scared her was her own depth of emotion. Seeing Kate on the ground and hurt had stirred up feelings like those she remembered from her trips to visit

Anna in the hospital. It was as if she herself were hurt, as if her heart was bruised with the effort of being in love.

Love. Jamie repeated the word to herself, waiting to panic. Did she love Kate? For once, she wanted to stick around and find out. To be with Kate, learn about her, share stories with her. Without business and the sponsorship looming over them and getting in the way. She was attracted to Kate, sexually and intellectually, and she was surprised by the cautious excitement that welled up inside when she imagined being in a relationship with her. She wanted to take Kate to a movie, out to dinner, on another boat ride.

But what did Kate want? Not Jamie, not a life here in Oregon. Kate wanted the stallion and a chance at the fame and success he could offer. Jamie might be tentative about claiming love, but she had no doubt she cared about Kate fiercely enough to want to protect her and see her happy. Kate thought the horse and a shot at the Olympics would make her happy, so Jamie had to give them to her. Even though she doubted Kate would find joy and fulfillment in the driving ambition the stallion would require from her. Jamie couldn't make that decision for Kate. But she could decide to keep her growing thoughts of love deep inside so Kate could leave without guilt or doubt or remorse.

In between trips to the van, Jamie observed Kate interacting with her visitors. She was as composed as always in public, but there was something else, a hint of shyness or awe that tugged at Jamie. It was as if she had spent her life acting successful and sure of herself, and actually being those things caught her by surprise. Jamie felt a rush of pride in Kate's accomplishments, and she hoped Kate felt the same thing. Jamie winked when Kate glanced over and caught her staring, earning one of those genuine Kate smiles that had nothing to do with the rules of etiquette.

About an hour later, she finally caught Kate alone for a moment. Most of the people had left the show grounds, and they had just loaded the last horse into the van. Jamie helped Kate lift the heavy ramp and slide it into place while Kate secured it carefully, making sure the doors were firmly closed.

"I haven't had a chance to congratulate you yet," Jamie said, resting her shoulder against the van with her hands in her pockets. The vehicle swayed slightly as the horses inside shifted around. "I was very impressed today."

"Thank you," Kate said simply. She leaned against the van next to Jamie with a sigh and rubbed her fingers absently over the blisters on her palm. "It was the most exhausting show I've ever been to, but the most exciting, too."

"Do you like all of the attention?" Jamie asked, unsuccessfully telling herself to stop prying, to stop foolishly wishing that Kate would say the fame made her miserable. Kate wasn't going to stop wanting this dream, and Jamie could never ask her to give up the Olympics for a shaky relationship with a workaholic.

"It's fun because it's so different for me," Kate admitted. "But a horse like Blaze is a big deal around here. On the Grand Prix circuit, he'll be just another in a line-up of really talented horses. We'll have to work harder to get this sort of attention, to keep from blending in with the crowd."

Jamie wanted to ask if the effort was worth it, but she made herself shut up. She knew what Kate's answer would be. "I hope you realize you always stand out, even without that stallion," she said instead. "I've been watching you this weekend, and you're very popular here. Your students, other trainers and riders, they all go out of their way to be around you, to talk to you."

Kate looked at her in disbelief, and Jamie guessed she really had no idea how other people saw her. Before she embarrassed herself by saying she, too, could barely resist Kate's pull, she changed the subject. "I suppose you'll do this same routine in reverse back at your barn?" she asked, waving to indicate all the packing they had done.

"Most of it," Kate said with a weary smile. "But I'll leave some for tomorrow. It's been a long day."

Jamie patted her on the shoulder in what she hoped was a friendly, casual gesture. "Well, let's get going then. I'll meet you at your barn."

She turned to leave but Kate's voice stopped her. "You really don't need to come home with me. Myra and my kids will help."

Jamie just waved off her protests and headed out to the empty parking lot. This was the end of her relationship with Kate, but there was no reason she couldn't make the day last at least a few hours longer.

The trip back to Kate's farm was short but slow as Jamie joined the caravan of Kate's students following the large horse van. Once they arrived, Jamie once again helped haul piles of dirty tack and equipment into the barn, secretly relieved she wouldn't be the one cleaning all of it the next day. After the excitement of the show, she could sense the feeling of letdown among the riders, and they did most of the work with little conversation. Jamie was amazed at the amount of time it took to get the horses settled and fed, but she hung around until after Myra and the last of the students left.

Kate crammed an armload of sweaty saddle pads into the barn washing machine and shut the lid. She would take care of them tomorrow. She went into the yard and found Jamie there alone, stacking empty water buckets in the shed. "Thanks for helping, I really appreciate it," Kate said when Jamie approached her. She started walking toward the Mercedes to see Jamie off but stopped when she realized she wasn't following her. She stood there awkwardly when Jamie made no move to leave. "If you want to stick around, I have some saddles you can clean."

"No thanks, I'd hate to deprive you of that pleasure," Jamie said with a smile. "But I do think I should stay with you for a little longer. Someone should watch you in case you have a concussion."

"I landed on my hip, not my head," Kate said. "You don't have to—"

"Come on," Jamie waved toward the house. "You probably want a shower, and I'll see what I can make for dinner."

Kate hoped that was a joke, but Jamie started walking to the house without her. She jogged to catch up and tugged on Jamie's arm.

"Jamie, this is ridiculous. I don't need a babysitter."

Jamie stopped and faced her. "Kate. You don't look well and you're walking funny. I'm going to stay here while you get cleaned up and eat something, and then I will leave you alone. But I'm not going anywhere until I'm sure you're okay."

Kate was too tired and sore, too emotional and raw to deal with Jamie. She struggled against a ridiculous urge to cry as she read the concern on Jamie's face. The same concern she had heard in Jamie's voice after her fall, had felt in the arms that tried desperately to keep her on the ground and out of the saddle. Kate wanted to hate her, to hate the way she was acting, as overbearing and rude as she had been during their first interviews. Bossy. And unbearably sweet. Kate turned away to hide her threatening tears.

Jamie was prepared to argue all night, but Kate must have read the determination in her eyes because she stopped fighting and stomped toward the house, muttering under her breath. Jamie caught the words *overbearing* and *pigheaded*, but she ignored them. Her original intent had only been to make certain Kate got home and settled before she left, but she had grown increasingly concerned about her. Kate had done more than her share of unpacking, even though Jamie and Myra had conspired to do most of the heavy lifting. As the hours dragged on, Kate's skin had taken on a grayish hue, and she was obviously favoring her left side. She didn't show any signs of a concussion, but Jamie couldn't just go home and abandon Kate on the isolated farm.

Jamie followed Kate into the house where Kate stopped in the entryway and blocked her from going down the hall. "There's a bar in the living room," Kate pointed to her right. "And the kitchen's through there. Help yourself to whatever you want. I'm going back to shower and change, and I'll be sure to yell if I need your help."

Jamie noted the obvious command to remain in the front of the house, but she let it go. She wandered into the living room first and poured a small glass of scotch while she looked around. The walls were painted a light blue, and the décor was straight out of a magazine. Chintz fabric covered the overstuffed sofa and chairs, and the pastel florals blended perfectly with the walls and the mahogany furniture. The prints on the walls were vague pastoral scenes that reminded Jamie of the forgettable pictures found in hotel rooms. The bar was well stocked with high-end liquor, but most of the bottles were full and there was a light coat of dust on them. Jamie guessed the supply was more an attempt to have anything on hand a guest might request than for Kate's personal use. But a half-empty bourbon bottle stood at the front of the bar, and Jamie poured some of that for Kate.

She carried both glasses with her as she went toward the kitchen, passing a formal dining room on the way. Kate had decorated it with pale lilac paint and a dark cherry table and sideboard. The kitchen was slightly cheerier with its bright yellow paint, but its too-clean look hinted at an occupant who either frequently ate out or forgot to eat at all, not someone who needed eight dining room chairs and a full set of ornately decorated china. Jamie checked the fridge and found it as empty as she had expected. She wasn't surprised to discover the stash of takeout menus next to the phone, and she ordered some Chinese food from a nearby restaurant. With dinner on the way, she dropped a couple of ice cubes into Kate's bourbon and left her assigned part of the house.

Jamie pushed open a partially shut door and found Kate's den. The colors were brighter here, more vibrant, and the oak desk and shelves were stained a light gold. Several bookshelves were crammed with well-read horse books, quite a few of which were for kids and must have been Kate's childhood favorites. Several Hopper prints hung on the walls, including *Nighthawks*, one that hung in Jamie's bedroom as well. While the front rooms could have belonged to anyone, the contrast between the dark paintings of loners with the clear, lively colors in the den was definitely Kate. Jamie guessed Kate spent a lot of time here. The desk was covered with papers and magazines and prize lists for horse shows. Jamie poked through some of the piles and found invoices and lesson plans. The room was as full of Kate's personality as the front area of the house was devoid of it.

The sound of water splashing in the shower pulled Jamie out of the den and into Kate's bedroom, decorated in a springlike mix of greens, pinks, and blues, and accented with displays of photos as well as a bulletin board crammed with mementos. Jamie would have been tempted to snoop around more if she hadn't been so drawn by the thought of Kate naked in the shower. She tapped on the open door of the bathroom and Kate's head appeared around the shower curtain.

"You were supposed to stay out front," Kate said accusingly.

Jamie held up the glass. "I thought you could use a drink," she said. "And are you really surprised I didn't obey orders?"

Kate just rolled her eyes and disappeared back into the shower. Of course the appropriate thing for Jamie to do would be to return to the living room and wait for her. Instead, she set the drinks on the counter and walked over to twitch the curtain aside. Kate was rinsing shampoo from her hair with her back turned to Jamie.

"Jesus," she swore loudly when she saw the darkening bruise that covered Kate's left side from her ribs to her hip. It was almost enough to keep her from noticing the soapy stream that cascaded over her perfect ass. Almost. Jamie had expected Kate to be beautiful naked after watching her in those chaps, feeling her when they danced, but she hadn't expected her own body to respond so instantly. Jamie watched the water flow over Kate and felt it rush through her own body. Kate squeaked at the sound of Jamie's exclamation and turned to face her.

"I'm pale so I bruise easily," Kate said matter-of-factly, as if explaining some small mark.

Jamie pulled the curtain open more and ran a hand lightly over Kate's side. "We need to get you x-rayed. You might have some cracked ribs."

Kate shook her head. "I know what a cracked rib feels like, and this isn't it. My side is a little tender, though, so stop poking at me."

"I'm just checking," Jamie said, pressing gently against the discolored area. She watched her fingers spread and span Kate's ribs, tan against the pale flesh at the edge of her bruise. Skin on skin. For a brief moment this simple touch was enough. "Does this hurt?"

"What do you think?" Kate answered, slapping at Jamie's hand as it moved higher on her side. "Now get out of my shower," she added in an unconvincing tone.

Jamie's palm slid over to cup the underside of Kate's breast, and she watched, mesmerized, as Kate's nipple hardened in response.

"I'm not bruised *there*," Kate said with a frown, unable to hide her quiet gasp as Jamie's thumb grazed her erect nipple.

"Can't be too careful," Jamie murmured as she gently rolled the stiff peak between her thumb and forefinger. "I recommend a complete exam."

"Jamie, please…" A quiet moan interrupted her. Jamie wasn't sure if it was *please stop* or *please, more*.

"I still haven't heard a no," she said, hesitating briefly, prepared to let go if Kate asked her to. Instead, Kate sighed and threaded the fingers of both hands through Jamie's hair, pulling her forward for a soft kiss.

"Yes," she said with a half smile, as if she was as surprised by the word as Jamie. She captured Jamie's mouth in another kiss, this one hungry with need. She whimpered softly in protest when Jamie broke off the kiss, only to sigh and drop her head back as Jamie's lips moved slowly down her throat.

Jamie tugged gently on Kate's right hip and pulled her closer so her mouth could replace the hand she held at Kate's breast, teasing and sucking until Kate's fingers tangled more firmly in her hair and urged her closer. Jamie straightened out of her awkward position, half in and half out of the shower, and shed her clothes quickly before Kate could come to her senses and order her out of the room again. She stepped into the shower and pulled the curtain closed.

Jamie pushed Kate back until her shoulders were under the shower, and she followed the track of the water over Kate's breasts with just the tips of her fingers. She kept up her playfully light touch, enjoying the sight of Kate's eyes growing darker with arousal until they were a deep forest green. Kate whimpered and bit her lip, trying to arch closer to Jamie's hands. When Jamie didn't think either of them could wait much longer, she reached around Kate's waist, careful to avoid her bruises, and slid the other hand down Kate's thigh.

She tugged insistently, lifting Kate's leg so her foot rested on the lower shelf of the shower. Kate's fingers tightened on Jamie's shoulders as she shifted to find her balance, and Jamie moved so the length of her body was in contact with Kate's, supporting her. "Don't worry, baby," she whispered into Kate's ear, nibbling on her earlobe. "I won't let you fall."

Jamie thought she might drown in sensation as she slid her hand between Kate's parted thighs, feeling the wetness there that had nothing to do with the shower. Warm. Welcoming. Kate had invited her in. Jamie wasn't just skimming the surface of a one-night stand, but diving deep into everything Kate was. She struggled to move slowly, wanting to savor the smooth silk under her fingers, but Kate reached down and covered Jamie's hand with her own.

"Take me, Jamie. Harder," she growled in a voice heavy with desire. Jamie was only too happy to oblige, and she entered her firmly with two fingers while her thumb rubbed Kate's swollen clit. She settled on an insistent rhythm, urged on by Kate's hand on her wrist, driving Kate quickly to orgasm. She cried out loudly and jerked against Jamie's hand. Jamie held her in silence, her face buried in Kate's neck, until Kate dropped her leg back to the shower floor.

"And they say I'm the bossy one," Jamie commented, smiling as she pressed her lips to Kate's wet skin and gently stroked her back. Kate lifted her head to retort, but the sound of the doorbell stopped her.

"Chinese food," Jamie said, kissing her briefly on the lips. "I'll give him an extra tip for his impeccable timing."

She got out of the shower and pulled on her clothes, leaving her underthings on the floor. She hurried through the house, running a hand through her damp hair, and paid for the food before grabbing a couple of plates and carrying everything back to where Kate was hastily drying off.

"We can eat at the table," Kate offered, pulling on a robe.

"I am not sitting in that fancy dining room," Jamie told her. She quickly stripped again and slid under the covers of Kate's bed. She patted the place next to her, and Kate sighed before she took off the robe and joined her. She moved closer and kissed Jamie on the shoulder.

"Maybe we can eat a little later," Kate suggested. "I think I owe you something."

"Eleven sixty-three for your half of the food?" Jamie asked innocently. Kate slapped her on the arm and set the bag of food on the nightstand.

"Lie down," she insisted.

Jamie raised her eyebrows at the imperious tone, but she obeyed, lying back on the cool sheets and raising her arms toward Kate. She moaned as Kate settled between her legs, teasing Jamie's breasts with her own before settling her weight fully onto her. Kate dropped kisses on her cheeks and jawline before capturing her mouth and sliding an insistent tongue inside. Jamie rubbed her hands over Kate's body, circling around the bruised areas, as she lost herself in their kiss.

Kate eventually broke away from Jamie's mouth and licked her way down her neck and toward her small breasts. Jamie struggled between arousal as Kate's tongue whipped across her nipples and the almost overwhelming urge to stop Kate's determined progress. She couldn't remember the last time she had lain passively and allowed another woman to give her pleasure, and she fought the rising panic as Kate kissed her tense stomach muscles. But when she slid lower and brushed a feathery kiss over Jamie's inner thigh, reaching with her fingers to swirl through Jamie's wet center, the intensity was just too much. Jamie sat halfway up and grabbed Kate's wrist firmly.

"Not inside," she said roughly.

Kate raised her head and met Jamie's eyes, the expression on her face changing from dazed surprise to understanding.

"I won't, sweetheart," she said gently. When Jamie still didn't release her grip, she repeated herself. "I promise. I won't."

Jamie let go and dropped back on the bed, feeling a sense of loss as her earlier desire was overshadowed by tension. Kate anchored her hands firmly under Jamie's hips, as if to control them, and she lowered her mouth to nuzzle Jamie's curls. Her movements were unhurried as she kissed her way along Jamie's inner thighs, and Jamie groaned in surprise as her arousal returned full force. She clenched her fists in the sheets, letting go to the sensations as Kate's tongue finally breached her defenses and touched her soaking labia. Kate licked close to Jamie's clit, not touching it but never moving far enough away to cause Jamie to panic, until something snapped inside as Jamie realized she could trust this woman's word. Her legs spread farther apart and her head dropped back as she gave in and pressed her hips against Kate's mouth. As if recognizing her surrender, Kate closed her lips over Jamie's clit and sucked deeply, flicking her tongue rapidly over the stiff nerves until Jamie cried out her name and bucked underneath her.

Kate moved quickly to her side, wrapping her arms around Jamie and kissing her with an almost reverent gentleness. For the first time in too many years to count, Jamie tasted herself on another woman's mouth, and she was surprised to feel the stirring of rekindled desire.

She laughed quietly against Kate's mouth. "Mmm. You've made me very hungry."

"For dinner?" Kate asked, in between kisses.

"For you," Jamie corrected her, urging Kate onto her back.

Their dinner was cold by the time they straightened out the covers and sat up to eat. Kate leaned against the headboard as she struggled to capture a piece of chicken with her chopsticks. She couldn't remember a more exciting or challenging day than this, with her thrilling win in the Grand Prix and then a couple of hours of Jamie turning her inside out with pleasure. She could do without the aching hip, but she was no longer sure how much of the soreness was due to her fall and how much to her own straining toward Jamie's hand and mouth.

"I can get you a fork," Jamie offered as the chicken dropped out of the chopsticks halfway to Kate's mouth. Jamie deftly snagged it off Kate's plate with her own chopsticks.

"You're very good at that," Kate observed.

"I have dexterous fingers," Jamie informed her.

"I noticed," Kate said with a smile as she successfully transferred a pea pod from her plate to her mouth. Jamie leaned in for a kiss. "Don't," Kate warned. "I need to eat."

Jamie sighed and scooted back to her side of the bed. "I'm surprised you aren't better at eating like this," she said. "What if you need to impress an international sponsor?"

"God, don't say that to my parents," Kate said with a groan. "They'll sign me up for lessons."

Jamie laughed and expertly scooped up some rice. Kate watched her as she ate, so relaxed and at home in Kate's bed even though their professional relationship until this time had been nothing but strain and struggle. Jamie had been that way at first in their lovemaking, too, fighting to keep Kate at a distance, until she had apparently decided Kate wouldn't push beyond the boundaries she set.

"Was it your stepfather?" Kate continued her line of thought without realizing she was speaking out loud. Jamie stopped with a bite of food partway to her mouth. She carefully set her chopsticks on her plate, lining them up neatly.

"Yes."

"When you were caught with the neighbor girl?"

"Yes." Jamie met Kate's eyes for only a second before she dropped her gaze back to her plate. Kate kept silent as she watched Jamie visibly struggle with the choice of whether to fully answer Kate's question or not. For the second time that evening Kate could sense the exact moment when Jamie made a conscious decision to trust her, when she gave a small sigh and started to speak again.

"He said he wanted to prove to me that I'd prefer to be with a man rather than a woman. He seemed to enjoy it more than I did, though," she added with a humorless laugh. "It only happened a couple of times when my mother was there, but it got worse when Mom left us a few months later."

"She left because of that?" Kate asked. She didn't even try to keep the anger out of her voice. She felt a helpless desire to protect Jamie, to punish anyone who had hurt her.

"No, there were drug problems. Had been for a few years," Jamie shrugged it off as if it were no big deal. "Anyway, I didn't think I had a choice except to put up with it, until a couple of years later when my health teacher gave us one of those talks in school. You know, the 'no one should touch you there' lecture. She saved my life," Jamie said quietly. "She'll never know it, but she did."

Kate watched Jamie's face as she talked, their food forgotten. Even Jamie's speech patterns seemed to be reverting to her teen years as she dredged up these memories. Kate wanted to reach out to her, but she sensed that Jamie needed to talk more than she needed to be touched.

"I had just turned fifteen, and one day I went to a friend's after he had…" Jamie waved off the rest of the sentence. "I had her take pictures of the bruises and stuff, and I had two copies made. I put one set in a safe deposit box at the bank and I gave the other to my stepdad. I said either he helped me get my own place, or I'd take the evidence to the police or CPS."

"Why didn't you just do that in the first place?"

Jamie looked up at her in surprise, as if she had forgotten someone else was in the room. "They would have separated me and Sara. She was only seven, and I thought she needed me." She shook her head. "Typical coward, he begged me not to tell, said he had just been trying to help me. All I wanted was his signature. He signed the lease on my first apartment, and later for a school loan, and then he was out of my life completely. I worked nights as a waitress while I finished high school, then I went to a voc-tech to learn to be a bank teller. I got a job in the same bank where I had my deposit box and paid my own way through college and grad school."

As much as her own parents' values were skewed, Kate had never doubted their love and devotion to her. She had always been safe with them. She couldn't imagine her fifteen-year-old self, with her cheerleader pompoms and homecoming queen aspirations, going apartment and job hunting. "That was very brave for a young girl to—"

"Not brave," Jamie interrupted, her voice growing cold and adult again. "Foolish. Sara would have been better off in a foster home. I tried to give her security, to keep her safe from him, but nothing I did was enough. I could provide a home, but I couldn't love her like a parent. She was a typical rebellious teen, but with more reason than most, and I guess she had the whole high school experience for the both of us. Wild parties, drinking, sex. She was pregnant at nineteen. Until then, she'd lived with me on and off. After, she'd bring Anna with her to visit me when she needed cash, but most of the time she kept me out of her life."

Kate set her plate on the nightstand and reached for Jamie's as well. She snuggled closer, feeling Jamie's arms circle around her tightly as she spoke.

"We were arguing that night, about how she was raising Anna. She said she gave her daughter more love than I had ever given *her*, and she stormed out. It was the last time I saw her alive. She was right though, and I've done the same thing with Anna. I buy her what she needs, things she wants, but it's just not enough."

Kate sat up and reached for Jamie's chin, forcing her to meet her eyes. "She wasn't right. You did the best you could at fifteen. You gave up your own childhood to protect hers. Maybe you made mistakes, but you're not a young girl anymore, and you can make it better with Anna. You already are."

Jamie pulled Kate to her roughly and kissed her as if trying to blot out the memories. Soon her lips softened and the kiss eased back into one of simple desire. Kate slid a hand down and cupped Jamie gently.

"This part of you is so beautiful, so special to me," she whispered. "I will *never* touch you anywhere unless you want me to."

Jamie closed her eyes and pressed Kate onto the bed, burrowing into her embrace. They remained that way for a long time, touching without moving beyond intimacy to sex, until neither one could hold back the desire they brought out in each other.

❖

Jamie woke up with a start, unable to recall where she was for several moments. Then Kate stirred against her with a small whimpering sigh, and the night came back to Jamie in a rush. She settled closer to Kate's back, her thigh warm and damp where it nestled between Kate's legs. In her usual bargain, Jamie decided to allow herself just a few more minutes like this before she got up and left.

Surprisingly, she didn't regret her actions of the night before. Touching Kate, making love with her, had been more than Jamie had anticipated. Even talking to her about the past had felt strangely okay, and that shocked Jamie more than anything. Since confiding in her friend in middle school, she had never spoken of her stepdad to another person, not even to Sara, although in hindsight that might have been another mistake. Jamie wondered if things would have been different if Sara had understood why Jamie had dragged her away from the only family she knew. Maybe, maybe not. Her younger self had no chance of replacing the mother who'd abandoned a five-year-old daughter, so perhaps Sara had been set on her course even before Jamie had the chance to screw her up even more.

Jamie buried her face in Kate's soft blond hair, memorizing her scent and trying to imprint the feel of holding her into her mind. So many things Jamie had experienced with Kate, because of Kate, were brand-new to her. Rationally thinking about Sara and what had happened between them seemed to be an important step forward. She had talked to Kate about her past, had set some limits to their intimacy, but she hadn't fallen apart or cried or even pushed Kate away. Yet. Jamie decided there might be some hope for her, maybe not in a relationship with a lover, but definitely with Anna. Kate had forced her to shift her way of thinking, open herself up to some different possibilities. And just like her long-ago teacher, Kate could never know what she had done.

Part of Jamie wanted to wake Kate and thank her, share some of her thoughts and plans, but a larger part knew that couldn't happen. She had seen the way Kate looked at her last night. Compassionate Kate, loving and so quick to connect and empathize with other people, had already gotten far too tangled and emotionally involved in Jamie's screwed-up life. Jamie was certain she could convince Kate to stay with her, to give up her Olympic dreams and remain here in Oregon. But that wouldn't be fair to Kate, and Jamie had to fight temptation with all of her self-taught discipline. Jamie had made choices for Sara, changed the course of her life, and limited her possibilities. She wouldn't do the same thing to Kate. She had already been almost unbearably selfish in sharing her past, allowing their intimacy to extend beyond something purely physical. Now she had to think of Kate's needs before her own.

Jamie sighed. That meant she had to leave. Not just walk out, but make certain Kate would never try to follow her. She slid her leg out from under Kate, debated internally about stealing one last time together as her desire rose again, and then steeled herself to get away.

Jamie got out of the warm bed and started hunting for her clothes, trying to look as if she was sneaking out while still making enough noise to wake Kate. Jamie felt her breath catch as she stood still and watched Kate reach for where she had been lying just moments before and murmur her name.

The biggest problem with letting feelings in was you felt every crack as your heart broke.

Kate rolled over. "You have to go?" she asked in a sleepy voice.

"Yes," Jamie said. She came over to the bed and kissed Kate on the forehead.

"You're sure you can't stay for just a little longer?" Kate snaked her arms around Jamie's waist and tugged her onto the bed. Jamie resisted her pulling, and Kate sat up and kissed her.

Jamie somehow summoned enough willpower to break free. "I really have to go," she said, taking hold of Kate's wrists and sliding out of her embrace. "I'm due at the office early. But thanks for last night, it was fun."

Kate frowned as if fun wasn't the word she would have chosen. "Yes, it was. I'm glad you stayed."

"Me, too. You saved me a trip to a bar last night. I could get used to this mixing business and pleasure idea. It's a lot less effort."

"Multitasking," Kate said with a distant smile. Jamie was surprised at how quickly she had erected her usual barriers, but Jamie could see past them to Kate's pain and confusion. "Glad I could be of service."

"It'll reflect well in my evaluation," Jamie said with a wink, slapping Kate lightly on the hip that wasn't bruised.

Jamie walked out of the room. She could feel Kate's eyes on her, and she could clearly picture the hurt look in them without needing to turn around and see it. She moved quickly through the house and shut the front door behind her, leaning against it as she fought the urge to go back inside. She knew Kate would hate her for being so cavalier about their lovemaking, and she would just assume that was how Jamie treated every woman she slept with. And that wasn't true at all. Jamie might not have relationships that lasted longer than the average movie, but she always made sure the women involved clearly understood the rules of the game. She couldn't say the same for Kate, and she had stepped into that shower knowing full well Kate wasn't a one-night stand type of woman. And Jamie had talked about her past in a way that would make any woman expect there to be a possibility of a future between them. Finally, sinking into her guilt, Jamie pushed away from the door and walked to her car, driving away without a backward glance.

CHAPTER SIXTEEN

By the time Jenn arrived at the office Monday morning, Jamie had already been there for a couple of hours. She hadn't gone straight home after leaving Kate but had instead driven Portland's empty streets until it was time for Anna to get up. Then she went back to the condo for breakfast with Anna and Elaine before taking a quick shower and going to work.

Jenn came into the office and replaced Jamie's cold coffee with a fresh cup. Jamie thanked her and handed over a thick folder.

"I need you to get this to the PR department," she said. "Priority."

"Is this about Kaitlyn Brown's sponsorship?" Jenn asked, hesitating by the desk.

Jamie sighed and turned away from her computer screen. "I've recommended we give her the money," she said and then looked back at the stock analysis displayed on her screen. "Like you weren't going to read it yourself on the way to PR."

Jenn didn't acknowledge the muttered comment. "Well, I'm glad you decided in her favor," she said, walking toward the door as she spoke. "Now we can get back to normal around here. No more going out to lunch, or spending weekends with friends and family, or dressing up and having fun at parties…"

Jenn shut the door firmly before Jamie had a chance to comment. That was just as well. Jenn's usual response to any criticism from Jamie was laughter, but Jamie couldn't complain. The reason she kept her as an assistant was because Jamie could pretend she was boss and Jenn would constantly prove she really wasn't. Jamie sighed and tried to follow the numbers in front of her as she prepared for the conference call with Brenda Colton's investment club.

She blamed her inattention on a lack of sleep, but mainly it was the cause of her sleepless night that kept her from focusing. Images of Kate in the shower, in bed, at the show, kept flowing through her mind. She put a hand on her stomach, unaccustomed to the clenching desire she felt when she pictured Kate between her legs. Sex had always been about controlling another woman's pleasure and finding a quick release for herself. She had never submitted so completely to someone's touch as she had with Kate, had never imagined she would be able to. She turned her chair around and stared out at the Willamette. She had missed her usual morning rowing session and that was never good for her mood. She was tempted to fight the crowds and go now, but there were too many larger boats motoring up and down the river to let her have a safe run.

Jamie gave up on the investment portfolio for the moment, unwilling to give it less than her full concentration, and turned instead to putting the final touches on the loan request from the owner of the Taj Mahal. She recommended Davison and Burke accept this application as well, with a few provisions. Her research showed the city seemed able to support another Indian restaurant, and she had been impressed by the owner's cooking skills and menu. But his accounting practices were haphazard and amateur, and Jamie suggested the bank give him capital for one new restaurant instead of the two he had originally wanted them to fund. If he complied with her other requirements—taking a few business classes and working closely with one of their financial advisors—then she thought they should help him open the third. His enthusiasm and work ethic were strongly in his favor, and Jamie was looking forward to being at the new restaurant on opening night. She just wouldn't order one of everything this time, she thought with a fond smile as she remembered her lunch with Kate.

Damn, did everything have to remind her of Kate? She dropped the completed folder on Jenn's desk for delivery, ignoring her comment that the rest of the world used interoffice e-mail to transmit reports rather than handwriting them and making overworked assistants haul them around. Jamie prowled around the office, staring out at the river more than at her computer screen. Finally, she gave up pretending to work, called Elaine, and asked her to bring Anna for an after-school picnic in the park that ran along the Willamette. She only suggested the outing to get her mind off Kate, but she refused to let herself feel guilty. No matter what her initial motivation, any step toward a relationship with Anna had to be a good thing. Maybe it wasn't really Kate she loved after all, Jamie tried to convince herself as she picked up a sack of hamburgers at a local diner. Maybe she had simply enjoyed a new sense of companionship over the past couple of weeks, a change from her usual social isolation. She walked down to the river and sat on a bench to wait for Anna and Elaine. Or maybe she should just focus on not jumping into the flowing water and letting it drag her out to sea.

Kate spent Monday morning busily scrubbing saddles, unpacking trunks, and washing a huge pile of saddle pads and stable bandages. Her entire body ached from the fall and from two days of riding the powerful stallion, but the soreness only reminded her of sex with Jamie. Unfortunately, everything around her reminded her of sex with Jamie. She was furious for letting herself be used by a self-proclaimed womanizer and embarrassed for falling into bed so easily with a woman who obviously was incapable of caring for anyone.

She knew deep inside that she wasn't being entirely fair, but her fuming helped her get past those humiliating moments when she too clearly pictured herself screaming Jamie's name, begging for her touch, demanding more. Jamie had never claimed to want more than a casual fling, and if Kate thought their night together meant more than that, it was her own fault. They had fought and flirted their way through the past few weeks, and if Kate had been stupid enough to fall in love…

"You are not in love with her," she said out loud as she slapped a sponge full of saddle soap onto her saddle. Of course she wasn't. She respected Jamie's business sense and her successful career. She even enjoyed spending time with her on those rare occasions when they managed to communicate. And she found her somewhat attractive. Kate shook her head and tried to dislodge the memory of Jamie wet and naked in her shower, wet and naked in her bed. That had nothing to do with love, at least not in Kate's experience.

She had to admit that the intense physical attraction she felt for Jamie was the main quality missing from all of her previous relationships. Her walls had been in place for too many years, walls designed to protect her parents, walls carefully constructed so they only showed the appropriate version of Kate and her family. She had longed for someone to come along with enough strength and passion to help her tear them down, since she couldn't do it by herself. Jamie was the only one who had been able to do that, but when she saw the real Kate, she ran away. Bossy Kate. The Kate who was messy and a little wild under her controlled façade.

Kate felt tears sting her eyes as she realized what that meant. She had trusted Jamie with her defenseless self, and Jamie had rejected her. She felt betrayed, but the expectations of love had only been on her side. All Jamie wanted from the relationship was an hour or two of sex. She tried to blame her aching heart on bruised ribs, but she knew the truth. She knew sex didn't always have to lead to a commitment in relationships, but she had let Jamie inside somehow, and once she got in, she'd trashed the place.

Kate wiped the saddle off with a dry towel and carried it over to Topper's stall. She quickly groomed her horse and tossed the saddle, still sticky from the soap, onto his back. They set off along the trail that followed the outer perimeter of the housing development. Although the grassy path led past houses and yards, the trees and heavy shrubbery gave Kate the illusion of privacy. Kate always welcomed the chance to get away from people and enclosed arenas, and she especially appreciated it now when her emotions were far too close to the surface for her to be able to hide them from anyone.

A few minutes in the saddle helped settle her, at least physically. The ache in her hip eased with the gentle sway of Topper's stride, and after her week with Blaze it was a pleasure to simply ride without a constant battle for control. She walked for fifteen minutes, doing the same stretching routines she used in some of her therapy lessons, until the only pain left came from her wounded ego. She urged Topper into a faster gait, and they trotted along under the bright summer sun until she came to a series of jumps she had set up when she'd first moved to this barn. Then she picked up a canter and sent Topper over the first one, pushing him faster at each one. Her pace was a little reckless, but she knew she could trust her horse, and the fast gallop helped clear her head. By the time she pulled Topper back to a walk, she could even think of Jamie without wanting to club her over the head. At least not too hard.

She loosened her reins and let her horse stretch his neck out as they headed back to the barn. Jamie was still not far from her mind, and she tentatively let herself bring up the question of love again. She had to ask herself if what she really felt was love or simply her typical urge to help anyone who was hurting. Yes, she felt sorry for what Jamie had experienced as a child, but mostly she was awed by the drive and self-sufficiency Jamie had shown. And Kate admired how hard Jamie was trying to improve her relationship with Anna, even though it seemed difficult for her to accept any degree of intimacy with another person.

Now that Kate was thinking more clearly, she knew that fact was the one thing most confusing about Jamie's overnight change. She couldn't reconcile the woman who had talked about such a significant event from her past with the breezy swinger who'd left her alone in bed with a wink and a slap. And there was no way Jamie's confession had been some sort of seduction routine. So why open herself up to Kate if she was only planning to leave at the first opportunity?

Perhaps Jamie had run away from more than her. Maybe she couldn't handle the intimacy of sharing more than just a night of sex. If this was Jamie's way of putting emotional distance between them, then no matter how much it hurt Kate, she would have to respect her decision. She made a promise last night that she wouldn't push past the boundaries Jamie set, and she would keep that promise. And anyway, if all went well, she'd be heading east and she could nurse her hurt feelings far away from this city, and far away from Jamie.

CHAPTER SEVENTEEN

Kate sat back in her desk chair and watched the pages of the grant proposal slide out of her printer. She had made the changes Jamie had recommended, grudgingly agreeing that her original draft was much too ambitious for the amount of time Myra would be able to devote to the program. Still, her fingers tapped idly on the binder containing the more complete version as she imagined how much she could expand the existing therapy sessions with the foundation's grant at her disposal. More horses, more time, specialized speech and physical therapists. She sighed as the final pages dropped into the printer's tray and she tucked them neatly into a manila envelope. She had spent months writing detailed plans for the program's growth, ever since she had first started looking for funding for the stallion and Myra had offered to keep her lessons going. She had gotten a little carried away, and it was difficult to scale back her vision.

After tomorrow, though, she would officially be endorsed by Davison and Burke, and she would be leaving for Canada to compete within a month. A representative from the PR department had called this morning with their formal offer, and she would be signing the contract tomorrow. After that, an official press release would go out, and she would be heading to Calgary for the Masters Tournament. The huge Canadian show would be her first experience competing against some of the top international riders on the circuit. Kate was sure the excitement would kick in after a couple of days.

The only reason she felt so deflated was it was difficult to accept that she had finally made it.

Kate quickly pulled her hair into a ponytail and grabbed the grant proposal on her way out to the therapy lesson. She waved as Elaine's van pulled in, not surprised that Jamie was nowhere in sight. Her first reaction to the call about her sponsorship had been disbelief that Jamie hadn't rejected it after their night together, but deep inside she knew Jamie had integrity in her business life, if nowhere else. Kate was certain her endorsement had nothing to do with guilt or sex. It would have been based solely on her belief that Kate would represent the company well, and the realization gave her an unexpected sense of pride. Earning Jamie's respect wasn't an easy accomplishment, and Kate hated how much it meant to her.

Kate stopped by the small barn to check Blaze's water, mainly as a delaying tactic. She wanted to put off this lesson as long as possible, since it would be the last therapy group she'd teach here, and starting next week she would be one of Myra's volunteers until she left town. She lingered in the stall, rubbing Blaze's forehead until he got bored and walked away. Their ride this morning had been uneventful, which was a good thing with this horse. She and the stallion were getting more comfortable together. He would never be as easygoing and willing to please as Topper, but his drive and charisma were part of what made him Olympic material. They were qualities Kate had always thought she wanted in a horse. So far, though, his energy seemed to sap hers, and she hoped that at the end of her five-year campaign she wouldn't be shriveled to nothing.

The sound of footsteps broke her introspection. "You okay?" Myra asked, leaning on Blaze's door. Kate turned and gave her a sad smile.

"Just overwhelmed," she said. She handed Myra the grant proposal. "The arrogant bitch decided to approve my sponsorship."

Myra caught her friend in an enthusiastic hug. "That's great. You really deserve it."

"Thanks," Kate said. "I guess I'm just a little sad because this will be my last time to teach the group."

"You have a few weeks before you go, so let's enjoy them," Myra said, draping an arm over Kate's shoulders as they walked. "You can cry all you want on the last day."

Kate reached around Myra's waist and gave her a squeeze, and they walked together toward the arena. She was going to miss having someone like Myra to talk to, someone who knew her so well.

"So, was the sex at least good while it lasted?" Myra asked when they were still out of earshot of the students and volunteers. Kate came to a halt and pulled away.

"I don't know what you're talking about," she said, but Myra only laughed.

"Please, she went from 'Jamie' to 'arrogant bitch' in a couple of days. And now you're blushing brighter than Chris's T-shirt. You're really not so difficult to read."

Myra walked away laughing, leaving Kate standing speechless, trying to control her thoughts before she approached her riders. She was embarrassed Myra knew about her and Jamie, something she had hoped to keep secret forever, and as if that weren't bad enough, now she was thinking about sex again. Remembering Jamie's touch in the shower, so gentle on her bruised ribs but so firm where Kate needed her. And Jamie's strength, as she supported Kate after her orgasm and later allowed herself to turn to liquid under Kate's tongue. Kate had labored to exorcise the memory of that night with Jamie from her mind, but at the slightest provocation it came rushing back. Maybe she wouldn't miss Myra as much as she had thought.

"My, you look like you've been getting too much sun," Elaine commented, pushing Anna's chair toward her.

"I forgot sunscreen this morning," Kate latched on to the handy explanation of her blush. She wasn't sure how she'd explain when it magically disappeared, and she covered her embarrassment by crouching down to speak to Anna. Unfortunately, the little girl's main topic of conversation was yesterday's picnic with her aunt by the river. Kate sighed as she listened, hoping Canada would prove to be far enough to run to get away from Jamie.

"Jamie said she walked with one of the riders at Anna's last lesson," Elaine said as they joined the rest of the group. "I'm not sure if I'll be as much help as she was, but I'm happy to learn."

Kate thought for a moment and then noticed Gwen sitting stiffly on a bench by the arena door. It looked as if she might be having a difficult day with her MS.

"Maybe you could walk with Gwen and help with her exercises. She doesn't need to be supported on the horse, but when she's hurting, a ground person can get her to stretch a little deeper."

She introduced Elaine to Gwen, and the two seemed comfortable with each other. As Elaine started to check Gwen's range of motion, she left them and went over to the group waiting for her by the mounting block. Myra and Chris were chatting with Bev, and Kate smiled at her before turning to Alex. She knelt by the boy who seemed lost in his own world.

"Hi, Alex," she said, lifting his hand to her cheek and tapping it lightly to try to get his attention. It didn't always work, but today he briefly focused on her face.

"Kate," he said quietly before he turned inward again. She let his hand drop and blinked rapidly to ease the sudden ache of tears. Just one small word, from a child who hadn't spoken at all before he started coming around the horses, and it was enough to make her cry like a little girl. She felt a little foolish until she looked up to meet Bev's gaze.

"He likes you," Alex's mom said with a satisfied smile, clearly unashamed of the tears in her own perpetually tired-looking eyes.

"Cool, dude," Chris said with a nod of approval as he walked over to untie Frosty and Myra squeezed Kate wordlessly on her shoulder before she led Alex to the mounting block. Kate watched her friends and students getting ready for the lesson in a routine so familiar Kate had stopped noticing it. Somehow, while she had been searching for some vision of success that was always out of reach, someplace to really feel she belonged, she had managed to surround herself with people who saw value in the same things she did. This was home, her family, a place where she could be herself. Even without a mirror, she could imagine the expression on her own face. It would be the same one Jamie had seen when she first came to Kate's barn, when she had stood so close and looked at her with those eyes that managed to see into Kate's soul. *You don't want to go.*

"I don't want to go," Kate echoed quietly as she stood in place and watched her friends and students getting ready for the lesson. She walked past Anna who was chatting with a couple of Kate's other students about the hobby they now shared. She met Anna's eyes and gave her a quick wink as she walked past, suddenly glad to be exactly where she was.

❖

One, two, three. Jamie started counting the strokes on the catch as her oars entered the water. The simple progression of numbers helped her focus more quickly so nothing would distract her mind from the efficiency of the movement. She was careful to barely skim the surface with her oars so they propelled the scull forward, and not let them cut too deeply and waste her energy pushing through the water. Three days since she last saw Kate. Not that she was counting. Jamie's scull veered off course and she carefully corrected her stroke.

Twenty-six, twenty-seven, twenty-eight. She drove the oars through the water as if she were in a race, trying desperately to outrun her memory of Kate's arm reaching over to her side of the bed after Jamie had slipped away from her. Kate murmuring her name in a sleepy voice laced with desire, a call so strong that Jamie felt her whole body respond even now. She shoved harder with the oars which only managed to break her rhythm, and she made herself listen to the numbers instead of Kate's imagined voice.

Forty-three, forty-four, forty-five. A gentle release and recovery so the oars left neatly spaced, tiny puddles in her wake. Although she was facing away from her goal, Jamie could picture every detail of the Hawthorne Bridge. She, Anna, and Elaine had eaten their picnic near it on Monday, and she had spent the whole damned time wishing she could have asked Kate to join them. It was one thing to long for Kate when she was in bed at night, but to miss her at a simple meal? To want her there to share something so trivial? Simple sexual attraction was easy for Jamie to understand and to dismiss, but this went well beyond that. Somehow Kate was everywhere in her life, and there wasn't a single part of it that felt complete without her.

One, two, three. Jamie lost count somewhere, but she started from the beginning. What mattered to her wasn't the numbers themselves, but their ability to take up the space in her mind that Kate occupied. Last night over dinner, Kate and the riding lesson had been all Anna and Elaine could talk about. Jamie listened to them and she wished she had gone with them, not just to see Kate but to share the afternoon with her niece. Anna had trotted a few steps on Spot, and Jamie hated that she hadn't been there to see it. She knew how much it meant to Anna to do such a seemingly simple thing, and she was surprised to realize how important it had become to her, too. That damned Kate had helped her to open up just enough to miss what she didn't have.

Jamie stopped rowing and rested her head briefly on her bent knees. She had been driving herself toward some destination she couldn't see, and suddenly it didn't seem worth the effort. She was tired of fighting against the current when all she wanted was to be back drifting on the lake with Kate's bare feet propped next to her, her low drawl talking about anything at all. Jamie dunked one oar in the water and turned the scull back toward the boathouse. Her numbers had failed her, and she had nearly run her boat into a pylon, so it was time to give up.

A few hours later, she prowled back and forth in her office, watching the clock and ignoring her work. Kate would be arriving soon, to meet with the PR representatives and sign her contract. This weekend there would be a party at Carl Burke's house following the official press release, and there was no legitimate way Jamie could back out of it. Her name had become linked with Kate's here at Davison and Burke, and she would be expected to help Kate through her first function with her new sponsors. Kate would be in her element at the party, not needing any assistance and certainly not welcoming any from Jamie after the way she had left Sunday night. Still, it would be their last time together, and Jamie hoped they might be able to talk civilly and leave their relationship on a better note.

Jamie ran her hands through her hair. She couldn't count how many times in the past few weeks she had pinpointed a moment that would be her last time to see Kate only to find some excuse to require yet another meeting. So what was one more?

She sat at her desk and stared at the legal pad in front of her that was covered with bulleted lists, most of them crossed out in frustration. The hastily scribbled notes were the result of two hours of hopeless planning, a search for an option that would let her and Kate try to make a relationship work. She had spent the morning researching medical facilities in various areas, as well as job opportunities for her, and comparing them with the scheduled competitions on the Grand Prix circuit. But even if she were willing to move Anna across the country, they wouldn't be able to follow Kate as she traveled to shows and went abroad for months at a time.

Jamie tossed the pad aside and ran her fingers through her hair again. She knew Kate would be under enough stress as her whole life turned upside down over the next month, and she didn't want to add to it. So she had tried to treat their relationship like a business deal. She'd decided if she could come up with one or two viable solutions to the problem of a long-distance relationship, then she would approach Kate with her proposition. All of her calculations about travel times and mileage charts left her with one conclusion. She didn't have an answer, a way to make a relationship with Kate work. But the only thing her notes told her for certain was she desperately wanted it to work.

Jamie had let Kate close, had trusted Kate with her body, her past. Jamie's childhood pain, her memories, her barriers were familiar. She had survived them and would continue to, even without Kate. Even if putting her future in Kate's hands were logistically possible, she would have to accept the risk of being hurt in a whole new way. And she didn't know if she could face those consequences alone. But she could no longer hide behind her numbers, behind the safety of her scars.

The thought of suggesting a relationship to Kate without having a plan to make it work was as ludicrous as telling a potential client she hoped she'd eventually find a way to invest their money wisely. But it was her only option. Jamie stood up and slid the legal pad off her desk and into the wastepaper basket.

"I have to pick up a contract from the legal department," she said as she walked past Jenn's desk.

"She's not there," Jenn informed her, not looking up from the letter she was typing.

"Who's not where?"

Jenn gave a long-suffering sigh and turned away from her computer, frowning as she examined Jamie. "What happened to your hair? Anyway, Kate called Ben Simon this morning and withdrew her application for sponsorship. If you're heading to PR, she's not there."

"I was heading to legal, not PR," Jamie halfheartedly protested. She stood by Jenn's desk, tapping her fingers on it as she tried to sort through the emotions washing over her. She felt confusion, of course, and curiosity about why Kate would suddenly abandon her dream. Most of all, though, she felt a foreign sense of happiness.

Jamie went back into her office and grabbed her coat and keys before heading out. "Are you expecting it to be cold in legal?" Jenn called after her innocently.

"Shut up," Jamie said with a grin. She expected a chilly reception but finally dared to hope it would heat up quickly.

CHAPTER EIGHTEEN

Jamie drove a little faster than usual on her way to Wilsonville, smiling at the thought of how some of her turns would have made Kate grab the dashboard. She slowed to an impatient crawl through the neighborhood surrounding Kate's barn and finally pulled to a stop near the house.

The stables were quiet, with no other cars in the lot and most of the horses lounging in their paddocks. Jamie first knocked on the door and then went searching for Kate in the barn. She found her halfway down the aisle, mucking out a stall with her back to Jamie.

"Hey," Jamie said, lounging casually against the open door.

Kate jumped and turned to face Jamie, her expression quickly turning from surprise to an unwelcoming frown. "I should have known *you'd* come," she said, flinging a pile of manure into the wheelbarrow next to Jamie.

"Office grapevine says you've retracted your application," Jamie said, refusing to move even though she knew there was a good chance the next rake full would land on her head.

"And you're here to what? Talk me out of it? Yell at me for wasting your precious company's time?"

Jamie had been expecting a more joyous reunion than this, but she made herself recall the last words she had spoken to Kate. She deserved all the anger this woman wanted to throw her way.

"Maybe I just want to know why."

Kate stabbed the rake into the shavings. "I don't want to leave here. I don't want to ride that horse for the next five years," she said, not meeting Jamie's eyes. "And I don't expect you to understand."

"Try me," Jamie insisted.

"I didn't realize I owed you an explanation," Kate said as she pushed past Jamie and headed to the next stall.

Jamie followed, undeterred when Kate ran the wheelbarrow over her foot. It was heavier than Jamie had expected but she didn't change her expression. She'd accept the physical pain as punishment for hurting Kate after their night together. "As a matter of fact, you do. I spent a lot of time working on this project."

"So bill me, and we'll be even."

"You really want to pay my hourly rate?" Kate shrugged and Jamie started ticking off numbers on her hand. "Okay, there's time I spent doing research, two trips out here to watch you ride, the Hadley party, the Country Classic. I'll deduct the hours I spent on other business while I was there, of course. I'm over thirty hours already, plus expenses. Do you want me to go on?"

Kate stepped closer. "If you add the time we spent having sex to that list, I *will* throw something at you. And you probably wouldn't like any of the options I have at hand right now."

"Don't worry," Jamie said, straightening out of her casual pose. "I consider myself well compensated for that night."

They glared at each other while Jamie struggled to find a way to fix whatever was going horribly wrong with this conversation. She rubbed a hand wearily over her eyes. "I didn't come here to fight with you or to get your money."

"Then why did you come?"

"To see you," Jamie said vaguely. "To understand why you're staying. To find out if it's because of me…of us."

"I sent in the grant proposal," Kate said after an apparent struggle with herself. "The way I originally wrote it, so I can expand the therapy program."

"I see," Jamie said, feeling a small surge of irrational anger that Kate hadn't told her about this. Not because she really cared about the time and effort she had put into analyzing the sponsorship application. She simply felt hurt because Kate hadn't sought her out to talk.

"I told you that you wouldn't understand," Kate said, sounding frustrated at Jamie's clipped tone. "I figured out it meant more to me than any medal could. I know that would never make sense to someone like you."

Jamie spoke in a softer voice. "I saw you teaching Anna's lesson, Kate. I could tell what it meant to you. I just wish you had trusted me enough to tell me in person. Like I said at the show, I only want you to succeed. In whatever you decide to do."

Kate picked at the wooden handle of the rake with her thumbnail. Her anger, prompted by Jamie's imperious attitude, dissipated as Jamie's irritation became more obvious. Kate had been anticipating and dreading this encounter, and now she could see Jamie wasn't as indifferent as she pretended to be. A tiny thrill of hope shuddered through Kate. Jamie had run away from her, but now she had come back. But Kate was afraid to bring up more personal topics until she could figure out how Jamie really felt. "Then would this be a good time to ask you to be a reference on the grant application?"

Jamie raised her eyebrows. "Should I assume you already listed me as one?"

"I thought you might put Anna's needs ahead of your own. The improvements I want to make will help her, too."

Jamie laughed and stepped closer, reaching over to brush her fingers under Kate's chin and drawing her eyes to Jamie's. "So you aren't staying because of me?"

"Change my life plans because of one night of sex?" Kate evaded the question for the second time. She refused to let Jamie know how close she had come to doing just that. "Of course not."

"Good. As long as we're clear about where we stand," Jamie said as she stepped away. The loss of Jamie's touch was almost painful, and Kate barely stopped herself from involuntarily moving to reestablish their contact. She thought Jamie might have smiled as she swayed slightly before catching herself.

"Very clear," Kate said, recovering smoothly.

"So you chose to stay here on your own, and our professional relationship is over?"

"Yes," Kate said simply, returning to her work. Jamie watched her silently. "So why are you still here?" Kate finally asked.

"Have dinner with me."

Kate stopped cleaning and stared at her. "What?"

"I'm asking you on a date," Jamie said, enunciating each word. She was asking for so much more, but she was afraid to let Kate know yet. "Please have dinner with me."

"You're asking me on a date?"

"I thought I was pretty clear on that point."

Jamie held her breath. No stock trade or investment deal had ever made her so anxious. Her future hinged on Kate's answer.

"Okay."

"Good. Tonight?"

"I'm done teaching by seven," Kate said. Jamie just nodded and turned to leave but Kate called her back. "Can I drive?"

"Your truck?" Jamie asked with a frown.

"No, *your* car."

"I'll have to think about that," Jamie said as she left, even though she knew there was nothing Kate could ask that she would deny her.

Kate managed to change outfits several times between her last lesson and Jamie's prompt arrival at seven. She didn't dwell too long on the question of why she cared how she looked for Jamie, let alone why she had agreed to go out with her. Still, she couldn't stop her answering smile when she opened the door and saw the look in Jamie's eyes as her gaze traveled over the form-fitting burgundy dress Kate had finally decided to wear. Kate had spent her life dressing for roles, playing parts. But she could feel Jamie's gaze on her, slowly stripping away her clothes, her masks. Jamie saw *her* in a dress—not an image Kate was trying to project. For once, clothes didn't matter. Except as something to be torn off at the end of the evening. Jamie kissed her on the cheek and let her arms slip around Kate's waist in a brief hug before she stepped away. The touch was chaste, but Kate could feel Jamie's desire as clearly as her own.

"I made reservations at La Riviera," Jamie said, holding her keys out to Kate. "You'll be careful?"

Kate snatched the keys out of her hand. "Of course," she said. "I'm sure I can drive at least as well as you can."

She got to the end of her driveway and the GPS voice instructed her to turn right. Kate flicked it off impatiently. "I know where the restaurant is," she said. She kept her speed low at first until she was comfortable handling the car, but she accelerated rapidly as they merged onto the freeway.

"It's a V-8, so you don't have to push on the gas so hard," Jamie observed casually as her own foot audibly pushed against a nonexistent brake pedal on the passenger side.

Kate waved at the speedometer. "I'm going slower than you were when we went to Lake Oswego."

"Yes, but *I* was driving. That's different."

"Oh, there's a surprise. You have control issues," Kate said with a laugh, almost unconsciously letting her hand wander to Jamie's thigh where it had itched to go since they'd gotten in the car. "You're going to need to get past that."

Jamie clasped Kate's hand and then set it on the steering wheel. "Much as I enjoy having you touch me, I think I'll feel safer if you remember the rule about having both hands on the wheel."

Kate easily maneuvered through the city streets, parallel parking near the waterfront restaurant. After her old pickup, the sports car was simple to handle, but Jamie grabbed the keys back from her as soon as they were out of the car. She put her hand on Kate's back as they walked into the restaurant, and Kate felt Jamie's fingers slide over the satiny material of her dress as they waited for the maître d' to seat them. The thin barrier only heightened the excitement of Jamie's touch.

"Ah, Ms. Callahan, good to see you again," he said smoothly, his eyes assessing them quickly. "If you and your lovely companion would follow me please."

"You apparently come here often," Kate murmured in a low voice once they were seated. They were in a quiet corner of the restaurant, with a view of the Willamette and Mount Hood, and all of the staff knew Jamie by name.

"Only on business," Jamie said, glancing over the wine list. "We have a company account and entertain a lot of our out-of-town clients here. I've never brought a date before."

Kate kept her eyes on the menu, refusing to be fooled by Jamie's easy charm. She had no doubt Jamie wanted her, but Kate didn't know if Jamie's interest in her went deeper than sex. She refused to be simply a convenient bed partner just because she had decided to stay in town. "You need to stop calling it that. We're just having dinner. I don't know if I like you enough to date you."

"Of course you do," Jamie said with her usual maddening smile. "You're just angry with me right now."

The waiter arrived before Kate could answer, and she suspected Jamie had somehow timed it that way. They placed their orders and Jamie asked about Anna's lesson. Kate chatted about Anna's progress and some of the exercises Elaine, a retired nurse, had suggested for Gwen. She mentioned Alex saying her name, not expecting Jamie to recognize how significant that had been.

"Wow, he recognized you? That must have felt great," Jamie said. "I hope Bev was there so she could hear him."

Jamie was pouring more wine in their glasses as she spoke, and she looked up when Kate didn't answer her. "What's wrong?"

Kate shrugged and kept her eyes on the window. "I just didn't think you'd care about something like that."

"I know how much it means to you and to his mom and…Oh, I see," she said with a nod, finally uncovering Kate's secret.

"What?"

"That's what made you snap and decide to stay, isn't it?" Jamie nodded again, not needing an answer since Kate's expression clearly proved her right. "I knew you had doubts, but I wasn't sure what happened to finally push you to make this choice."

Kate visibly struggled with that for a moment. "How did you know I had any doubts? I thought I convinced you I wanted this. Hell, I believed it myself until this week."

"At first I wasn't sure, but I guess I got better at reading you. Or you were less careful how you acted around me and let your mask slip sometimes."

"And you were still prepared to give me the money?"

"Of course," Jamie said, hesitating as their food was delivered and then resuming the conversation when the waiter left the table. "I could see you were willing to give up what you have here to chase your dream. I knew you would give it your all if you went, even though I didn't believe it would make you happy. I made the right business decision."

Kate took a bite of her filet mignon. "I see, so you didn't care about me enough to—"

"Didn't care?" Jamie leaned forward and spoke in a low, but forceful voice. She couldn't let Kate think it had been easy for her to leave. Nothing but love would have pulled her out of Kate's bed that night. "Didn't care enough to tell you to give up your dream? I couldn't do that to you. If you wanted to go, I had no choice but to let you. That's why I left Sunday night, even though I thought it might kill me."

Kate put down her fork and leaned toward Jamie. She could see the other diners' attention being drawn to the intensity of their muted conversation, but she didn't care. "You left because I was just a fling. Just another in a long line of women who share your bed for a moment before you run away."

"No," Jamie said, reaching over to cover Kate's hand with her own. "It was never like that with you. I just didn't want you to feel like you had to stay because…"

Now it was Jamie's turn to look uncomfortable, and Kate tried to figure out the rest of her sentence. "Because I was falling in love with you?"

"No," Jamie said. "Because you felt sorry for me. Wait, what did you say?"

"I'd sooner feel sorry for a shark in a koi pond," Kate said, ignoring Jamie's question. She pulled her hand away and returned to her food. She expected Jamie to get up and leave the table since she had brought up love, but instead she sat there and watched Kate with a bemused expression. "Good steak," Kate said, taking a sip of her wine.

Jamie winked at her and started eating her own meal. "Yes, I love their food. Love the wine. And love you, too, by the way."

Kate stared at her plate, unable to stop her smile as it spread across her face. She looked up to see Jamie's answering grin. For just a moment, Kate considered walking over and climbing into her lap, not caring how fancy the restaurant. Jamie must have read her expression because she cleared her throat and took a drink of water.

"Maybe we should talk about something less…um, personal before we embarrass ourselves," she suggested. Kate nodded, her face heating. Jamie reached across the table and grazed her thumb over Kate's cheek. "God, I love it when you do that."

"That sounds personal," Kate warned, leaning into Jamie's touch. The contact was fleeting, but Kate could feel Jamie's promises. Sex. Love. A future.

"Believe me," Jamie said quietly, withdrawing her hand. "Of all the thoughts on my mind right now, that was the most appropriate one to say in public."

❖

Jamie searched her mind for conversation topics that didn't involve Kate naked or Kate kissing her. She brought up the trips to California and Washington she was planning to take with Anna now that she had signed Brenda Colton's investment group, only slipping once or twice when she used the pronoun "we," as if she assumed Kate would be going with them. At least the first one was accidental, but it made Kate flush such a gorgeous shade of red that Jamie had to try it again.

It seemed to take an interminable amount of time for the waiter to bring their check, and Jamie even told a couple of work stories to fill the time, though neither of them seemed interested. She contemplated sweeping the table clean and lifting Kate onto it, but the bill finally arrived. She dropped her card on the check before the waiter could walk away again. Then she poured the rest of the wine into Kate's glass.

"Are you trying to get me drunk?" Kate asked with suspicion, clearly aware of the track Jamie's thoughts had been taking.

"Only enough so you can't drive my car home," Jamie said with a teasing smile.

"Coward," Kate said, finishing off the wine.

Jamie held Kate's coat for her when they finally were able to leave the restaurant. She held the door for Kate, and then the car door, doing her best to stay close without actually touching her. Once she did, she wasn't planning to stop, so she wanted to at least make it back to Kate's house first. She had some making up to do.

Jamie left her hand resting on the gearshift on the drive to Wilsonville. As if understanding her desire to be close, but also afraid to touch, Kate leaned her elbow on the console so their forearms were only an inch or so apart. Jamie downshifted in a tight turn and felt the brush of Kate's arm travel directly to her groin. She shifted in her seat and glanced over to see Kate's smug smile.

"You like making me uncomfortable, don't you?" Jamie asked, her eyes returning to the road.

She could see Kate's shrug out of the corner of her eye. "You always have so much control, I do enjoy watching it slip now and then. It's good for you."

"I think you're good for me," Jamie said. She finally reached over and captured Kate's hand, interlacing their fingers and settling their joined hands on Kate's lap. "And I might have control issues in some areas, but if I remember correctly, you're more than my match in that department in the bedroom. Not that I'd dare complain about it."

"Good, because I know what I want and I'm not going to be afraid to tell you."

Jamie caught an undercurrent in Kate's tone, and she knew this wasn't a joking matter to her. "So tell me," she said softly.

Kate hesitated. "Don't *ever* treat me like some one-night stand you picked up in a bar, like someone who doesn't matter to you. You made me feel like I wasn't good enough, and that's not acceptable."

Jamie felt as if she had been punched in the stomach, but Kate's anger was no less than she deserved. And no worse than what she had said to herself over the past couple of days. She parked next to Kate's house and turned off the ignition before facing Kate.

"I'm sorry for what I said when I left on Sunday. None of it was true, but that doesn't make it right." She paused and ran a careless hand through her hair. "I wanted you to be free to go without feeling guilty because I told you about my past. If I had thought there was any chance you loved me, I would have stayed. I've been trying to come up with a way to work things out. Five years isn't forever."

Kate sighed and leaned back in the leather seat. "I wanted you to ask me not to go. I hated you for not asking, but I suppose in a way I'm glad you didn't. I had to make this decision on my own." She laughed. "Damn. It's hard to stay mad at you when I have to admit you did the right thing. You weren't very nice about it, but still..."

Jamie grinned, glad to be able to put that night behind them and start over. She liked the word *start*, she decided. She had spent a lot of her life ending relationships. Now she had a chance for some beginnings. With Kate, and with Anna. She leaned over and kissed the side of Kate's neck. "Can you stay mad while I'm doing this?" she asked as she used her teeth to gently tug on a dangling earring. She ran her tongue over Kate's ear and smiled at their simultaneous intake of breath at the contact.

"Why don't we go inside?" Jamie suggested.

"Not if you're planning to run away again," Kate said.

"I can't stay all night since I need to be home before Anna wakes up," Jamie said. "Until I can talk to her about what's going on between us, I don't want to confuse her. But I'm not going to run away from us."

"That's fine," Kate said with a nod, getting out of the car and heading to her door. She paused before she let Jamie inside. "But if you slap me on the rear when you go and say thanks like I'm a hooker, I swear I'll kill you."

"You're not going to let that go, are you?" Jamie asked with a shake of her head as they went inside. "You said I was right to leave, but I'm still in trouble?"

"Welcome to a relationship," Kate said with a grin. "Stop expecting logic." She locked her front door and grabbed Jamie's lapels, pulling her close so their lips met.

Jamie recovered quickly from the sudden move, and she pushed Kate against the door and kissed her back forcefully. She might not be comfortable apologizing with words, but she was confident her mouth could do a damned good job in other ways. Her tongue explored Kate's mouth and neck and shoulders, and the small sounds Kate made as Jamie licked her were driving her crazy. Jamie slid her hands up Kate's thighs, pulling her dress around her waist, and then hooked her fingers in Kate's panties. She abruptly broke their contact, feeling Kate rock toward her before she leaned back against the door for support. Jamie knelt and slowly removed Kate's damp, lacy underwear, letting her mouth resume its leisurely sampling around Kate's thighs and hips.

"Maybe we should…oh God…go into the bedroom," Kate gasped as Jamie's fingers insistently parted her thighs. Kate groaned when Jamie's mouth moved to her wetness, driving her harder against the door.

"You want the bedroom?" Jamie asked as she pulled away briefly, meeting Kate's eyes.

Kate shook her head no and caught her hands in Jamie's hair. "Don't stop," she said.

Jamie recognized an order when she heard one, and for once she didn't even consider disobeying. She ran her tongue over Kate, relishing the taste she had thought was lost to her forever, before taking hold of her clit with teeth and lips. She thought she might come herself when Kate gave a wordless cry as an orgasm quickly caught her, her hands pressing Jamie firmly to her hips. She slid down the door and into Jamie's arms.

"Hello there," Jamie said, her arms wrapping around Kate in support. "You okay?"

"Not bad," Kate said with a weak laugh. "You?"

"Getting a little uncomfortable," Jamie admitted. Kate smiled and kissed her.

"Let's go into the bedroom, and I can help with that," she said. Jamie stood and pulled Kate along with her.

Their pace slowed once they made it to Kate's bed. They stripped, sliding under the covers and meeting in a gentle kiss, as if their urgency had found release when Kate had. Jamie let Kate push her onto her back, and her fingers sifted through platinum hair as Kate softly sucked her breast. Kate's touch was intimate and playful, with none of the rushed fervor they had shown at the front door. Jamie was surprised by the waves of desire that came over her at such teasing caresses, and she could feel the rest of her control slipping away.

"Kate," she whispered, her voice breathless. She had never asked to be touched but had always avoided it, refused it.

Kate reached her hand up to brush through Jamie's hair. "Don't worry, sweetheart. I won't…"

"I know," Jamie interrupted. "But someday. I want you to touch me tonight, Kate. I want your hands on me."

Kate propped herself on one elbow and met Jamie's eyes. "Are you sure? You know I'd never push…"

"I know," Jamie said, reassured by Kate's hesitation. Kate understood what this meant to her, what a big step it was to simply lie back and allow someone else to touch her. She lifted a hand and brushed Kate's cheek. "Please."

Kate nodded. She draped her thigh over Jamie's and lowered her head. Her kiss was teasing, her lips touching and pulling back until Jamie was moving restlessly underneath her, wanting more. Kate placed her palm on Jamie's breastbone and pressed gently, finally deepening her kiss.

Jamie opened her mouth and welcomed Kate's tongue even as her breath caught. She felt panic rising at the soft pressure on her chest, and she raised her hand and grasped Kate's wrist. She was about to push Kate off, flip her on her back, and take care of the aching need between her legs in her own way. Kate stopped kissing her.

"No," Kate said, her voice soft. Jamie heard the order behind the single word but knew the choice was hers. She looked at Kate for a long moment, fighting against the walls she had erected to keep herself safe and alone. But this was Kate. Jamie loved her. Trusted her. Her grip loosened on Kate's wrist, and then she let go, her arm dropping to the bed.

Kate buried her face against Jamie's neck, kissing her rapidly beating pulse. She slid her hand down Jamie's torso, and Jamie gasped in surprise as she felt her own hips rise to meet Kate's hand. As Jamie had come to expect, Kate seemed to sense the moment when she truly surrendered. Kate's fingers brushed against her clit, with a touch as teasing and light as her earlier kisses had been. Kate pressed harder, and Jamie forgot to breathe for a moment, until she felt the coolness of Kate's breath on her neck. She exhaled, and then there was Kate, touching her everywhere, and Jamie couldn't have stopped what was happening even if she had wanted to. She thought she heard a choked sob from Kate, and then her orgasm hit with the suddenness of being tossed off a cliff. She felt a momentary panic, a need to hang on, before she let go and fell.

Kate moved her hand to Jamie's hip and lay close against her side, giving Jamie time to catch her breath. Jamie felt so strong but so fragile in her arms. Kate expected Jamie would go now. Make some excuse about work, or simply say Kate's touch was more than she could handle. Kate stayed as still as she could, wanting to put off Jamie's departure as long as possible.

"Kate?" Jamie whispered. "Are you holding your breath?"

"A little."

Kate felt Jamie's laugh against her hair. "I'm not a wild animal that will panic and run if you move."

Kate lifted her head. "Are you sure? I shouldn't have…it's too soon."

Jamie raised her index finger to wipe tears from Kate's cheek, and Kate saw Jamie's hand trembling and the tears that were in Jamie's eyes as well. "Not too soon," Jamie said. "I love you, Kate. If we're going to make this work, there can't be any barriers between us. We'll tear them down one at a time."

"Together," Kate said. "And I love you, too." She wrapped her arms tightly around Jamie's neck and uncurled her body so she could press it against Jamie's. Jamie shifted without pulling out of their embrace and pushed Kate onto her back. Her hand slipped between them and she entered Kate firmly and without preamble. Kate arched against her and tightened her hold around Jamie's neck. The wonder at Jamie's ability to read how she needed to be touched only added to Kate's arousal.

Jamie drew her head back just enough to meet Kate's gaze, her fingers slowly stroking through her wetness. "Kate, when you made love to me, when you touched me, you were the only one there."

"I'm so glad." Kate smiled and raised a hand to caress Jamie's cheek. Jamie had eased the worry Kate had been afraid to voice, that Jamie's memories would always be between them. Her relief at Jamie's words rushed through her just before her eyes slid shut as Jamie's ever more insistent touch brought her to a shuddering climax.

Jamie draped her thigh over Kate's, settling her close as she pulled the covers over them. She listened as Kate's breathing grew deeper and more even before she let her own eyes slip shut. This was the moment when she would usually tell herself she had five more minutes to relax and then she would make her escape. The moment that had always been an ending. Jamie snuggled even closer to the warmth of Kate—her beginning, her future—and she dropped into a dreamless sleep.

Chapter Nineteen

Jamie came around the corner of the show stables at Spruce Meadows, the Calgary site of the Masters Competition, and stopped to enjoy the view when she saw Kate at the end of the aisle. Kate had removed her riding jacket and shirt, and she was spraying the stallion with a hose while wearing a tank top and old sweats over her breeches. Her blond ponytail was damp and flattened from her helmet, and Jamie's breath caught at how sexy this woman could be even when she was sweaty and dusty from a long day of showing. She could have stood there and watched Kate for hours, but she finally made herself move.

Kate glanced at her with a smile and then returned her attention to the sweat marks on Blaze's back. "Is it all done?" she asked.

"Yes. They signed the papers and they'll be taking him home tonight," Jamie said, trying to read Kate's expression. "Are you sure you're okay with this?"

"You've asked me that every day for a month now," Kate said. "And yes, I'm fine with it. I don't regret my decision at all, and I'm kind of glad Blaze'll be moving on so I can concentrate on expanding the therapy program. But really, you're done with the meetings and everything?"

Jamie frowned. "Yes, everything's official and he's sold. Why?"

"Just because I hate how you always look so cool and put together while I'm such a sweaty mess," Kate said before she arced the spray of her hose in Jamie's direction, soaking her midsection. "There. Much better."

"Very juvenile," Jamie observed, wiping futilely at her wet slacks. "You know you don't need a hose to get me wet. But speaking of small children, where's Anna?"

"She and Elaine went back to the trade fair to shop. They're meeting us for lunch in half an hour."

The large Canadian show hosted a tent full of vendors who sold anything even remotely horse-related. Jamie thought Anna had spent more time there than watching the actual animals. Secretly Jamie didn't mind, especially after last night when she and Kate had sat with Anna on her hotel bed and looked through her new horse books together. Like a family. "Great, there goes all my profit," she muttered as Kate turned off the water and bent to coil the hose. The stallion took that opportunity to shake like a dog, dousing Kate in the process as she shrieked and tried to get out of the way.

"I am going to miss that big guy," Jamie said with a smile. Kate just rolled her eyes and used a metal sweat scraper to remove some of the excess water from his shining chestnut coat.

"I don't know how you managed to arrange this, but I sure appreciate it. Today was a blast," Kate said as she worked. Jamie had used all her powers of persuasion to convince the executives at Davison and Burke to buy the stallion as planned, but as a quick turnover investment instead of a long-term PR project. The venture might not have had the same publicity value as the original sponsorship would have provided, but it managed to link their company name with the equestrian world. The young stallion had sold for a handsome profit after his and Kate's spectacular fifth-place finish as an unknown team against top international competition. So Jamie got a healthy commission, and Kate was well compensated for her time training and riding the horse, plus Kate was once again the darling of Davison and Burke. Most important to Jamie, she was able to give Kate a chance to ride the talented horse at a prestigious show. Her only worry was that the experience would reveal to Kate exactly what she had given up and make her second-guess her decision to stay in Oregon.

"It's just my job," Jamie said with a shrug, although the deal had required more finesse than she would let on. "See that fence post over there? I could have it earning its keep by sundown."

"I have to admit you're very good at what you do. At everything you do," Kate added with a grin as she locked the horse in his stall. Her voice turned serious again. "I hated to think I was cheating you out of a commission by changing my mind at the last minute."

"Believe me, my hourly fee has been paid in full," Jamie said. She came up behind Kate and wrapped her arms around her waist, resting her chin on Kate's shoulder. The touch, the closeness felt natural to Jamie now, but she still experienced a sense of wonder every time she held Kate. "And you couldn't pay me enough to make me give up these past few weeks with you."

Kate leaned against her. "And this is just the beginning..." she said, her head tilting back as Jamie kissed her way along Kate's neck. "Because I love you."

"I love you, too," Jamie said, turning Kate in her arms and lowering her head until their lips were just a breath apart. "And I don't intend to stop."

About the Author

Karis Walsh is a horseback riding instructor who lives on a small farm in the Pacific Northwest. When she isn't teaching or writing, she enjoys spending time outside with her animals, reading, playing the viola, and riding with friends.

Books Available from Bold Strokes Books

Worth the Risk by Karis Walsh. Investment analyst Jamie Callahan and Grand Prix show jumper Kaitlyn Brown are willing to risk it all in their careers—can they face a greater challenge and take a chance on love? (978-1-60282-587-1)

Bloody Claws by Winter Pennington. In the midst of aiding the police, Preternatural Private Investigator Kassandra Lyall finally finds herself at serious odds with Sheila Morris, the local werewolf pack's Alpha female, when Sheila abuses someone Kassandra has sworn to protect. (978-1-60282-588-8)

Awake Unto Me by Kathleen Knowles. In turn of the century San Francisco, two young women fight for love in a world where women are often invisible and passion is the privilege of the powerful. (978-1-60282-589-5)

Initiation by Desire by MJ Williamz. Jaded Sue and innocent Tulley find forbidden love and passion within the inhibiting confines of a sorority house filled with nosy sisters. (978-1-60282-590-1)

Toughskins by William Masswa. John and Bret are two twenty-something athletes who find that love can begin in the most unlikely of places, including a "mom and pop shop" wrestling league. (978-1-60282-591-8)

me@you.com by K.E. Payne. Is it possible to fall in love with someone you've never met? Imogen Summers thinks so because it's happened to her. (978-1-60282-592-5)

High Impact by Kim Baldwin. Thrill seeker Emery Lawson and Adventure Outfitter Pasha Dunn learn you can never truly appreciate what's important and what you're capable of until faced with a sudden and stark reminder of your own mortality. (978-1-60282-580-2)

Snowbound by Cari Hunter. "The policewoman got shot and she's bleeding everywhere. Get someone here in one hour or I'm going to put her out of her misery." It's an ultimatum that will forever change the lives of police officer Sam Lucas and Dr. Kate Myles. (978-1-60282-581-9)

Rescue Me by Julie Cannon. Tyler Logan reluctantly agrees to pose as the girlfriend of her in-the-closet gay BFF at his company's annual retreat, but she didn't count on falling for Kristin, the boss's wife. (978-1-60282-582-6)

Murder in the Irish Channel by Greg Herren. Chanse MacLeod investigates the disappearance of a female activist fighting the Archdiocese of New Orleans and a powerful real estate syndicate. (978-1-60282-584-0)

Franky Gets Real by Mel Bossa. A four day getaway. Five childhood friends. Five shattering confessions…and a forgotten love unearthed. (978-1-60282-585-7)

Riding the Rails: Locomotive Lust and Carnal Cabooses edited by Jerry Wheeler. Some of the hottest writers of gay erotica spin tales of Riding the Rails. (978-1-60282-586-4)

Sheltering Dunes by Radclyffe. The seventh in the award-winning Provincetown Tales. The pasts, presents, and futures of three women collide in a single moment that will alter all their lives forever. (978-1-60282-573-4)

Holy Rollers by Rob Byrnes. Partners in life and crime Grant Lambert and Chase LaMarca assemble a team of gay and lesbian criminals to steal millions from a right-wing mega-church, but the gang's plans are complicated by an "ex-gay" conference, the FBI, and a corrupt reverend with his own plans for the cash. (978-1-60282-578-9)

History's Passion: Stories of Sex Before Stonewall edited by Richard Labonté. Four acclaimed erotic authors re-imagine the past…Welcome to the hidden queer history of men loving men not so very long—and centuries—ago. (978-1-60282-576-5)

Lucky Loser by Yolanda Wallace. Top tennis pros Sinjin Smythe and Laure Fortescue reach Wimbledon desperate to claim tennis's crown jewel, but will their feelings for each other get in the way? (978-1-60282-575-8)

Mystery of The Tempest: A Fisher Key Adventure by Sam Cameron. Twin brothers Denny and Steven Anderson love helping people and fighting crime alongside their sheriff dad on sun-drenched Fisher Key, Florida, but Denny doesn't dare tell anyone he's gay, and Steven has secrets of his own to keep. (978-1-60282-579-6)

Better Off Red: Vampire Sorority Sisters Book 1 by Rebekah Weatherspoon. Every sorority has its secrets, and college freshman Ginger Carmichael soon discovers that her pledge is more than a bond of sisterhood—it's a lifelong pact to serve six bloodthirsty demons with a lot more than nutritional needs. (978-1-60282-574-1)

Detours by Jeffrey Ricker. Joel Patterson is heading to Maine for his mother's funeral, and his high school friend Lincoln has invited himself along on the ride—and into Joel's bed—but when the ghost of Joel's mother joins the trip, the route is likely to be anything but straight. (978-1-60282-577-2)

Three Days by L.T. Marie. In a town like Vegas where anything can happen, Shawn and Dakota find that the stakes are love at all costs, and it's a gamble neither can afford to lose. (978-1-60282-569-7)

Swimming to Chicago by David-Matthew Barnes. As the lives of the adults around them unravel, high school students Alex and

Robby form an unbreakable bond, vowing to do anything to stay together—even if it means leaving everything behind. (978-1-60282-572-7)

Hostage Moon by AJ Quinn. Hunter Roswell thought she had left her past behind, until a serial killer begins stalking her. Can FBI profiler Sara Wilder help her find her connection to the killer before he strikes on blood moon? (978-1-60282-568-0)

Erotica Exotica: Tales of Sex, Magic, and the Supernatural edited by Richard Labonté. Today's top gay erotica authors offer sexual thrills and perverse arousal, spooky chills, and magical orgasms in these stories exploring arcane mystery, supernatural seduction, and sex that haunts in a manner both weird and wondrous. (978-1-60282-570-3)

Blue by Russ Gregory. Matt and Thatcher find themselves in the crosshairs of a psychotic killer stalking gay men in the streets of Austin, and only a 103-year-old nursing home resident holds the key to solving the murders—but can she give up her secrets in time to save them? (978-1-60282-571-0)

Balance of Forces: Toujours Ici by Ali Vali. Immortal Kendal Richoux's life began during the reign of Egypt's only female pharaoh, and history has taught her the dangers of getting too close to anyone who hasn't harnessed the power of time, but as she prepares for the most important battle of her long life, can she resist her attraction to Piper Marmande? (978-1-60282-567-3)

Wings: Subversive Gay Angel Erotica edited by Todd Gregory. A collection of powerfully written tales of passion and desire centered on the aching beauty of angels. (978-1-60282-565-9)

Contemporary Gay Romances by Felice Picano. These works of short fiction from legendary novelist and memoirist Felice Picano are as different from any standard "romances" as you can get, but they will linger in the mind and memory. (978-1-60282-639-7)

Pirate's Fortune: Supreme Constellations Book Four by Gun Brooke. Set against the backdrop of war, captured mercenary Weiss Kyakh is persuaded to work undercover with bio-android Madisyn Pimm, which foils her plans to escape, but kindles unexpected love. (978-1-60282-563-5)

Sex and Skateboards by Ashley Bartlett. Sex and skateboards and surfing on the California coast. What more could anyone want? Alden McKenna thinks that's all she needs, until she meets Weston Duvall. (978-1-60282-562-8)